Another Family Reunion Novel
In the Wisdom of the Ancestors Series
— Book 18 —

An Ulterior MOTIVE

ALEX-MONT KIDS SAGA, Episode 1

ANN JEFFRIES

Published and Distributed By
New View Literature
820 67th Avenue N, #7603
Myrtle Beach, South Carolina 29572
www.newviewliterature.com
annjeffries@newviewliterature.com

Cover and Interior design: TWA Solutions
ISBN: Print 978-1-941603-16-1
ISBN: eBook 978-1-941603-15-4
Library of Congress Control Number: 2017903338

Seconod printing January 2020

For inquiries, contact the publisher.

Acknowledgments

I bow in humble appreciation to:

The Creator
The Ancestors
Jenetha Hollis, Editor
Jessica Tilles, Creative Designer
The Carolina Forest Authors' Group
Carolina Forest Public Library, Horry County, SC
Family, friends, and fans

The journey continues and the struggle for literary
perfection shall never end.

I remain faithfully yours,

Ann Jeffries

Titles in the
Ann Jeffries
Family Reunion–Wisdom of the Ancestors Series

In paperback and e-book formats:

Southern Exposures
Another Point of View
Northern Exposures
Uncommon Choices
An Unguarded Moment
Moments To Remember
The Better Part of Valor
Walking on Uneven Ground
Ask Me No Questions . . . I'll Tell You No Lies
Touch Me In The Morning
All Goodbyes Aren't Gone
A Different Frame of Mind
Judicial Indiscretion
Crystal Clear Persuasion
Sweet Justice
Bittersweet Memories
All in the Family

In the Audiobook Format:

Southern Exposures Produced by Ginger Walton
Another Point of View Produced by Glen Pavlovich
Northern Exposures Produced by CJ McAlister
Uncommon Choices Produced by Kelley Hazen
An Unguarded Moment Produced by Richard Dennis Johnson
Moments To Remember Produced by Richard Dennis Johnson
The Better Part of Valor Produced by Richard Dennis Johnson
Walking on Uneven Ground Produced by Richard Dennis Johnson
Ask Me No Questions . . . I'll Tell You No Lies Produced by Pam Dougherty
Touch Me In The Morning Produced by Ginger Walton
All Goodbyes Aren't Gone Produced by Julian Thomas
A Different Frame of Mind Produced by CJ McAlister
Judicial Indiscretion Produced by Kelley Hazen
Crystal Clear Persuasion Produced by CJ McAlister
Sweet Justice Produced by CJ McAlister
Bittersweet Memories Produced by Kelley Hazen
All in the Family Produced by Kelley Hazen

In Production:

An Ulterior Motive

"...Recognize the disguises of the hunter,
Some might carry smiles...
With a quick slap on your back.
That's been carefully prepared...
To slip on a custom made trap that fits.
While socializing with those exposed,
With ulterior motives for selections they've chosen..."

by Lawrence S. Pertillar

Prologue

He watched her as she twirled unbelievably fast on pointed toes. She was in the spotlights which followed her across the big, empty, otherwise darkened stage. The hushed audience seemed to be held in a state of suspended animation. Those sitting close to him had their eyes riveted on her and gleaming in the lowered theatre lights. He had seen her performances on ice, too, but never tired of repeat performances. She was perfect in every dimension; tall, proportionally slim with perfect, strong, muscular arms, legs, and thighs. Her carriage was high, tight, and regal. Yet, she was as graceful as the swan her character portrayed.

The classical ballet, Swan Lake, by Pyotr Ilyich Tchaikovski would not have been a performance he would have opted to attend. Were it not for another chance to observe the world-renowned prima ballerina known as The Black Swan, Linda Lewis, he would have been at a concert performance for NSYNC. Generally, his taste went more to a performance by Beyoncé and others like her. However, Linda was the only reason he put out the astronomical fee for a ticket to be in the audience of this grand, old theater watching her perform. A presentation which was sold out for months in advance.

Still, this was not the first venue he spent an inordinate amount of money on. Rather, he watched her performance in Paris, France; Madrid and Barcelona, Spain; Lisbon, Portugal; and Tokyo, Japan. Each time, her routine was flawless; a masterpiece of motion. Incomprehensible. On each occasion, he tried to get close to her but failed. Her world tour took her to other renowned theatres over the last six months, but he could only follow at certain times. Her security was top-notch, so he didn't want to be conspicuous or draw attention to himself too soon, if at all.

Now she was ending her world tour here in New York City, and tonight was her final performance for a while. He needed to get close to her, but he spotted members of her extensive family in the audience. They were hard to miss, so he resolved that tonight would not be the night he could approach her. She would be living with her uncle in New York City, so he relocated too. Then he'd find a way to get to her.

The curtains came down while the audience quickly rose in clamorous applause. Slowly he rose, but applauded just as vigorously. There were unabashed tears in the eyes of some of the people around him. Her performances always rung heartfelt emotions from her fans and other spectators, including him.

During intermission, while in the lobby, he closely watched her family. Her father, Dr. Charles Patrick Montgomery, was a Johnny Depp look-a-like, with a pelt of shoulder-length, brown hair tied in a queue at the nape of his neck. He sported a diamond winking in his left earlobe, a modern affectation, though he wore dressy Texas cowboy garb and stood nearly seven feet tall to her mother's five-ten height. Her father was out of a family of eleven children, and he was the youngest boy. His siblings still lived in Monroe County, Pennsylvania, a farming community, and practiced their crafts in the building trades as plumbers, electricians, carpenters, etc., as they each farmed their own lands.

Linda's mother, US Supreme Court Judge Vivian Lynn Alexander, Esquire, at a distance looked like the youthful image of the actress Jada Pinkett Smith. Her short, shiny, pin-curly, dark-brown hair was plastered flat to her scalp. Her family was also large and hydroponic farmers in the Town of Goodwill in Summer County, South Carolina. Vivian was the middle child of five, the oldest girl. She won Olympic Gold playing basketball while in college. As a member of an elite, advanced scholars program at Georgetown Law Center, she scored in the upper one percent of her graduating class. Later, right after graduation, she and five of her classmates started the Alexander, Carter, Chandler, Charles, Lightfoot, and Towson law firm. Though Vivian was selected first as a judge on the

Federal Circuit Court of Appeals and then the US Supreme Court, the law firm still carried her name and remained one of the most prestigious in the country.

As he continued to observe, he saw Linda's uncles, aunts, and cousins from all sides of her family, who like her and her siblings, were an array of shades from ivory to ebony and very prosperous in their own right. All of her grandparents were active and involved people of stature. He had secretly taken pictures of each family member and close friends. He placed the pictures in a collage on his walls, intently studying them so that he could easily pick them out of a crowd. He had what he thought of as deep background intelligence on each one.

She had what he considered a regimen of siblings who also resembled a rainbow coalition. Like Linda, many, if not most, of her brothers and sisters were adopted by her first and second set of parents. Still, were it not for the differences genetics bestowed, the siblings were a more tightly-knit group than biological siblings would likely be. He didn't personally know about that. He didn't have anyone in his life to rival what he sensed she had in hers.

Oddly, he thought as he continued to observe them, *her family liked to laugh*. He hadn't caught a picture of any one of them when they weren't smiling or laughing. They also seemed to do everything together, providing unfailing moral support for one another. It was apparent that they cared about each other, but he sensed they actually *liked* each other, too. At least that's what he found in his research of the people around Linda. He amassed a great deal of information and studied her closely beginning from the day she was born; particularly during the time she was a young girl.

In classical ballets or on the ice when she skated, she did so with such precision and heart, combined with technical skill. Her celebrity began at an early age. He learned from interviews she granted that in her youth, she was torn between focusing on ballet or figure skating. Both were equally important to her and she had a slew of awards, including a bronze for her Olympic performance at the age of twelve. Her parents' support and encouragement allowed her the freedom to pursue her dreams no matter where those endeavors took her. In each interview, she always gave thanks to her family for her successes.

Indeed, she was a member of a family of high achievers. Her first adoptive father, Derrick Jackson, a man of color, was a multibillionaire basketball icon, and then a renowned pediatric surgeon before he suddenly died of a heart attack. Early in his medical career, he devised a treatment using both hardware and software, which revolutionized pediatric medicine. Linda was one of his earliest patients and success stories.

Her second adoptive father, Charles Montgomery, a Caucasian, was also a multibillionaire and notable basketball figure who later became an emergency room doctor. A number of years ago, he opened his own Physicians' Hospital with a group of other doctors in a rural area in Maryland near Washington, DC. It was one of the few hospitals in the world which specialized in surgical techniques to separate conjoined twins using Derrick's innovative surgical technique and had a high success rate. Some of those twins were abandoned by their biological parents but ended up being adopted by Dr. Montgomery and his wife, Vivian, Linda's parents.

Both Derrick Jackson and Charles Montgomery, who were the best of friends since adolescence pimpled their skins, the Gayle Sayers and Brian Piccolo of their time, married the young attorney Vivian Alexander. Now Linda's adoptive mother was the youngest and wealthiest person ever to be appointed a member of the US Supreme Court. Her mother was still in her mid-thirties and, together with her husband, was raising, at last count, more than twenty-five children of various ages and ethnicities. Vivian had one biological son with her former husband, Derrick Jalon Jackson, Jr., and five biological children with Charles. Together they continued to adopt orphaned or abandoned babies and some older children with ongoing health challenges. These were youngsters who, because of their high medical bills, health care costs, and expenses, no one else wanted.

He recorded the family's interview on the Sweet Justice show and every piece of film or video footage he could find on the family and their close friends. The Alexander-Montgomery wife and husband team were long-time, close friends of some very notable people, including Constantina Justice, owner and operator of the Sweet Justice TV Network Channels and her husband, Nicholas Collins, a giant in the business world. The Hawkins' heiresses, LaiLoni Hawkins, aka, Dakota Sinclair, wife of Ambassador Emeritus Jefferson Logan, and JaiHonnah Hawkins, wife of J. Roderick Baylor, former basketball icon and head of Baylor and Baylor Design and Developers. The heiresses were the daughters of Ambassador Jake Hawkins, the titular head of BlackHawk Global, one of the wealthiest conglomerates in the world. Judge Kristin Catherine Bryant and her wealthy husband, international law expert Thomas Ashton Marshall, were in the Alexander-Montgomery inner circle, just to name a few notables.

Oh, yes, he had spent a considerable amount of time and money studying Linda Lewis, all the while planning when and how to approach her when he could get her alone. He even moved to the United States to track her. For the past week, he followed her and her security team to a converted fire station in the SoHo area of New York City. It was one of the homes owned by her uncle, the Wall Street phenom and basketball great, Gregory Alexander, known in sports and financial circles as Alexander the Great. All indications were her uncle would be leaving after the casts' wrap party tonight at Angelique's Restaurant and Club to go to South Carolina and leaving Linda alone in his home.

With her family, close friends, and so many notables in attendance, he was sure he would not be allowed past her security team or be permitted inside the restaurant, so he would bide his time a little longer. He had to get her alone soon though. His time was running out.

Chapter 1

"Linda?" called out Angelique Menendez-Gaza from the common area outside the eight-bedroom suites. A formerly-active fashion supermodel, actress, and now a Le Cordon Bleu certified chef and restauranteur, she and Uncle Gregory were engaged and planning their wedding during the Juneteenth family reunion holiday in South Carolina. They were both ecstatic about their upcoming nuptials, but holding off being intimate until their wedding night. Gregory, nearly eight years older than Angelique, wanted to give her time to be sure marriage to him was what she was committed to for the rest of their lives.

"Coming," Linda called back. She shifted the long, wide strap of her duffel bag over her head and across her body as she hurried. Her Uncle Gregory was getting one of his cars out of the garage to take her and Angelique to drop off in different locations in the city."

"Have you got everything?" Angelique teased, motioning to Linda's large duffle.

Linda laughed. "I'm not carrying the kitchen sink, but that's probably the only thing I don't have in here." They headed down the wide, open, ultra-modern, iron and teak wood, floating stairs to the interior access garage door just as Gregory pressed a button that rolled up one of the three garage bay door exits to the exterior.

When they were settled in the SUV, Gregory pulled out of the garage onto the parking pad and waited until the garage door rolled closed and locked before he merged into the wet, rainy traffic. It was still fairly early in the morning; only half past five, and the uptown traffic wasn't at a standstill yet. Sitting in the back seat, Linda put in her earbuds to listen to her cousin Adelaide Jackson's latest novel; another in her Firelight Love series. The series was on the hot and steamy side of the romantic suspense genre and climbing the best seller list. It gave Linda a voyeuristic glimpse of what love with the right man might be and to live vicariously through the audiobook version of each novel. Now that she was back in the United States for a while, she planned to go visit Adelaide and the rest of her dads' families, the Jacksons and the Montgomerys in Pennsylvania, maybe for Easter.

So far, Linda mused as she listened to a particularly juicy scene in the novel, she hadn't found anyone she trusted, respected, and loved enough to share her body with. Not like her cousin and BFF Whitney Ivy Alexander. She had the incredibly handsome and genially nice Tucker Cavanaugh as her newly-minted fiancée. Tucker admitted he was instantly in love when he first saw Whitney Ivy jogging across the Georgetown University campus where they were both enrolled. They had been dating for two years now. Whitney Ivy was in her last year of law school, and Tucker, an active-duty Marine, was in his second year of residency as a medical doctor. On New Year's Eve, he went down on bended knee and presented an engagement ring to Whitney Ivy at their family's annual holiday party. No one among their family and friends was surprised when she accepted. Although they planned to wait to marry until they were both established professionally, their parents, families, and close friends were there to celebrate the upcoming union. Linda had never seen two people more in love and happy.

Well, of course, there was her Aunt Aretha Grace and her guy friend, Russell Greene. They were involved for more than ten years but had not chosen to become formally engaged yet. Her aunt admitted they didn't have time for a full-time commitment. They were both in their twenties and very busy. Russell, an extraordinary artist, was either touring the globe for art shows given in his honor or working on new masterpieces. Aunt Aretha was working on another doctorate at Oxford University in England and volunteered with the Peace Corp during the summers, spending a lot of time helping people in Third World countries improve their living conditions. Yet, Aunt Aretha and Russell were content to be together when time permitted.

Then, of course, there was Uncle Gregory and Angelique. She got a lot of opportunities to observe them while she was living in New York in Gregory's home.

Still, Linda longed to find a relationship she could enjoy. Preferably with a man who had a stationary career and had the positive qualities exhibited by the men in her family or in Adelaide's novels. She realized she would need to settle down in one spot herself and couldn't continue to put the stresses on her body that ballet and professional figure skating demanded. Eventually, she would have to find a new career. At the moment, she didn't have a clue what she would do once the cheering stopped.

"Hey, kiddo, what's on your mind?" Gregory asked his niece as he turned around in his seat to look at her. He'd already dropped Angelique off at her restaurant and pulled into the parking garage of Indulgences, the sports and health center owned and operated by his friend Will Hamilton. He knew something was bothering Linda. She was too quiet lately and introspective. Very unlike his usually lively and vivacious niece. He would delay his trip back to Atlantic Beach, South Carolina, for a day or two in order to figure out what was up with Linda.

"Nothing, much, Uncle Greg," she said in answer to his question and smiled at him.

However, in his view, her smile didn't quite reach her pretty, dark-green eyes. Something wasn't right with her. She had lived with him for too many years for him not to spot a subtle change in her demeanor. Yes, he would call his great-grandaunt Hanna Ivy in South Carolina and let her know he would be delayed. Next, he would call his basketball league office and alert them to his need to delay a group of meetings with the team owners. His staff at the Summer County Bank and Trust he was establishing could do without him for a few more days as well. He pulled his phone from his pocket as they got out of the SUV to walk into the sports facility and began to make the calls necessary to change his schedule.

Uh oh, Linda thought as she overheard bits and pieces of her uncle's conversations. He was delaying his departure by a few more days. She never could put anything over on him or anyone else in her family for that matter. Her parents were human bloodhounds. They could sniff out problems long before they became issues. It didn't help that she wore her feelings on her face. Her uncle must have sensed something was going on with her and he wouldn't leave until he knew what it was. If he became too concerned, he'd report her behavior to his older sister and brother-in-law, her mother and father. Then there would be more family members, including her grandparents, involved until she was forced to confess her fears about her uncertain future.

She and her Uncle Greg were the best of pals, so she had no concerns about talking with him. He was a good listener and gave good advice only when he was asked. Still, she was growing up and knew she had to learn to stand on her own two feet like an adult. However, she hadn't quite figured it all out in her own mind yet.

Uncle Gregory carried his sport's bag on his left shoulder and slung his right arm around her shoulders as they moved into the health, sports, and fitness facility's lobby.

Linda noticed two youngsters; a boy of about seven or eight, and a girl who appeared to be younger, about five or six years old. They were sitting in the plush chairs of the well-appointed black-granite lobby but didn't seem to be the least bit happy about something. The boy was sporting a shiner around his left eye. Linda didn't see any adults in the vicinity and would have mentioned it to her uncle, but they were joined by an extremely handsome, athletically fit man.

"I heard about the accident. I'm sorry for your loss, Will."

"Thanks, Greg. I admit it's been hard losing my older brother, Harold, and sister-in-law so suddenly. Now, I have their children, my young nephew and niece, to raise along with my younger brother. At least Drew is twenty-five and in his last year of grad school at City College, but Eugene and Violet are only eight and six. I've never been married, and I don't have children. I'm out of my element, but Drew and I are almost all the family they have. My sister-in-law was an only child and her parents are deceased. Her paternal grandparents raised her and are still living, but they're in the early eighties. They offered to help financially with their great-grandchildren but felt they couldn't take on the responsibility of raising them. They want to be a part of their lives, so I agreed to periodically bring them to Portland, Oregon, to visit."

"That's understandable. Although I've never been married or had children of my own either, I do have a gang of nephews and nieces and a lot of experience. So, if there is anything I can do to help, let me know."

"Thanks, Greg. I know you're busy, but I'm going to tap you for guidance. If you have time later, let me know. I could use your advice. Right now, though, I have a customer waiting." He looked around as if searching for someone. "My brother should have been on early desk duty this morning to help this customer."

Greg laughed. "Yes, she is a customer and she's a very patient one. Will Hamilton, this is one of my many nieces, Linda Jackson Montgomery. Linda, Will Hamilton owns and operates Indulgences, this health, fitness, sports club, and spa."

She extended her hand, still transfixed by the man's Brian McKnight good looks. *Now, this was a man whose rugged appeal fueled the lusty images in romance novels*, she thought. "It's a pleasure to meet you, Mr. Hamilton. You played baseball in the pros, am I right?" she asked.

He smiled at her, surprised and amused. He wondered how a gorgeous and sophisticated young woman like her would know things like that about him. "I did, yes, many years ago. It's kind of you to remember and, please, call me Will. You must have been a kid when I played."

She shrugged. "Not so long ago as I recall. You set records that haven't been broken." She went on to mention some of his stats.

Impressed with her knowledge and memory, he took a moment longer to appreciate what a poised and attractive young woman she is. She had luminous dark green eyes and a killer body with a subtle musculature and . . . something began to dawn on him. He snapped his finger when recognition came. "The Black Swan! You're Linda Lewis!"

She inclined her head in acknowledgment, a smile rimming her mouth.

"I didn't know you were a patron of the arts, Will," said Gregory, laughing.

"Generally, I'm not, but I escorted someone to the theatre last month. She had front-row tickets and the show was Swan Lake. Although I'm not a particular fan of classical ballet, I remembered the star ballerina. Recognition probably would have come sooner, but your niece was wearing face paint during her performance.

"My date made a big issue out of wanting your autograph after the show, but the crowd at the stage door was too large to wait. Nevertheless, your performance was flawless. I still have the playbill from that performance. Your picture is prominently displayed on the program."

Although later that night he was balls deep in Jolie Jance, that evening's companion, he remembered the beautiful face of a prima ballerina and couldn't get her out of his head even days later.

"Thank you. I hope your date enjoyed the show, too. I'd be happy to give the autograph to her she didn't get that night."

"That's very gracious of you, but she and I aren't still in contact," he said though he knew Jolie wanted it otherwise. He enjoyed having sex with her over a period of about six months. She was talented in that respect, but had an aversion to his nephew and niece, and children in general. So, he knew pursuing a relationship with Jolie would be an exercise in futility. "I see you must be carrying your workout gear in your duffle. Are you here for the spa or the health and fitness facilities?"

"Both. Uncle Greg signed me up for the works today as a guest under his membership. He brought me in early to show the facility to me before my appointments."

"How about a month-long, complimentary membership in your own name so you can use it to visit the facility anytime you like?"

"That's very kind of you, Will. Thank you, I'd like that. However, I prefer not to use my stage name, if you don't mind."

"Great. It's not a problem. Several celebrities, who are members here, prefer to keep their association with Indulgences private. They don't want to be bothered when they come to work out and relax. Let me get my brother to sign you in and get your membership card," he said, picking up a desk phone.

Moments later a tall, well-built younger version of Will Hamilton or Brian McKnight swaggered up to the front desk. He looked a little the worse for wear; his eyes a bit bloodshot. Still, his musculature in the black T-shirt with **INDULGENCES** emblazoned in white lettering over his heart and well-defined pecs was admirable. Yet, Linda's attention was riveted on Will.

"Whoa!" said Drew Hamilton expressively when he spotted the woman standing with his brother and the six-foot, ten-inch, super jock, Greg Alexander. He had seen Alexander's equally beautiful super, high-fashion model and actress girlfriend, Angelique, and, although stunning, this babe wasn't her. The sports' jocks always scored the finest babes. He didn't get it. His brother and his fellow athletes always had arm candy while men, like him, got their leftovers or cast offs. Okay, so he didn't play a sport or have big-time name recognition, but he could shoot pool with the best of them. If it weren't for his brother putting his foot down, holding the purse strings, forcing him to work at Indulgences, while he finished college and grad school, he'd be in Vegas, Monte Carlo or other places where big money could be found in the pool halls around the globe. Soon he'd be out from under Will's iron fist and on his own. Then he could score babes who looked like this woman who must be Alexander's new or side piece.

"Drew, this is Linda Montgomery. Would you set her up with our Platinum Complimentary Membership and then give her a guided tour of the facility? I would do it myself, but I have to take Eugene and Violet to school and deal with the suspension the school wants to give Eugene for fighting."

"Yeah, you go on and do that. I'll be happy to show Ms. Montgomery the place…and anything else she wants to see."

Will didn't appreciate the way his brother was scrutinizing Linda's body. He had heard from others that his brother was doing more for the female members than his job at Indulgences required. He'd have to speak with Drew about that when he returned from dropping off the children at school.

He spoke with Gregory a few more moments after Drew left with Linda, then gathered the children. They went into the garage where his car was parked in his assigned space and headed for the private school. An hour later, he and Eugene returned. His mission to convince the school to rescind the week-long suspension failed. The school had a no-tolerance policy for fighting. As an additional punishment, Eugene was expected to complete all of his in-school and homework assignments and the extra work he was given. Will could only shake his head. That meant he or Drew would have to spend even longer than they already did every night going over Eugene's assignments and then delivering the work to the school the next day. For now, he didn't have an alternative other than to bring Eugene to work with him every day this week. He didn't have a sitter or a housekeeper. No backup except Drew when he wasn't in one of his classes in grad school. Eugene wasn't pleased with the prospect of sitting in the office with Will all day either.

Things didn't improve when he had a heart-to-heart conversation with Drew about his behavior toward Linda and other female members of Indulgences.

"You should talk, brother," grinned Drew. "I know for a fact you've dipped into the membership pool of women from time to time to get your rocks off. Jolie Jance bends my ear about you every time she's in here."

"That's different, and it's not the point. Jolie joined Indulgences *after* we stopped dating. I didn't meet her here. The women who come here are customers not a dating pool for your convenience."

"Hey, brother, what can I say? The women come to me and, according to you, the customer is always right," he smugly boasted.

"Don't screw around, Drew. Particularly not with Ms. Montgomery," Will cautioned.

"Just because she's your pal's side piece, doesn't mean she's not fair game, brother. Besides she's closer to my age than you over-thirty jocks."

"You are wrong on so many levels, Drew. Don't make me have this conversation with you again," he said and turned away to answer his phone.

He didn't see his brother flip him the bird before sauntering away.

Chapter 2

It was half noon when Linda left the dressing room after her Pilates'
class and a shower. The class was intense and gave her a great workout.
She sweated right through her one-piece leotard and after her shower,
put on the club's long, thick, terrycloth robe and slippers that everyone
else wore. Earlier, she participated in a spin class, then an aerobics session
before she hit the gym equipment. Now, she was hungry and ready for
her spa treatments. She headed for one of the cafés in the facility Drew
had shown her on her early morning tour. She chose the ingredients for
her frappé and looked around for a place to sit in the crowded bar. In
the corner, she noticed Will's young nephew sitting alone with his chin
braced on his stacked hands, a textbook under his nose, and moved in
his direction.

"Hi," she said brightly to the young boy. "My name is Linda. You're
Will Hamilton's nephew, Eugene Hamilton, aren't you?"

He gave her an absent shrug, lifted his eyes, but never lifted his head
from his hands.

"It's pretty crowded in here. May I sit with you for a while?"

He shrugged again in answer. She took the absent motion as assent
and sat down across from him.

"I noticed your black eye. Is that a new kind of fashion statement or
were you in a fight?" She knew it was the latter and that as a result he
was on suspension.

This time he did look up at her and said "Yeah?" with suspicion
evident in his voice.

"A fight then. What did the other guy look like?"

"I gave him a bloody nose and I knocked his front tooth out," he said morosely.

"Gee, what did he do to deserve that?"

"Nothing."

"Oh, so you're a bully who goes around beating up on little kids, huh?"

Obviously incensed, he sat up. "Nu-uh, I didn't start it," he stridently argued. "He's bigger than me and he's always pushing other kids around. I wasn't going to fight him or anything, but he called me names and then pushed Violet down."

"What name did he call you?"

"He said I was a pansy and a pussy."

"Why would he call you that?"

"I don't know," he shrugged. "Maybe because I like to dance. You see, it was like this. I was picked to dance in the school play, The Nutcracker Suite. He said only girls dance in plays and wear tights."

"I sure don't agree with that. I've known some famous men who dance classical ballet and other forms of dance and they look really good in tights."

"Really?" He enthused, obviously warming to their topic of discussion. He sat up straighter and intently listened as she listed names of the men she had partnered with in various performances she had as a ballerina and figure skater and one of her male mentors. His eyes got as big as silver dollars and he became very animated about the subject. She was thrilled to talk with a young boy so interested in the performing arts and the conversation sparked an idea growing in her head.

"This was before your time and mine, but Rudolf Nureyev toured with the Grand Ballet du Marquis de Cuevas. Donnie Burns is a Scottish professional who specializes in Latin dance. He's the President of the World Dance Council, and I'm a member. He helped me a lot and talked with me about how he was teased in school just like you. Although he didn't want to, he often had to fight off bullies." She leaned across the table and conspiratorially whispered, "Women call Joaquin

Cortes sex on legs. He's a Flamenco dancer." She nodded seriously to Eugene's wide-open eyes and mouth.

"Really?" he asked almost breathless.

"Yes, and there are many more men who can dance any bully right off a stage," she boastfully assured him. "Dancers have to work harder than big, strong football players. They can't keep up with the exercises dancers have to do every day."

Linda and Eugene were so focused on their conversation, they didn't notice they were being watched.

Will wasn't the only one who watched the lively and obviously engrossing conversation going on between his nephew and Linda Montgomery. He hadn't seen the boy this engaged ever. Of course, it had only been a few months since Eugene's parents died, and the child psychologist he hired said the children may never recover fully from their loss. Violet seemed introspective, but she was coping with the changes in her life better than her brother. Yet, whatever Eugene and Linda were discussing had a light shining in the boy's eyes. Will's heart swelled with appreciation. He'd have to find a way to thank Linda for her kindness.

Of course, looking at Linda was a pleasure at any age. She seemed grounded and self-possessed for someone so young. He actually took time out of his busy schedule to Google her and was surprised at all she had accomplished. Linda's biological father was killed in Iraq. She was Violet's age when she was in a fatal car accident that took the life of her mother and younger brother. She was hospitalized for two years with fractures that should have rendered her unable to walk let alone dance or ice skate. Yet, according to what he read, her doctor, a pediatric surgeon, Derrick Jackson, stuck with her and through many surgeries used a webbing material he developed and revolutionary technique that knitted her young bones back together stronger than they were before the accident. Based on what he read, over time, Linda learned to walk again and then began to train her body to dance and ice skate.

Dr. Jackson and his new, young wife, Vivian Alexander, adopted Linda and other orphans who had health challenges. Before Derrick died, they adopted or began adoption proceedings on eight children and gave birth to one biological son, Derrick Junior.

Will looked at Linda now and never would have believed she was the victim of a near-death experience. She could certainly relate to Eugene in ways he could not. They both tragically lost their parents in fatal car crashes. Will recalled that he hadn't lost his parents suddenly. Rather, when he began to earn money playing professional baseball in the big leagues, his parents quit their jobs and began to party all the time, booze it up, and use illegal drugs. Even after he kicked them off the gravy train and demanded they enter a rehab program, they were too far gone and died of overdoses within a few years of one another. Their deaths took the life out of the game for him. Still, he and Harold had Drew to look after. When Drew was in high school, Harold married and moved to Oregon. They rarely saw each other after that, and his family just seemed to fall apart. Now, with Harold's death, he was left with the sole responsibility of taking care of Drew who was a handful then and now and his nephew and niece.

When Will's phone vibrated in his pocket, he realized he wouldn't have time to spend talking with Eugene over lunch. Still, he was pleased the boy was having a seemingly fun experience with Linda. Will regretted that he didn't have time to join them, but duty called. He had a business to run.

Linda was comfortably relaxed after her spa experience and was waiting in the lobby for her uncle to pick her up. They planned to have an early dinner at Angelique's Restaurant and then go to a Broadway show, just the two of them. Angelique had to work, so she couldn't join them, but they would pick her up after the show and she would spend the night with them at Gregory's home in SoHo.

As Linda stood waiting in the lobby, she noticed that a building across the street was dark amid the bright lights and activities of other buildings and stores in the block. Taking out her phone, she did a Google Earth search on the address and got information about the square footage and ownership. It was twelve stories high and had not been renovated above the first few levels. She knew anything in Midtown Manhattan would be expensive, but she was not without resources.

After speaking with Eugene during lunch, an idea began to germinate in her very fertile mind. Now the answer to her question of "what next" seemed to be staring her right in the face. When her phone chimed in her hand, she noted the picture of her uncle on the screen.

"Are you going to stand there looking wise and otherwise or are you coming out anytime soon?" Gregory teased.

She laughed, picked up her duffel, slinging it over her left shoulder, dug her hands in the pockets of her jeans, and walked out to her uncle's SUV. She tossed her bag in the back seat, got into the front, and exchanged a kiss with her uncle before she strapped in.

"Uncle Greg, don't pull off yet. Look at the building across the street, the one that's dark and boarded up and tell me what you think."

He left the car idling, let down his window, silenced the audiobook he was listening to, and peered at the building in question. It was an old building, built sometime before the turn of the century, but had a certain characteristic charm about it on the front façade. It was extra wide and roomy from what he could see from his car. It resembled a neighborhood library with the large, double-wide front door; two granite steps up from street level with a stoop not big enough to be called a porch. The stone banisters were massive, chunky, carved brownstone edifices bordering the steps and stoop. The building had large front windows on the first floor which were boarded up with remnants of posters and flyers tacked to the board over the windows and doors. He could see there was probably a basement from the squat windows at and below street level. From the brownstone's exterior, at least it didn't appear to be ready for the wrecking ball, but he hadn't a clue what she was thinking.

"Okay, I see a turn of the century building of about two to three thousand square feet per floor and twelve stories high, not including what I think is a full-height basement. Likely a backyard or parking pad with rear entrance. The building probably has been used for storage since it has no recent signage on the front. The question is what is it that you see?"

"I see a dance studio and school with an upper floor residence."

Greg relaxed in his seat and stared at his niece for a humming moment before turning his head to look at the building again. Slowly he nodded. "Yeah, I see that, too. Does this mean you're going to hire someone to operate it for you?"

Slowly she shook her head warming to her idea. "No, I think I see a new career objective."

"You're scheduled to begin a new Broadway show in the fall and rehearsals begin in a few months, don't they?"

"Maybe I'll make this next show my swan song."

"Is this what's been bugging you? Figuring out what to do with the rest of your life?"

"Some. I can't perform the way I used to, Uncle Greg. I have repetitive motion stress fractures I feel when I dance. My muscles are still strong and firm, but my bones are weakening." The tears began to flood her eyes. "I have to look at alternative means of taking care of myself and planning for my future."

She really didn't have financial worries, he knew. His firm handled her financial portofolio. She was already a multimillionaire in her own right from her contract appearances and her parents established a trust fund for her and each of her siblings that insured they would be taken care of for the rest of their lives. Greg palmed her face and smoothed away the tears with his thumbs before cocooning her in his strong embrace. "Well, you could always learn to cook and become my maid and housekeeper for when Mrs. Joyner marries or move back home and live off the fat of the land," he deadpanned and made her laugh as he had hoped.

She sat up and faced him, searching his eyes. "I can do this, Uncle Greg. It would be a lot of work, but I know I can do this."

He sobered and earnestly looked at her, nodding. "I know you can do it, too. You've accomplished every task you've set for yourself. Then again, you have a venture capitalist in the family who happens to love you fiercely. So, do we have a deal? If you decide to go forward, will you let me help you do this?"

She nodded smiling. "You'll tell Dad and Mom about it, too, won't you, Uncle Greg?" she wheedled.

"*Ha!* Not on a bet, delinquent. You talk with your parents and grands. I'm staying out of harm's way."

"What kind of favorite uncle are you?" Linda asked.

"A smart kind," he said laughing, as he put the car in drive and pulled into the stream of traffic. "I'm hungry. Let's go to Angelique's to eat and talk about your ideas."

"Uh, first tell me what you know about Will Hamilton."

Gregory quickly glimpsed his niece as he drove. "I presume you mean the personal stuff."

"I do, yes."

Gregory shrugged. "He's single, never married, and about my age. He doesn't have children. You know he played baseball professionally and, while still in the game, he opened Indulgences. After that, he retired from baseball. From time to time just like me, he does the color commentary during the baseball season for local, regional or national sports news outlets.

"I didn't know his parents, but I met his older brother, Harold, before he married a woman from Oregon and moved there so she could be close to her elderly grandparents who raised her. Unfortunately, Harold and his wife, who had two children, were killed late last year in an auto accident. Will and his younger brother brought Harold's children to New York after he closed up and sold their home in Oregon.

"I consider him a good friend and business associate. He works hard at keeping Indulgences on the cutting edge of the health and sports businesses. He's turning a good profit and keeping his costs low in the process. You haven't had much time to evaluate his operation, but it speaks volumes for the type of person he is. Membership is expensive, but not too expensive for the type of services he offers to his customers.

"As you probably already know, he has medical staff on duty 24/7 and top notch, licensed exercise and orthopedic technicians. He offers rehab and chiropractic services for people with sports or other muscular injuries. I like that I can get a haircut and full-body massage all at the same place where I can work out. The Olympic-sized pool and exercise equipment are always kept in good order. Both men and women can feel comfortable in the facility because it's so well managed and security is tight."

"Is he involved with anyone? A woman, I mean."

Greg laughed. "I wouldn't know that information, but he's the type of person I believe would only date one woman at a time. I know he's not gun shy. We've been out and about a time or two, when we, and guys from my office, like Adam Adderley and your Uncle Troy, were bachelors on a lost weekend, but not that often.

"You're a good judge of character, Linda. You should get to know him and decide for yourself. If you're interested, he would be quick to tell you if his light isn't on or if he's just not into you. We've gone out in groups where women have consistently hit on him, but he didn't seem to gravitate toward anyone in particular or any particular type of woman. He's sociable and will dance with anyone, but he doesn't drink to excess or become loud or belligerent after a few beers or glasses of wine. I've never seen him get plastered." Greg shrugged. "He's a man of simple tastes, needs or wants and generally a good guy. I wouldn't have a problem with it if you're interested in dating him, but with your schedule, you probably don't have much time to invest in a relationship. I'm confident you're not into one-night stands. I know you haven't done so before."

"Thanks, Uncle Greg. I appreciate your advice and, as you suggested, I'll get to know him better. There's just something about Will Hamilton I like . . . a lot."

Chapter 3

"Well?" Linda asked a few weeks later while studying her parents' faces. They stood on the first floor of the building she planned to purchase. After their dinner discussion, her uncle wasted no time getting started on her plans. In the intervening weeks, the appraiser's opinion on the fair market value of the property nearly stopped Linda's heart. She also took a deep breath and closed her eyes when the Baylor and Baylor architectural and construction inspector listed, in detail, the likely costs of the renovations needed to turn this twenty-four thousand square foot building into a mixed-use property for a school, dance studio, and residence on the top three floors with a rooftop garden.

She wouldn't do anything without her parents' approval, and she impatiently waited with her fingers crossed for them to say something. The whole crew, her siblings, were here climbing up and down the stairs and, undaunted, exploring each nook and cranny through a half inch of dust and grime. It was Saturday morning and they had flown in just to see for themselves the size of the project she was proposing.

Of course, her Uncle Greg weighed in on her side. He was arranging the settlement through his bank and choosing the oversight business team she would work with for the first five years of operation. She had already picked out a name: New York Academy of Dance. Though she had not attended a traditional college, she was tutored and intended for her students to receive an education equal to a four-year private high school and two-year preparatory college. That's why she was glad that her grandparents, her sister, Dena, and her Aunt Aretha were also here.

They were the education gurus of the family and would help her devise a curriculum like the one in operation in Summer County, South Carolina.

In its former life, the building was a private library with beautiful, wide-planked, hardwood floors. There were exquisitely carved bookcases and priceless books everywhere. Her uncle was right, the building was once used as a storage facility by the family who previously owned the library. Fine pieces of furniture were left on all floors with large library tables and large smoking-room chairs. Ornate picture frames of bygone eras were left stacked everywhere. Abandoned boxes of china, crystal, and cutlery, some of it priceless and forgotten. Museum quality pieces she planned to keep.

Her maternal grandfather, Bernard Alexander, a woodworking hobbyist, was salivating over certain furniture pieces. As they toured each floor of the building, for her, he named the species of wood used to construct the fine pieces of artistry while she took notes. When she told him he could have anything he wanted, tears formed in his eyes.

He took her in his arms and said, "Bless you, my child, but these pieces belong here. They're a part of the legacy of this fine old place you've discovered. I would like to catalog each piece and help restore them to their former glory. Anything that you don't want or can't use, we'll ship down to The Summer House to display as your contribution to the family reunion."

That's all it took for her tears to well up and overflow.

It would be easy to achieve the open-concept, industrial-look, minimalist goals she wanted with lacquered brick walls so as not to distract from the art she would use from what she religiously collected during her travels. Her art pieces were currently packed away in her uncle's storage space. She couldn't wait to unpack and place them in her new home.

The structural, twelve-foot, beamed ceiling would be painted black and left uncovered with miniature, directional lights like stars installed and reversible ceiling fans strategically placed to keep a balanced temperature on each level. The spaces would have a decidedly industrial look, she knew, but it wouldn't look cold or uninviting with the revitalized hardwood floors. The art and wood furniture would add warmth and vibrancy, too. She liked the raw beauty of the spaces and with the hardwood floors and minimal distractions from the art she would introduce, it would be perfect.

Robotic walls and furniture would fit nicely into her design ideas for her private space. Bedrooms, the dining room, living room, and kitchen complete with furniture and appliances would disappear into the walls and be revealed only when required for use. She was thrilled at the prospects she and her architects, JaiHonnah, and Fiona Lizette, Jai's younger cousin, discussed and were planning to install. She couldn't wait to get started picking out pieces from her storage bins.

Chuck Montgomery could barely contain the pride he felt for the daughter of his heart. Though she was not his by blood, she was his by love. He watched her struggle through adolescence, her body bent and broken from the accident that took the life of her biological mother and baby brother. Linda had no one except Chuck's best friend since childhood, Derrick Jackson, to champion her cause and need to rise above her disabilities and health challenges. Then Vivian suggested that she and Derrick adopt little Linda Lewis, and the rest was history.

Five years after Derrick's death, he and Vivian continued to raise all of the children she adopted before and after Derrick's death and the new ones they continued to adopt. They had not been successful with saving all of the young lives and had lost some in the process. Undaunted, they continued to reach out and see what they could do to love and protect other abandoned children, usually babies, who had health challenges and no one to care for them. Many of them, through no fault of their own, were born addicted to drugs. The children they had now still had health challenges but were thriving and were, like Linda, his and his wife's pride and joy.

Linda was the first child adopted, the oldest at eight years old, and the first to step out of the family cocoon to spread her wings. She would be home from time to time, but she would never be in the household on a full-time basis again. He and Vivian had talked about this eventuality where their children were concerned and, intellectually, they accepted the inevitable. Still, the reality would take a little getting used to. He assumed he and Vivian were preparing themselves for this since Linda traveled extensively, sharing her talent domestically and abroad. At least, she would be making a home in New York where Gregory was close by rather than abroad.

Having completed a thorough inspection of the place with his brothers who were all in the building trades and getting a thumbs-up from them, Chuck took an envelope from his chest pocket and handed it to Linda. Her facial expression held curiosity as she opened it and pulled out the check. Her jaw dropped and her eyes widened tearing to overflowing. She grabbed her mother and him violently crying as she tightly squeezed them in her arms.

"Now, enough of that, my daughter," said her mother, Vivian. "You're still expected to be home on the first weekend of every month for the traditional birthday celebrations. Juneteenth is reserved for the family reunion in South Carolina, and we claim Thanksgiving, Christmas and New Years as our time together. Every other Easter and Thanksgiving is negotiable should you find a young man worthy of your time and attention and we are forced to share you with his family."

"Mom, you're the best! You and Dad have given me so much with which to build a life. You've been the wind beneath my wings every step of the way. When I was a little kid and thought I couldn't make it another step, you and the dads were all there to give me the boost I needed. I love you fiercely and forever. I am so enormously proud to be your daughter," she said with tears choking her voice with emotion. "I promise I'll do everything to make you even more proud of me."

"You already have, baby," said Vivian hugging her tightly "but your entire family will always be in your corner rooting for you to succeed no matter what. Never forget that."

"With this investment, I'll do a great job and more."

"It's a gift, Linda," said Chuck. "You have already given us a return on our investment in you and you are a gift to our family. Now, it's your responsibility to help the next generation when and where you can."

"Thank you, Dad."

With a check in hand that would completely pay for the cost of renovations, Linda looked at the drab and dilapidated conditions with enhanced energy and began to dream.

Immediately after settlement on Monday morning, she got the keys and the building was hers…and her uncle's banks. The workmen from Baylor and Baylor Design and Developers caravanned in with two big, roll-off dumpsters; one positioned on the street and the other in the backyard off the alley and got to work. Others carried the pieces she wanted to keep to the basement for temporary storage until the project was completed. An eighteen-wheeler waited to accept the furniture and other precious pieces she was shipping to her grandfather in Goodwill, South Carolina.

It was raining and, not wanting to get in the way, Linda parked herself across the street in the comfortable lobby of Indulgences to watch the deconstruction and demolition. She enjoyed the facility so much she bought a two-year membership. Again, she took a deep breath and paid the cost.

That's where Will found her on one of his passes through the lobby after settling a dispute Drew should have handled the day before. However, Drew had been eager to go out and party with his friends and left certain tasks undone. In addition to getting Eugene and Violet up, dressed, fed, double checking homework, and ready for school, Will had to hit the ground running to clean up what Drew failed to do.

He supposed the kid got lucky because he hadn't come home last night and wasn't at work on time this morning. He couldn't fault his brother for wanting to take a breather. Between his college courses, helping with his nephew and niece, and work at Indulgences, Drew had little time to himself. Still, he should have taken the time to complete all of his tasks before he left the building. Will sighed. He needed a breather, too, so he went to sit next to Linda.

"Well, good morning. Are you early for an appointment?" Will asked her.

When she turned, the smile she gave him would have lit up every dark corner of the universe.

"I'm sitting here wondering just how insane I am. I'm probably certifiable."

Will chuckled at that. "Does insanity run in your family?"

She nodded. "Yes, in fact, it does. It's a pandemic."

"Then, from what I've read about your family, you're in good company."

Interest bloomed first in her expressive eyes and then a smile edged her lips. "You've read about my family?"

He shrugged and the little affectation reminded her of his nephew.

"Not in-depth research or anything. I Googled you."

She laughed and her face transformed from merely beautiful into something glorious, thought Will. She looked like the actress Regina King. Through the curtain of natural thick lashes, she had the most amazing moss-green eyes.

"You have no idea how funny that sounded."

He thought a moment longer and found himself laughing along with her. "You're right. It does sound a bit off color. I wasn't trying to imply anything. I mean I wouldn't approach you with a lewd comment or . . . Oh, hell, you're laughing at me. I mean, I used to be good at talking with women, but somehow I get tongue-tied when I'm around you."

She couldn't help it. She laughed more. He looked so adorable all flustered and a little tired. "Not getting much rest, huh?"

"I," he said and hesitated. Did Linda think he was out partying all night like his brother? He certainly wanted to dispel *that* thought. "No, I'm not. I admit I'm at a complete loss as to what to do for Eugene and Violet most of the time. I don't want to screw up their lives, but I'm operating outside of my comfort zone." He looked earnestly at her. "A few weeks ago, I noticed you seemed to be having a good conversation with Eugene. How did you do it?"

"Oh, that was fairly simple. Eugene needed to vent. He's holding a lot inside. Did you ever ask him what the fight was about?" Linda asked

"Well, no. At the time my objective was to get him back in school." Will's brows knitted in question.

"He was defending himself and Violet against a bully," Linda supplied.

Properly chagrined, Will sighed. "I never thought to ask," he said rubbing his face in frustration.

"He's a little person, Will. That's all. Little people have things to say just like big people do. Give him the opening, the encouragement, and he'll be more comfortable sharing his concerns with you. So will Violet. You're a big person, an authority figure, and your size alone probably seems a little intimidating to them. From what he told me, he and Violet never met you until you came to take custody of them and to arrange the funeral for their parents. After the funeral, you and Drew packed up their home and brought them to New York.

"They're still a little shell-shocked by all that happened in such a short period of time," Linda said and continued. "One day they had breakfast with their parents and went to school. When the school day ended, no one came to pick them up. The principal called the emergency contact number and late that night you showed up. They didn't know what happened to their parents until you told them. You, Drew, and your brother, Harold, apparently, look enough alike that you didn't frighten them, but it's apparent that Eugene and Violet cling to each other for moral support instead of you or Drew. Right now, they are a little apprehensive about depending on anyone other than each other for fear they will lose someone else. Let them open the dialogue that will make things better and easier between you."

"You know, Linda, I like your kind of crazy. Thanks," Will said meaningfully.

"You're welcome. Now, you can help me figure out why I bought the building across the street."

Surprised, he looked at her askance. "You did *what?*"

"I forked over a lot of American dollars to purchase and begin construction on a dream. Now is that crazy or what?" Linda said wryly.

Will laughed at her deadpanned delivery. "I vote for '*or what.*' So, tell me why you bought it."

So, she did, sharing her dream of opening a school for dance. He was a good, active listener, she found. He didn't interrupt her with inane questions or put her off even when his phone signaled incoming text messages. He continued to talk with her. They sat with their heads together going over the preliminary renovation plans she showed to him on her iPad. Architects and structural engineers JaiHonnah Baylor and her cousin, Fiona Lizette Lowry, devised the layout in a relatively short period of time. JaiHonnah and Fiona were working on other aspects of the buildout including electrical, plumbing, and HVAC systems with Chuck's six brothers who were also in the building trades in Monroe County, Pennsylvania.

The electronics would be important because the students would all be working on iPads instead of paper textbooks. So, her Wi-Fi system had to be top of the line and hack-proof. Her Uncle Kenneth Alexander's company, CompuCorrect Global, a telecommunications and internet provider was designing the systems and Slade Richardson's company, Richardson Investigations and Security, was handling the installation of smart house technology. Richardson's provided her personal security service since she began to travel and perform, and they were the best in the business, bar none.

She told Will about the highlights of her plans. Her Uncle Gregory was not only handling the insurance coverage through his Wall Street firm, Compliant Trading and Investments, but also the accounting and financial aspects of her new business. Her uncle worked out the numbers so that all costs associated with participation in the school included the price of admission and tuition. For need-based students, her family established a not-for-profit foundation in her name, donations to which qualified as write-offs under federal tax laws. Using her connections in the entertainment industry, she would launch a full-blown campaign here and abroad to raise funds for students who would need financial assistance to attend the school.

The school's cafeteria would only stock healthy and nutritional food for breakfast, lunch, and dinner. Angelique, a Le Cordon Bleu certified chef, a former supermodel, and actress would determine the menu.

Her primary role was to find and hire teachers for both the academics and for each form of dance instruction she would offer. She knew she could tap both male and female dancers who had the ability to instruct different age groups. There would also be the novices who wanted to learn various forms of dance for exercise and proficiency. Ballroom dancing and competitions were very popular in the city. Then there were the professionals who would come to rent studio space and time for themselves or to work with private clients. Ideas were popping up like balls in a Lotto game.

"You seem to have everything covered," commented Will. He was fascinated with her and her very creative ideas for her future. She was very much like him when he left his comfort zone in baseball and chose to open Indulgences; a health and fitness industry entity he knew little to nothing about eight years ago. Thanks to Greg Alexander, his baseball earnings were well invested and turned a substantial profit sufficient to get the business off the ground. Now, with Greg's continued guidance, and the addition of another major investor, Nico Collins, a former NFL legend, the business was thriving with a steadily increasing clientele.

Also, Greg's suggestion about instituting a financial industry pro-am basketball tournament brought in both male and female big money members from Wall Street and professional athletes. Each team was made up of five men and five women and there were sixty teams who played on the five-court, round-robin tournament, simultaneously between 10:00 A.M. and 2:30 P.M. weekdays.

With her uncle's guidance, Will believed Linda would be equally successful and wanted to hear more. "Do you have plans for dinner tonight?" he spontaneously asked, surprising himself.

Momentarily she was stunned by the question. "No, as a matter of fact, I'm solo for the next few weeks. Uncle Gregory left for South Carolina early this morning."

"Then, would you be willing to have dinner with the children and me tonight? Maybe your presence will help bridge the gap I've been trying to close."

"Yes, I'd enjoy that. What time?"

"We generally eat at six. Would that work for you?"

"It would, yes."

"Great. If you'll let me have your phone, I'll put my contact info in it."

She passed it over to him.

"Well, well, well, isn't this cozy?" drawled Drew as he approached Linda and Will, malevolently eyeing Will.

Will vividly remembered their conversation about not having a relationship with the clientele outside of work. *Busted*, he thought, *but couldn't regret it.* It wasn't a date, *per se.* He asked Linda to dinner for purely platonic reasons. He had no ulterior motive, so he rose from his comfortable seat next to Linda and headed to their business offices to deal with his brother on other issues.

Once in the privacy of his office, Will turned to Drew studying him. "Where have you been? You didn't get the grocery orders in yesterday and you didn't order the extra sheets and towels for the spa. Then there is the matter of over-booking several of the hair salon operators, cosmetologists, and barbers. They are not happy about that."

"I delegated those tasks to others, to the section managers. If they didn't handle their responsibilities, it's not my fault."

"The buck stops here, Drew. They report to you and you are responsible for reporting to me. You don't leave your work for others to handle. Why weren't you here to start your shift on time this morning?"

"Damn, Will, I had a date last night and the woman in question wanted me to stay for breakfast. You act like this is some big deal," he flashed. "It's not like I'm dipping into the company pool the way you are with your pal's extra lady. At least my woman *de jour* isn't a member of Indulgences."

"Stop jumping to the wrong conclusions. Linda is coming to dinner to help us communicate better with Eugene and Violet. She's Gregory Alexander's niece, not his piece, so stop referring to her negatively."

"His niece? Well, hell, in that case, if you're not into her, she's on the market."

"Get real, Drew. She's a client and she's not that type of lady. Don't disrespect her."

"Me? Ha! I wouldn't think of it, but that doesn't mean I can't take her out for a good time."

"That's exactly what it does mean. We don't date employees or clients."

Will actually had no right to dictate to Drew who he could or could not date, but he drew the line at dating women connected to Indulgences. However, he selfishly hoped, if Drew asked her out, Linda would turn Drew down. He refused to question why he felt that way.

Chapter 4

Will didn't understand why he was so nervous. The children's rooms and Drew's room were immaculately clean as was his master suite because he checked each one twice. Not that he planned to take Linda on a tour of his bedroom. Drew and he agreed not to bring over-night dates here around the children. If they wanted to be alone with a woman, they generally went to her place or a hotel. He checked the common areas of his home several times assuring that all unnecessary things were put away. He had the cleaning company come in again today to make sure nothing was amiss.

When he and his brothers sold their parents' place in the heart of Harlem to a friend, Jackson Chase, they purchased this home. The house had six bedrooms and five and a half baths. It gave them another place to restart their lives with a clean slate away from the bad memories of their parents' drug lives and deaths.

The first floor was a traditionally-arranged space which would likely be the only area Linda would see. The new dining table was nicely dressed. The smell of good food coming from the warming drawers in the kitchen at the back of the house permeated the air. He ordered everything from Angelique's, including the table set up. He had help selecting what to serve from the chef herself; one of Linda's best friends. It was heavy on fresh vegetables and light on the starches. They had a choice of meat dishes and desserts. Angelique even had her sommelier select the wines to serve with each course and sparkling cider for the children.

He wasn't sure what music to play before or with the meal. He would have to rely on Drew for that. Lately, his brother played a lot of the music from the singing group known as Ivy. He imagined Linda would like that type of music, too. His brother was closer to Linda's age than he. Thanks to modern technology, a push of a button could provide a variety of sounds. Those were his thoughts when he heard the front door chimes.

Carefully, he looked around the spaces again before heading through the wide vestibule to the front door. He took a deep breath and let it out in a huff before opening it and there she was. Linda turned to wave to her security team who sat idling in their town car, but when she turned back to face him, his heart shuddered at the beauty of her smile.

They stood regarding each other for ponderous moments before Will had the presence of mind to ask her to come in. That's when he noticed she was carrying a dome-covered, gift-wrapped package.

"Wow, what do you have there?" he asked reaching for it while she took off her poncho-like wrap.

"Just a little somethin' somethin'," she teased, as she exchanged her wrap with him for the gift.

"You've certainly piqued my curiosity," he said hanging her wrap in his hall closet. It was so soft and lightweight, and it smelled of her special intoxicating scent.

"Good! Then I'm halfway to my goal. Are the children around?"

"They are, yes. Eugene and Violet are in their rooms doing homework, but they should be finished by now. They're looking forward to your visit." He led her into the living room before saying, "Have a seat. I'll get them."

While Will went to get the children, Linda set the gift on a coffee table and roamed the spacious living room. She could see the large dining room across the vestibule and sensed the spaces were designed and decorated by a professional. However, it didn't hold anything that looked or felt personal or related to a good memory. The furnishings were of very good quality, but sparse as if selected from an Architectural Digest magazine catalog. He and his brother were bachelors, after all, and from what she gathered about Will, he spent the majority of his time and energy at his facility. The place was perfect for him and Drew; comfortable and functional, but it held no warmth, energy or vitality.

In contrast, her uncle's converted fire station was beautifully designed by him and held tastefully decorated spaces that conjured up good memories and wonderful times spent with family, close friends, and warmth galore. Everywhere in his home, Gregory had sturdy furniture his great-grandfather, grandfather, father, and brother, Kenneth, built with their hands. Sofas, tables, chairs, cabinets, the works were slices of home and family.

She wanted to achieve the same feeling of safety, security, warmth, and comfort in the space she was designing for the first home she would have of her own.

Linda turned at the sound of feet on the grand staircase. The first face she saw was Drew's, who came forward taking her into his arms and, had she not turned her head fractionally, he would have kissed her on her mouth. As it was, he stood with his right arm possessively around her shoulders. To dislodge his grip, she stooped to greet the children. She didn't want to touch them unless or until they felt comfortable with the contact. So, she smiled and was delighted when both children smiled back at her.

"How's the homework going?" she asked them.

"It's okay. It's not that hard," said Eugene.

"How about you, Violet? Have you cracked the calculus code yet?" she teased.

"Nuh uh," she bashfully said with a little shake of her head, but her smile bloomed on her pretty face. Her hair was intricately designed in pretty cornrows with long, thick braids and cowrie shells at the tips. They set off a musical tone when she shook her head.

"No? Well, then I guess you're going to have three guesses each to figure out what's in here," Linda said moving out of the way and motioning toward the covered gift.

"Wow! Is it a palace like at Disney World?" Violet excitedly piped up.

"No, but close."

They continued to guess but couldn't figure it out. So, Linda had the children close their eyes while she lifted the cover to reveal a miniature town made of fresh fruit pieces under a dome similar to Edible Arrangements. There were strawberries; blueberries; raspberries; peaches; pineapple; red, purple, and green seedless grapes; orange slices and an array of other delectable pieces including white and dark chocolates.

Linda was pleased with the children's stunned expressions and the expression on Will's face. Drew seemed less enamored but was probably a little miffed from his inability to kiss her, she surmised. From the time spent with Drew, she sensed there was a bit of sibling rivalry or angst he felt toward Will. However, she didn't get the same vibe from Will toward Drew. Nevertheless, she watched as Will interacted with the children over her gift, pointing out different aspects of the town she said was called Goodwill.

"Where did you find this?" asked Will.

"I made it this afternoon," said Linda.

He looked at her in wonder. "You're kidding, right?"

"Nope," she said, laughing. "I actually made it at my uncle's place. Have you ever been there?"

"No, I haven't even though he's asked me several times to come. I never found or made the time."

"Then you don't know that he has a fresh fruit and vegetable hydroponics garden in his basement. I picked the fruit today."

"Unbelievable. You're very gifted and creative," offered Will.

"I can't take the credit. Before this, I lived with my parents and siblings on a working farm in rural Maryland. They operate a hydroponics facility and fishery on the farm, and my aunts, my father's sisters, taught my siblings and me to make these displays as gifts. With so many of us, Dad and Mom found lots of creative ways to keep us busy and entertained."

"Can you teach me?" piped up Violet.

"I certainly can anytime your uncle says it's okay with him."

The children turned and looked up at Will. He playfully put up both hands in mock surrender.

Warming to the idea, she suggested, "How about Saturday morning about ten o'clock?"

"I can make that work," Will agreed while checking his schedule on his phone for the date and time. "Drew doesn't have Saturday classes. You're scheduled to manage Indulgences that day, aren't you?" Will asked his brother.

"I am, so I guess Linda and I will have to pick another date and time when I can come to her place for a visit and private demonstration," Drew said and lasciviously grinned.

"Sure, you're welcome to come and bring Eugene and Violet anytime they are available," Linda parried.

Will breathed an easy sigh of relief. Linda was quick on her feet. He felt more confident she would be able to skillfully handle Drew. Though he didn't want to question why he felt possessive of her. He just was and he wasn't sure how to get over it or whether he wanted to.

Dinner was a roaring success, thought Will later after Linda left. He had to laugh to himself. Drew tried every trick in the book to draw Linda's attention to him to no avail. He even offered to take her home and was loath to discover she had a security team and car service to pick her up. It baffled Will as well. He knew Linda's celebrity probably made her a target, but a car service was usually all that was needed; not armed security. Yet, she had both and it appeared this was not a new occurrence. He didn't want to pry, but his curiosity was piqued.

This was new, the man thought as he watched Linda wave goodbye to the owner of Indulgences and two young children. He bought a membership in the high-end sports and fitness facility just because Linda was spending a lot of her time there when she wasn't touring the building across the street. He learned from the workmen that the former library building was being converted into a school and dance studio with a residence for the owner on the upper floors. He even got a look inside, particularly upstairs where she planned to live. He took his time going from floor to floor around the workmen because he knew Linda and her agent, Bill Chandler, were meeting with the executive producer of her next ballet, The Nutcracker on Broadway. She would take the leading role during the fall and winter theatre seasons.

Next, she was scheduled to do a week-long guest appearance in Holiday on Ice for a fundraiser to aid the World Children's Fund. This appearance was to be performed as a prelude to the Olympic trials. He wondered whether she would enter the Olympic Games again or go on tour as a figure skater at the beginning of next year.

For now, since she seemed to be settling in, he bought a condo on the same block where her school and residence would be located. He was having the space painted, the floors stripped, and ordering furniture before he moved in. He didn't have time to have his things shipped from Europe, and he wasn't sure he wanted to. She wasn't scheduled to move into her space for a while, and he had not yet found a casual way to make her acquaintance.

When she was alone at her uncle's home, an older woman and her grandsons were usually around visiting. The woman was Greg Alexander's housekeeper who lived in and managed a condo building Alexander owned up the block from his residence. Linda's uncle was also mentoring the housekeeper's grandsons. When the grandmother was out for an evening, her grandsons would stay at the house with Linda and Gregory. Apparently, the housekeeper was engaged to be married to a former Marine who happened to be the doorman and night watchman at Angelique's Restaurant.

Then, too, Angelique or any number of Linda's family and friends might show up and spend the night while her uncle was away. Getting close to her was getting more difficult and he had less time to accomplish his goals with regard to Linda.

Chapter 5

"Wow! This space is so large it should have its own zip code," Will commented the following weekend as he stood on the first level of Gregory's converted fire-station home. It was completely renovated inside and was comfortably furnished. He stood at the front windows and could see clear to the rear over a basketball-court-sized hardwood floor.

Eugene and Violet were taken away to explore by the housekeeper's, Mrs. Janie Joyner's grandsons, Keaton and Dejon Joyner. She was there to clean the house as she usually did on Saturday mornings whether Gregory was there or not. He was still in South Carolina, but Angelique spent most of her nights there in Gregory's home after she closed her restaurant at one o'clock in the morning. Angelique was on her way out when Will and his charges arrived.

Sometimes, Linda would wait for Angelique to come in and they would laugh and talk for hours, especially when they didn't have to be up early the next day. Although Linda was a few years older than Angelique, they were BFFs, enjoyed each other's company, and would often laze around in their PJs. As a talented chef and restauranteur, Angelique would often whip up something delicious for them to eat or they would cajole Mrs. Joyner into feeding them with her Caribbean island dishes.

Today, Mrs. Joyner made a manicotti, half-meat-and-half-cheese casserole, a loaf of crusty, onion-and-garlic bread, and a fresh, field-greens salad for Linda to serve for lunch with Will and the children. Shortly, after Mrs. Joyner completed her housekeeping duties, she would leave for her hair and nails appointments and then do the household grocery shopping for Gregory and for herself. Her grandsons would remain with Linda until she returned in the late afternoon to deliver the groceries and any clothing she picked up for Gregory from the dry cleaners.

Linda was anticipating the time she would get to spend alone with Will, getting to know him better. Beyond the handsome face and great physique, he interested her as no other man had. She liked how she felt around him and thoroughly enjoyed spending time with his nephew and niece. Her uncle was right. Will was a genuinely nice guy.

"How about we start the tour on the rooftop level?" she suggested.

"Sure, I didn't want to ask, but please, lead the way," he said. When she turned her back, he was hard-pressed to take his eyes off of her long legs in a pair of black leggings and bare feet. She wore a white loose-fitting man's tailored dress shirt over it with a snug T-shirt underneath. Her hair was down around her shoulders and he noticed, for the first time, how curly and thick it was. She usually wore it pinned up like a wrap around her head and out of her way whenever he saw her at his facility. Now it was shiny, loose, and perfectly framed her face.

He followed her onto an elevator that took them up to a glass-enclosed, rooftop deck. There was a swimming pool surrounded by real grass, trees, and flowering bushes. It was a spacious slice of a park-like setting with comfortable outdoor furniture, a kitchenette, and surround-sound video and audio system. Will listened as Linda explained that the glass enclosure was moveable and was closed for the season to allow the use of the pool during the colder months. She pointed out the solar panels used to provide energy to the residence, offsetting electric service use and costs from the power company and to heat the household water. There was also a rain-barrel system used to collect rainwater, filter it, and provide for its use in the hydroponics farm, laundry, and to flush toilets. She went on to explain that some of the water was diverted for further filtration to use for showers, baths, and a third filtration system for potable water used for cooking and drinking. The tile floor was heated, making the space comfortable on what was a cold day outside the enclosure. She described the innovations she planned to use in her mixed-use facility to offset the costs of utilities.

Next, they went down a flight of stairs to a game room across from Gregory's master bedroom suite. The children were there enjoying an array of activities and working model electric trains on tracks. Linda and Will left them there and went down another level to where eight bedrooms with en-suites, a kitchenette, and open lounge space were located. *The bedroom she used smelled of her; warm and exotic,* Will thought *and could imagine her sleeping in the king-sized bed with the mountain of pillows surrounding her.* The suite had a fairly large, religiously neat walk-around closet with a vast array of shoes and clothes. There was both a large, free-standing shower and double-wide whirlpool tub in the adjoining bathroom. Will fought to keep images of Linda wet and warm from the shower or bath out of his head.

They bypassed the main level that contained the kitchen, dining, living, media areas, and a restroom going straight to the ground level where Gregory parked a number of cars; some of which were vintage that he was restoring as birthday gifts for his nephews and nieces. Down a long hallway were doors leading into a room holding thousands of bottles of wine Gregory purchased from wine sellers worldwide. In another room were shelves holding barrels of home-made wine. Gregory enjoyed experimenting with making wines, jams and preserves. He was quite good at it.

However, across the hall was Gregory's hydroponics gardens. There was a wide array of healthy-looking fruits and vegetables growing on vines and stalks with the roots in troughs of running water under sun-bright lighting.

Will wandered through the expansive space amazed at what he saw. "You weren't kidding about this. He has everything here one could imagine. It looks like the Garden of Eden."

"Here, try this," she suggested breaking off a fat, juicy strawberry from a vine and holding it up to his lips to sample.

He held her hand in his with the fruit between her fingertips and sampled the treat. "Delicious," he said, his eyes riveted on hers.

Linda felt the earth move when Will's lips captured the strawberry from her fingertips. She rubbed her thumb across his bottom lip to capture an errant drop of juice. "Yes, it is, isn't it?" she said just above a whisper. "Would you like another?"

"I would, yes. I could eat a whole bushel full, but we'd better save it for the little people," he said purposefully using her reference to his nephew and niece. He didn't recognize the lower timber of his own voice.

Thankfully, the door opened, and the children trooped in, forcing him to let go of Linda's hand. He was dangerously close to sampling more fruit from her fingers and nibbling on her lips.

Linda took time to show Eugene and Violet around, giving them each a basket to collect the fruits and vegetables they wanted. When their baskets were full, Keaton and Dejon led the way, showing the indoor basketball court and exercise room before going upstairs. They went to a long, quartz-topped kitchen island and began to construct their village on thick Styrofoam pads. When completed, the kids wanted to go for a swim before lunch. Though the Joyner boys were excellent swimmers, Linda didn't want the children to be alone in the pool. With Will's consent, she found swimwear for her guests and donned one of her more demure, single-piece bathing suits.

The water was nice and warm in the rooftop pool. *Fortunately, Eugene and Violet were both good swimmers and were having the time of their lives,* Will thought. He had to admit, he was enjoying himself, too. This visit was a great departure from the staid weekend routine he established since the children came to live with him and Drew.

Although he did have an uncomfortable moment when Linda fed the strawberry to him. Given more time and privacy, he would have taken her up on her offer of more fruit or collected her in his arms and ravished her mouth. The light in her eyes and the smile on her lips did wonderfully strange things to all of his bodily systems. The simple swimsuit she wore wreaked havoc on him, too. He noticed the beautiful gold chain she wore around her neck that spelled FAMILY, but her body was a masterpiece from the top of her head to the bottom of her feet and took his attention away from the jewelry. She swam as if she was born in the ocean and enchanted his charges . . . and him.

After lunch, Linda dried Violet's hair and her own while the boys and Will cleared the table and loaded the dishwasher. Then the children went to the media room and curled up on the sofas to watch movies. Linda and Will sat on a divan in the living area before a picture window with a panoramic view of the East River and the Brooklyn and Manhattan Bridges.

"So, you're a native New Yorker?" Linda asked.

"Born and bred at 124th Street and Lenox Avenue across from Rice High School. It was a private, all-boys' Catholic school at one time. Closed now, but my father and all of the Hamilton brothers attended. My older brother, Harold, Eugene and Violet's father, lettered in basketball. I lettered in baseball, but Drew chose not to play a physical sport. He prefers shooting pool."

"Do you visit your old neighborhood anymore?"

"No," he said shrugging. "The property we lived in was in our family for several generations. From the turn of the century in fact. After my parents' deaths, we sold it to a friend of mine, Jackson Chase. He renovated it and converted it into four condos. He and his uncle lived in two of the condos and he leased the other two out. Since I was starting Indulgences, I purchased the place where we live now, and the three Hamilton brothers moved in. I don't have such great feelings about living in the heart of Harlem. My parents liked to party and ended up getting into the drug culture. Eventually, it killed them while I was away from home and still playing professionally. It's still hard to think of the old neighborhood without thinking about how drugs contributed to the destruction of so many families."

"I can't imagine how difficult it must have been to lose your parents after having them for so long. I lost my father while I was still very young and don't remember anything much about him. I only have pictures. I was about six years old when my biological mother and younger brother died in an auto accident we were all in. I was hospitalized for years, but then I was adopted. I lost my first adoptive father, Derrick Jackson suddenly, but you already know about that because you Googled me," she said, laughing.

"You're not going to let me live that down, are you?"

"Not on a bet, Pal," she teased.

He stretched out his long legs to pull his phone out of the pocket of his snug jeans and went through the process of Googling his name. He actually hadn't done it before and didn't bother to look at the resulting information on the screen before he handed his phone to her. "Now we're even," he boasted.

She laughed at him as he expected she would.

They continued to talk getting better acquainted and comfortable with each other. It wasn't hard to be in each other's company and both felt bereft when Mrs. Joyner returned. Linda wanted to take Eugene and Violet to see open-casting calls and auditions in preparation for the winter performance of The Nutcracker. She already planned to take Keaton and Dejon the following Saturday; the boys had been modeling for the past two years and were interested in expanding their repertoires with dance and acting. Will didn't even check his calendar and readily agreed to meet her for the outing. Linda was surprised and pleased when both Eugene and Violet hugged her upon leaving.

Will wanted his hands on her, too, but cautiously refrained for fear he would take it too far and not let her go.

He saw when the housekeeper, Mrs. Joyner, returned in a taxicab with groceries and made a note of it in his iPad. He also noted when Will Hamilton and the two young children he learned were Hamilton's orphaned nephew and niece, drove away right past him. The Joyners were still in the house with Linda and, apparently, were staying for dinner. It was getting late, he was hungry, tired, and needed a restroom break. He had been sitting in the car down the block most of the day watching for an opportunity to be with her. However, this was the type of neighborhood where people noticed such things and reported it to the police. Most of the homes and businesses on this street had security cameras. The Alexander home, a converted fire station, was a veritable fortress. He had casually strolled past it several times but couldn't afford to be considered a thief casing the joint.

He pulled out of his precious parking spot, which had an unobstructed view of Gregory Alexander's home, and drove away disappointed that again he failed in his goals regarding Linda.

Chapter 6

Drew noticed it was nearing one o'clock in the afternoon and Linda the Luscious, as he liked to privately call her, hadn't come in that day for her usual appointments. She was fairly conscientious about her workout sessions and he could set his watch by her appearance. However, he happened to be at the front desk that morning when he saw her enter the building under construction across the street. According to the clerks on lobby duty, they hadn't seen Linda leave. She was such a beauty, she was hard to miss. So, it was likely she was still inside the building.

He knew what she liked to have for lunch and had the café supervisor prepare a picnic basket for two. He checked to make sure his brother was booked solid with business meetings for the next few hours before he left the building and crossed the street. Workers were on every floor of the building under renovation, taking a break to have lunch. He asked several guys where he could find Linda and was directed upstairs. Carrying the picnic sack, he took the elevator up to the top floor. When the doors opened, there were workers there, too, but so was Linda with the super-model Angelique and two other raving beauties.

He salivated over the array of beautiful women but zeroed in on Linda. "Ladies," he announced around what he believed to be an ingratiating smile.

"Hello, Drew," Linda said tamping down the urge to smirk. "Were you looking for me?"

"I was, yes, however, I didn't know you were surrounded by the cream of the crop."

This time she did smirk. "Drew Hamilton, this is JaiHonnah Baylor and Fiona Lizette Lowry, my architects and interior designers, and my friend, Angelique Menendez-Gaza. Drew is the brother of Will Hamilton, owner and operator of Indulgences."

"Ah," intoned Angelique. "I thought you resembled him. I often see him at his facility. I have a membership there."

"Yes," Drew said annoyed yet again that the beautiful women sought Will out and not him. As many times as she was in and out of the facility, she didn't even recognize him. "I know."

Linda sensed his irritation, for what, she didn't know. Through a yawning silence, she asked, "What do you need to see me about?"

"I, uh, brought a picnic lunch."

"Oh," she said, perplexed. "Did Will send it? When I spoke with him earlier, I told him I have lunch plans today."

Now he was considered Will's delivery boy. Nonplussed, Drew said, "He must have forgotten. You know men of his advanced age become forgetful."

Linda laughed for form, but she knew Will could not have forgotten because she asked him whether he wanted to join them for lunch. He said he did but couldn't because of his heavy schedule of meetings that day. He suggested they have dinner out tonight instead. She agreed and they settled on a time and place. Nevertheless, she bypassed the uncomfortable moment with Drew and thanked him for bringing the lunch for her. Shortly thereafter, Drew said his farewells and beat a hasty retreat.

"Well," said Angelique coyly, "we know what that was about. Linda, my friend, I think you have a not-so-secret admirer."

"He's cute," commented Fiona Lizette, with tongue planted firmly in cheek.

"Yes, he is," said Angelique, "but his brother, Will, is drop-dead gorgeous."

"As you were saying, JaiHonnah," Linda deadpanned talking over her friend's comment. "If I want to put my bedroom up here on this rooftop level, it's doable, right?"

"It is, yes. You can have an operable, robotic wall of windows facing in this direction," JaiHonnah said pointing toward the south, "and have your solarium on an east-west axis."

"That way," added Fiona Lizette, "you'll have the benefit of a sunny, southern exposure year-round for a small hydroponics garden and park-like environment you want. Your windows will slide out of the way, and you'll have open-air access to the entire deck. We'll triple glaze your front windows against the harsh, cold north and west winds. You don't have the space Gregory has for his rooftop swimming pool, but JaiHonnah and I believe we can fit a six-foot deep, thirty-foot long, and five-foot-wide exercise pool against that wall."

"We'll landscape grass, small trees, and shrubs over there. You'll be able to fit outdoor lounge chairs, a chaise, and other furniture on this side of the pool, but not on the side against the wall. Your garden could be squeezed in on that side, but you'll only have limited access to it."

"Thanks, I think that should work. Just so I can get my exercise routine in every day and have a selection of fresh fruits and vegetables available."

"Well, you do have membership in a fitness center right across the street that's open twenty-four seven," offered Angelique. "They have an Olympic sized pool on the lower level. I'm sure Drew would be willing to show you the way."

"A lot more, too," teased Fiona Lizette.

"Uh, huh," retorted Linda, but she didn't let on that she was more interested in Will Hamilton than Drew.

"Unlike Greg's pool, yours will be only for your exclusive use . . . or anyone you choose to invite into your boudoir," said JaiHonnah with a gleam in her eyes. "Your private elevator will go to this level, but the other two elevators will only provide access to the school and studio spaces on the lower levels. Because of the depth of the pool, we shortened the space available for the guest bedrooms and baths directly below this rooftop level. However, your decision to make this rooftop serve as your master retreat allowed for more generous guest room spaces below. We were able to fit in the open stairwell you requested from the common areas of your residence. I'm glad you agreed to let us install soundproofing and electronics on all four sides of the building. For security purposes, you wouldn't want your neighbors to be able to drill directly into your building. This way, an alarm will sound if anyone tries to access your space from any direction or any floor."

Fiona Lizette picked up the conversation. "With the robotic walls and windows everything will tuck away nicely, and you'll have a completely open-floor space except for the powder room. We'll install your plumbing and cooking needs on the back wall with extra insulation and a little balcony off the back overlooking the courtyard. With a window over the sink, you'll get nice natural light from that southern exposure, too."

"JaiHonnah, you and Fiona Lizette have done an awesome job to accommodate all of my requests. I really appreciate it."

"Your design suggestions were well thought out and innovative," commented JaiHonnah. "It was easy to work with. We didn't have to do a lot to tweak the preliminary plans. The convertible spaces for the classrooms and studios work wonderfully into the final scheme. Now that the demolition phase is complete and all of the wall cavities are open, we can begin installing the utilities. The new staircases are being manufactured, but I don't want them installed until the project is near completion. The old elevators will also stay in place for a while to carry construction material and supplies up and down. However, your new, private elevator will be installed before the walls are closed up."

"You're ahead of schedule, it seems," said Linda, pleased.

"We are, yes," said Fiona. "Anytime we can throw these many hands at a task, the better. Your budget allowed us to bring more of our crews up to work with your Montgomery uncles from Pennsylvania and work in twelve-hour shifts. Added to the fact you knew what you wanted and didn't delay the process, we were off to a great start."

"The only thing that may slow us down is getting the city inspectors in to approve each step and stage. Once we're able to close in the utilities, that problem pretty much goes away," said JaiHonnah. "Then it's a sprint to the Occupancy Permit."

They started moving toward the open staircase and noticed a man moving quickly down the stairs ahead of them. *From behind, he didn't look like any of the workmen and he wasn't dressed as an inspector,* thought Linda. They hadn't heard anyone moving around other than the workmen with their hammering and buzz saws after they finished their lunches. There were always looky-lous, but it made Linda decidedly uncomfortable to know someone who didn't belong there was roaming around her property. She pressed her hand against the gold chain around her neck that read **FAMILY** to ensure it was still there if she needed it.

She was cautioned enough by her security team to trust her instincts. Her family was fervent about personal safety and security. It was only a few years earlier when a group of wealthy criminals participated in a human trafficking ring. Angelique was one of the people targeted for abduction. They got close and thought they had her, but had accidentally kidnapped her friend, Emery Arden, another supermodel and BFF instead. Fortunately, the authorities were onto the criminals and Arden was rescued almost immediately. The same thing happened to her cousin Whitney, but she, too, was rescued. There were still dangerous people out there, so she knew not to overlook even the slightest incident. She would report the occurrence to her security detail and have someone posted to the front and back entrances of the property for the duration. Baylor and Baylor's employees carried company identification. Her uncles did, too. IDs would have to be checked every time someone attempted to enter the building.

As they departed the property and got into the waiting limo on their way to lunch, Linda took her phone from her pocket and called in her concerns.

Well, that was uncomfortably close, thought the man. When he, quite by accident, saw Linda entering her building, he was down the block about to check on the progress of his own space. The painting was done in his unit. Only sanding the floors and applying several coats of polyurethane remained to be completed before he could move in. The furniture delivery was scheduled for the following week. He didn't need a lot; just a place to rest and his computer workstations.

For the present, he was making do with a few laptops, but he needed his full array of computer monitors and network connections. He had projects to start or complete, but his side task of hacking into Linda's computer had failed. Her firewall was the strongest he'd ever encountered. Each time he attempted to gain access, traps were set to capture and follow his trail. He had to be quicker to cover his tracks and back out of danger.

He wasn't as swift as he used to be, but he still had the skill. However, it was rare he would come up against someone more skillful than him. He had to be more careful in the future or his plans involving Linda would be discovered. He couldn't afford for that to happen.

Chapter 7

On Saturday morning at six, Will and the children met Linda, Dejon, and Keaton at the front of Rockefeller Center. The air had a little, unexpected chill for early spring, but the sun was out. They were warmly attired in sweats and carried what looked like heavy duffle bags over their shoulders. Eugene and Violet were so excited they ran forward to hug Linda. She greeted them just as enthusiastically before she stood and regarded Will.

"I'll take one of those hugs, too," he said grinning.

"I have several to spare," she said easily going up on her toes to accept his hug. He felt the smile on her lips as she kissed his cheek.

Sticking her arm through his, she said to all, "Let's go this way," and off they went to a side entrance where uniformed guards stood keeping a small crowd at bay.

"*There she is!*" shouted someone in the crowd. "*There's Linda Lewis!*"

Linda smiled and waved, but ensured the children and Will were protected while she stopped along the rope line to sign autographs, pose for pictures, and answer questions. One person shouted, asking whether Will was her husband and the children theirs. Linda didn't have to respond as someone else in the crowd shouted that she was not married, and Will Hamilton was a baseball icon. That bit of information brought on applause. She shook hands briefly with everyone who reached for her and then headed for the stage door being held open for her by one of the uniformed guards.

"Good morning, Ms. Lewis," her assistant draper, Felix Jones, greeted just inside the stage door.

"Mr. Jones," she acknowledged. "This is Will, Eugene, and Violet Hamilton. Please take care of them."

"Certainly," he said nodding to Will, then to Keaton and Dejon, he said, "You're in room eighteen."

"Okay," said the boys in unison and split off in a different direction while Mr. Jones continued to lead her with Will and the children to her dressing room.

Backstage was chaotic with people everywhere. Linda noted Eugene and Violet's eyes were wide as they turned from side to side trying to capture all the excitement. That would never happen. In all of her years since the age of nine, she still felt the thrill each and every time she entered the theatre as a performer. However, she enjoyed seeing the excitement on the faces of those who experienced it for the first time.

Mr. Jones led them to a dressing room that bore her name on the door. She knew Security would have already swept the room and the area before her arrival. They were very unobtrusive which made her feel secure and free to move about unafraid. Recently, Richardson used miniature drones to track her or protect the space she would inhabit.

"Mr. Maxton will be with you momentarily. He's retrieving your tutus," he said opening the door to her dressing room.

"Thank you, Mr. Jones," she said upon entering and ushering in Will and the children. "You can hang your coats in the closet and have a seat," she offered.

The room was fairly large, cold, and smelled of greasepaint, thought Will surveying the space. A full-length, three-way mirror stood against one wall next to an open door that appeared to be a bathroom. A dressing table with drawers on both sides stood unusually tall, its surface covered with pretty pots and jars of various sizes, shapes, and colors. Linda sat on the bare hardwood floor, her long, strong, shapely legs stretched out to her sides, feet and toes flexing. She dug into her duffle sharing its contents with Eugene and Violet who tried to mimic Linda's leg stretches.

Will marveled at her ability to stretch out as if boneless, arms extended to her sides while curving her back until the top of her head touched the floor behind her. Then using only her abs, she leaned forward to achieve the same feat with her upper body strength to maneuver into position. She talked with the children as she went through what must be a routine for her to limber her muscles using the floor exercises. Within a few moments, she rotated her upper body sweeping the floor in a circular motion with her arms still outstretched from her sides. His arms ached just from watching her hold that position.

"Why do you have so many pairs of pink ballet slippers?" asked Violet.

"Ah, they are called pointe shoes. I may change them as much as ten to fifteen times during a performance, but more often during rehearsals," she said picking out several pairs. "Do you feel how stiff they are?" she asked handing a pair to each child. "This is the most important part of my costume. So, I have them custom made to fit my feet every few months. If my shoes aren't right, I can't give the best performance. I think I have fifty pairs in my duffle and many more at home." She took a needle and baby pink thread from a case and began to sew the ribbons onto the shoes. Then she tried on the pointe shoes lacing the wide pink ribbons around her strong ankles and lower legs.

Each step and stage was precise, Will noted until she was finished with her floor routine, and then she stood to use the balance barre affixed to a wall to the right before a mirror. As she proceeded through dance positions, she identified each one for the children, and again they attempted to mimic her moves. She took time to watch the children go through the simple routine balancing front, back, and to the side with one leg and then turning to repeat the same exercise with the other leg. She only corrected their stances when necessary. Then she taught them a little more using the French pronunciation for each pose or movement. As they mastered each phase, she upped the tempo and changed up the movements as they followed her.

She was enjoying herself, Will realized. She was working her routine but enjoying teaching as she worked. She stood at the end of the balance barre instructing and praising them for their efforts. Indeed, the children were moving through each step and stage improving a little more each time.

"Demi *Plie* in first position, with your arm out to second," she instructed. "Keep your back straight. Now bend your knees out to the side, keeping them in line with your feet. Very good! Now, *Tendu* front slowly sliding your foot out from third position until just your pointed toes are in contact with the floor. Then return your foot to third. Excellent! *Dégagé* front. This movement is rather like the *Tendus* you've just practiced. The difference is, instead of keeping your pointed foot in contact with the floor, this time you will lift your pointed foot off the floor by a few inches. Yes! Yes! Perfect!" Linda gleefully said as the children mimicked her movements.

The serious expressions on Eugene and Violet's faces were enhanced by the light Will saw in their eyes at Linda's enthusiastic praise. Indeed, from what Will saw, they executed each position with little or no instruction. In the last twenty minutes, the children's progress was notable. He understood why she requested they wear sweats and thick sox instead of jeans. It was to keep their muscles warm so they could stretch comfortably. It was a little embarrassing having to explain to Violet why he had to purchase a jock strap for Eugene to wear when Violet asked what it was for. He wasn't sure he got it right. However, the children were enjoying this outing as much as Linda. He decided to add dance to their plans for Eugene's and Violet's summer vacation after they returned from visiting their great-grandparents. If they did well in the dance school's environment, he'd consider letting them attend for the full year.

"Okay, now the *Grande Battement* front, side, and back. Now switch to your left and repeat. This move is taking the *Dégagé* to the next level. You're going to be doing a slow kick up to roughly hip height, keeping your leg perfectly straight out in front of you, Eugene. That's right! Nicely done! Keep everything apart from your working leg perfectly still and your back straight," Linda cautioned as she performed the move and the children followed. "Come on, get that leg up a little higher and stretch those butt muscles," she encouraged.

"That's hard," said Eugene, but he was smiling when he said it.

"Stick with me, kid, and you'll be able to do this," she said effortlessly curling her long left leg up over her shoulder until the sole of her foot rested at the back of her head.

Will forced a purely masculine moan into a cough. Linda was so damn limber his imagination morphed into scenes to be repeated in the privacy of a bedroom. When she looked at him with a little Mona Lisa smile, he knew she had performed that last little maneuver to get a reaction out of him. Oh, yeah, she knew exactly what she was doing to him because she handed a bottle of water to him and a towel to mop his face of the sweat accumulating there in the cold, dressing room environment.

A knock at the door and it opened to reveal a tall, svelte middle-aged man and the assistant dresser, Mr. Jones, who wheeled in a rack of costume tutus.

"Mr. Maxton," Linda acknowledged and then introduced him to her guests.

"Let's see what we have here," he said as Linda slipped out of her sweats revealing a full-body, black, leotard suit with the feet cut out with stirrups, but the rest molding her body like seal skin. He pulled a cloth tape from around his neck and began to measure Linda's body. She stood with arms extended. "You've lost inches," Mr. Maxton said, seemingly annoyed. Linda said nothing, simply holding her position as if a manikin. "Number two," Mr. Maxton said causing the assistant draper to scramble among the rack of tutus for the right size.

"We only have Number three, Mr. Maxton," the assistant said tentatively.

Mr. Maxton huffed and rapidly snapped his fingers.

The draper handed over the costume and waited while Mr. Maxton fitted it on Linda, inside out then pinched and pleated until the tutu fit snugly to her body. Shortly, he and his assistant disappeared out the door.

"What's his major maladjustment?" asked Will.

Linda cut her eyes at the children who were entertaining themselves by going through the routines she taught them. Then she maneuvered close enough to whisper, "I have no real proof, because he's never verbalized it, but I think he's old school. He's not pleased that I'm not blue-eyed, and blond, yet he uses his seniority to demand to be my draper for any performance I have here in this theatre."

"Then he should seriously get over himself."

Linda merely shrugged, sat on the floor to remove her pointe shoes, and began to tape her toes.

"Why are you doing that?" asked Violet.

"Taping my toes prevents me from getting blisters. My feet will sweat during practice and rub against my shoes, creating friction. I wrap this cloth around them and use lamb's wool to pad my shoes. After long hours, my feet may become uncomfortable. There are twenty-one different performances in The Nutcracker and many wardrobe changes. I change my shoes each time."

"Wow! That's a lot!" exclaimed Eugene. "Do the boys have to do it, too?"

"They don't generally wear pointe shoes," she said chuckling. "They wear ballet or boot slippers.

"Uncle Will showed us videos of you when you were a little girl and won a silver medal at the winter Olympics for ice skating. You were wearing red boots and spinning really fast."

"Ah, yes, I danced the ballet 'Firebird' for my win. It's a ballet that's difficult to dance but it's harder to translate for figure skating. At the time, I was excited to try, and it worked. It's different when I have to carry around five to ten pair of ice skates versus different pointe shoes. Then the boots and blades are much heavier on my feet, so I have to compensate for that when I dance on ice versus when I dance on my pointe shoes."

Just then, Mr. Maxton returned and fitted the altered costume on Linda's body.

"Why do you have to have so many costumes to practice in?" asked Eugene.

Linda was surprised when Mr. Maxton answered. "The dancers sweat and the costumes can loosen when damp, stretch and chafe the skin with increased friction. Then the male dancers' hands have natural oils that rub off on the costumes when they lift a ballerina. They use powder to keep their hands dry. It could be dangerous if the costume moves too much and the male can't hold on. So, the costume has to be snug to minimize the amount of movement and friction. As a prima ballerina, Ms. Lewis is lifted many times during a performance. If her costume is too damp, I require that she change it for a dry one between acts. It's necessary to alter all of her costumes particularly when she shrinks an entire dress size. The way she performs she may lose another dress size with her robust performances." Seemingly pleased with the altered fit, he nodded his approval. "The stage director would like a word," said Mr. Maxton before opening the door and leading Linda and her guests out.

People in the crowded hallway nodded and spoke to Linda seemingly in awe of her, Will noted, as they traveled to a larger venue where applause greeted her arrival. Obviously, she was a member of the elite dance royalty. However, no one approached except a man wearing a headset who began an animated conversation with Linda. When finished, Linda closed her eyes and began to walk the stage area.

"What is she doing?" asked Violet.

"She's getting her bearings on the stage floor," whispered the assistant draper. "Sometimes she has to move very quickly, and she must maintain her spatial recognition at all times. If she doesn't, she could end up spinning off the stage into the orchestra pit. So, she walks the space with her eyes closed to judge where she is every minute she's on stage."

When she finished, she executed a few more exercises before the music started, and one-by-one the male dancers were introduced. They practiced for a few moments before they began to dance different segments of the ballet that called for Linda to be lifted or carried. By the tenth male introduced, Will got the impression the men were auditioning for the part of her partner. Linda was given no coaching, but the male dancers were. They had to lift her as if she were weightless. He could see the nervousness on some of the men's faces. Some turned their backs or looked at the floor, but were in constant motion while awaiting a chance to dance with her. Others practiced as the music played and intently watched each move.

When the stage manager called for a ten-minute break to check the lighting, Linda came directly to where he and the children were waiting on the sidelines. Violet and Eugene enthusiastically greeted Linda but kept their eyes on the male dancers who took advantage of the opportunity to practice on the central stage area.

The assistant draper was immediately there with a towel and bottled water.

"How are you holding up?" Linda asked smiling up at Will.

Close to her, he caught the faint scent of her early morning shower gel and sweat. "You're amazing," he said smiling down at her.

She laughed. "That was not quite the question I asked, but I'll take it nonetheless."

"I think it's one of the most monumental days I've ever had. I know Eugene and Violet feel the same way. Look at them. They're trying to mimic the steps the male dancers are doing."

"I am particularly glad that you're not bored . . ." she said trailing off as a camera crew approached shining a light in her eyes.

"Well, fancy meeting you here?" a woman's voice purred behind the bright lights.

Linda had to put a hand up to shield the light from her eyes in order to see who the speaker was. When she did, she noticed the attractive woman was speaking to Will and not her.

"Ms. Jance," the stage manager said, annoyed. "I asked that you not move your cameras around the area. Your lights are distorting our stage lighting and distracting our performers. Please turn the camera lights off or I'll have to ask you and your camera crew to leave."

The woman, who Linda now recognized as a local television station reporter, Jolie Jance, made a slashing motion across her throat and the cameras lights were immediately extinguished. The silence between them was enormous until Will made the introductions.

"Jolie Jance, I have the honor to present the world-renowned, prima ballerina, Ms. Linda Lewis."

"Yes, Will and I had the privilege of seeing your performance in Swan Lake."

"Ah, yes, he mentioned he had escorted someone to one of my performances. It's nice of you to come."

"I've been a patron of dance for many years. I'd like to do an in-depth interview with you."

"Are you familiar with Bill Chandler?"

"The fashion model, actor, and lawyer, yes, of course. Who isn't?"

"Good," Linda said while noting the signal to return to the stage. She nodded her acknowledgment to the stage manager and then started backing away from Will and Jolie Jance. "If you'll contact his office, he'll make the appropriate arrangements. It was a pleasure to meet you," she said with a significant look into Will's eyes as she moved further and further from his side.

Will watched her go as if she were deserting the field of battle. Indeed, she was when Jolie stepped into his line of vision.

"Charming *young* woman," Jolie said significantly.

"She is, yes," he answered.

"Known her long?"

He shrugged. "A while."

"Is that why you didn't want to wait for her autograph the night we went to the theatre? You've been seeing her while we were together."

"No, I didn't know her then. As I recall, you were the one who chose not to wait because there were too many people and it was cold outside."

"Actually, I was anxious to get you into my bed that night." She stepped closer and said with a lowered voice, "I'm keen to have you in my bed again. Why can't we make that happen tonight?"

"I'm unavailable, Jolie, and you know the reasons for it."

She looked over at Eugene and Violet. "Yes, I see. You still insist on keeping those children with you instead of putting them in a boarding school, as I suggested. I was at one of the most exclusive boarding schools in Switzerland from the age of five years old. It has done wonders for my social and professional life. I met people who will one day be world leaders."

"I thank you for the suggestion, but Eugene and Violet are my family and becoming my life. I don't want to part with them."

"So, you're sleeping with a baby you want to make a mama?"

He narrowed his eyes at her. "This from the woman who wants an interview? I should think you can behave with more class than that."

"I don't give a damn when she stands between me and something I want."

"Something you can't have, Jolie, so catch a clue. It has nothing to do with Linda Lewis. It's about your aversion to the change in my life. I wasn't a parent when we met. Now, I am and nothing this side of heaven or hell is going to change that. Stick a fork in it and consider it done."

Jolie's face contorted in anger before she turned and strode away. Will gave no more attention to her departure and returned to watching the audition. Linda was being lifted above a man's head and held up with one arm.

From across the stage, the man watched what appeared to be a contentious exchange between Will Hamilton and the reporter, Jolie Jance, before she left his presence in a huff. He had to laugh to himself and turn his face away when she strode away within a few feet of him. Jolie had been coming on to him since he joined Indulgences. They had been out a few times. Often, he found her annoying with her incessant questions about him and his business. However, his thoughts were not far from the fact he actually shook Linda's hand on the rope line outside the stage door. Quickly he found a connection of a connection or two or three times removed to help him gain entrance into the theatre during the open casting call.

Now he would be able to be on site whenever Linda was there to practice. She was not scheduled to start initial rehearsals with the over one-hundred-twenty performers until mid-July. Then, there would be the daily rehearsals beginning sixty days before opening night.

Of course, Linda danced in The Nutcracker many times as a principal performer, so there wasn't anything she didn't already know about the role she would perform. This would be the first time he was able to get this close to her during auditions. He carefully watched as she narrowed the field of men who would be her final choices as partners and who would understudy the role. Even in this informal setting, he held her skill and ability in awe.

Chapter 8

"Linda, you look lovely," said Will as he took her hand and escorted her from her chauffeured town car through the station to the waiting train. Indeed, she was a beautiful woman . . . and young, he reminded himself. However, clad in the simple, black, hip-hugging dress that fit her like liquid asphalt and the man-killer, stiletto ankle boots on those long, perfectly shaped legs, she looked like a walking wet dream come true. Her hair was down and a mass of thick, shiny curls around her face.

He fought hard to keep his touch impersonal and his eyes on her face and not let them drop to the deep décolletage which was only the beginning of her feminine assets. Her breasts were high on her rib cage, the perfect shape, and about the size of a pair of grapefruit. He recalled she must have tied down her breasts when she performed because she seemed almost flat-chested in costume. For a woman her size, he believed she'd fit perfectly in his arms.

Linda smiled at Will's compliment. The light in his eyes was exactly the effect she was striving for. Adept at using makeup to the best advantage, she worked hard to keep her enhancements to a minimum, but appropriate for this occasion. The scent she chose was nicely understated but memorable.

She was enjoying the time they were able to spend together. They always shared lively and interesting conversations. Not having traveled extensively outside of the United States, he encouraged her to talk about her many roles and places around the world where she performed. He had great stories about his time playing in the major leagues and simultaneously building his business. She enjoyed him most when he shared details about himself with her; things he never told anyone else.

Over the past couple of months, they were able to find time to share a meal a couple of times a week, usually with Drew, Eugene, and Violet at his home if on a school night and on weekends without Drew at her uncle's home. The children got a big kick out of visiting with her, Dejon, and Keaton, talking about dance, swimming in her uncle's pool, playing games in his game room, and watching movies in his media room.

Tonight, she and Will were on their own; out for a mystery theatre and dinner train ride from the city north into the countryside. During the first leg of the trip, they dined on delicious foods and sampled different wines. After the train reached its destination, they disembarked and, for an hour and a half, visited the winery which provided the wines they sampled while the train turned around in preparation for the return trip to the city. She purchased several cases of assorted wines and arranged to have them shipped. Her Uncle Gregory was a connoisseur and collector, so she often sent wines from places where she performed or visited. On the return leg of the trip, they were treated to an array of desserts and coffee while they watched or participated in an interactive murder mystery theatre play performed by the waitstaff who served the meal on the trip up to the winery.

It was a unique and delightful evening, and Linda was charmed when Will kissed her cheek and hugged her before exiting her town car at his front door. She had great dreams about Will that night. What she didn't know was that Will had great dreams of his own that same night about her.

During the spring, her Uncle Gregory coached the Joyner brothers' baseball team which was right up Will's alley. Will offered to become an assistant coach, and Gregory willingly accepted. Will paid for new baseball uniforms and equipment with the Indulgences logo over the breast pocket. New shoes and caps came with the uniforms and new equipment. Each kid would get to keep the gloves, bats, and balls after the season was over. So, every Saturday morning they would leave

Gregory's home after breakfast for the ten-minute walk to Battery Park, a twenty-five-acre green space, bikeway, and promenade where the games were held. After each game, they, with the baseball team, would walk to a neighborhood restaurant where Gregory would always spring for lunch for everyone.

Today, Will was sitting with Gregory talking at a table in Harry and Mike's; a restaurant with games galore, while Linda and Angelique treated the Joyner brothers and the Hamilton kids to an assortment of game machines while they waited for their lunches to be served. Greg and Will's baseball team was victorious that day and whether win, lose or draw, Greg treated his team to lunch at a different restaurant each time. Usually, the parents would also come along to join in the celebration. Today was no different. Parents were there enjoying themselves, too.

"Greg," said Will when they were relatively alone at the table, "I've been seeing Linda while you were away. I would like to know how you feel about it."

"I'm fine with it as long as you treat her with respect. I have no reason to think you wouldn't. However, I don't want her hurt in any way."

Will nodded his understanding. "I don't know where the relationship might go, but for now we're becoming good friends."

"Are you involved with anyone else on an intimate basis?" Gregory asked.

"No, not now. Earlier this year I was involved with Jolie Jance, but that ended a bit less than amicably."

"Jolie Jance, the television news reporter? What happened?"

"We were involved for about six months before my brother and sister-in-law died. She didn't care for the sudden appearance of my nephew and niece in my life or children in general. Her ultimatum was that I had to put them in a boarding school somewhere outside the area or it was over between us." He shrugged. "I chose Option Two. She's tried to rekindle the relationship, but I'm not open to renewing old acquaintances.

"I like Linda," he continued, "and I'd be lying if I said I didn't want to explore an intimate relationship with her, but I don't believe we're anywhere near that point at this time."

"Obviously, you know I love my niece, but more importantly I respect her. She began to live with me when she entered Julliard, and we are great friends. I trust her and her judgment. She has a very good head on her shoulders and she's thoughtful, open, and honest to a fault. I hope you can gauge your ground where she's concerned."

"You're right. If I don't read Linda's signals correctly, she could be the one to hurt me."

"Linda had a lot of life's experiences because she's travelled extensively since she was a pre-teen, but, to my knowledge, my niece has never been seriously involved with anyone. She hasn't had much time to develop a relationship because she's always busy pursuing her career. Just as we did when we were young athletes, she gets into a zone outside of time and space where nothing penetrates except her craft. As you probably know, she's going to start training soon for her next role and she'll likely withdraw a bit as a result. Linda's a perfectionist and lives in and breathes through her art until the final performance."

"I appreciate you for discussing her with me. Since the Joyner boys were contracted to perform in The Nutcracker, Eugene, Violet, and I have accompanied her to the theatre several times. I've spent quality time with her and recognize how special…and how young she is."

Gregory laughed. "I've learned from my father and the wisdom of my ancestors that age is nothing but a number. Although I realized I was in love with Angelique for a very long time, I denied my interest in her for years because of our age differences and substituted short-term relations with women as a result. Now that Angelique and I are engaged, we're holding off having sex until after the wedding. Angelique and Linda are best friends and about the same age, just as you and I are. I can predict you'll probably experience some tough times ahead, my friend."

Will smiled nodding in agreement and understanding. "I've already had to take a few cold showers after being around Linda."

"Yeah, no, that doesn't usually work for me with Angelique," Gregory said laughing.

"Me either," said Will while joining Gregory in laughter.

"I wonder what they're laughing about," questioned Angelique.

Linda turned her head momentarily to observe her Uncle Greg and Will at a table in the restaurant before she resumed play on the pinball machine, racking up the points. "Probably some ribald joke one of them came up with."

"Greg usually doesn't joke about sex," Angelique said as she turned to watch Linda play. "He avoids the subject all together around me. I decided it's my premarital duty to get him torqued up at every opportunity," she mischievously grinned. "The way Will Hamilton looks at you, I think he's torqued pretty tight, too."

Linda shrugged. "If he is, he hasn't done anything about it."

"Nothing?" Angelique asked, surprised.

"He took me on this wonderfully romantic train ride last week. I pulled out all the stops and gave him the green-light-go signal. At the end of the evening, he kissed me on the cheek and hugged me."

"Bummer," Angelique sympathized.

"Yeah, tell me," Linda agreed, frustrated.

"He touches you a lot. Like he did when we were walking here from the ballfield. He put his arm around your shoulders."

"Yeah, so does Uncle Greg," Linda deadpanned.

"Still, I think Will is interested in you," Angelique said, nodding in the affirmative.

"Maybe I'm not his type or he's involved with someone else. He, apparently, dated or is dating Jolie Jance, the television news reporter," Linda surmised.

"Scratch that," Angelique denied with a shake of her head. "I don't see him as the type of man who would date more than one woman at a time."

"Maybe he doesn't consider what we do as dating. He could see us as just friends."

Angelique shrugged. "Or it could be the age thing. Like Gregory, Will is about eight years your senior. Greg was hung up over that issue between us and he still is. He delayed our wedding for two years because he wanted to give me time to decide whether I wanted to be married to him for the rest of my life. It was totally unnecessary because I've been in love with him since before I strapped on my first training bra."

"How well I know," Linda said and grinned in agreement. "You talked about no one else since the day you met him. I think we were about nine or ten years old, but that's about the time you became a high fashion model. Your career went stellar and you were rarely able to be at home in DC and, of course, Gregory was at home in South Carolina until he went to college in Virginia."

"I know," Angelique agreed. "That was usually the only time I got to see him. Margo Chandler or my Aunt Joyce Montgomery would drive us to Charlottesville to see Gregory during football season or watch his home basketball games. When I was away, you and I had to have a strategy to hook up on several continents. We were like this pinball machine always bouncing here and there, but Gregory came home just to come to my Sweet Sixteen birthday bash. That was the first time he kissed me on the mouth, and it was almost platonic," she said smiling. "He was out of college and grad school then and playing professional basketball. I was off on one movie or modeling assignment after another."

"You still take modeling assignments from time to time," Linda acknowledged.

"You're still performing in the great theatres around the world," Angelique reminded Linda. "I usually only take an assignment if it's for a charity I support."

"Aren't you scheduled to do a movie later this year?" Linda asked.

"Oh, yes, but it's a short role for my brother. He's got the lead in another of the movies Tina Justice is producing and the character I play is Miguel's sister. How tough do you think that is?" Angelique asked laughing. "I don't mind doing stuff occasionally, but I love cooking, my restaurant, and living in one place most of the time. When Gregory and I marry, everything will be right with my world.

"You're doing the same thing by changing careers as I did by going to Le Cordon Bleu."

Linda nodded in agreement. "I'm not so much changing careers as I'm adding a career. I still love dance and I want to continue to perform for as long as I can."

"You never said what made you decide to add the school and studio to your career objectives."

"It was a thought I had after talking with Will's nephew, Eugene. He was being taunted and teased at his private school because he liked to dance. I remember one of my male mentors telling me what he endured during his childhood. He was traumatized by the name calling and accused of being gay when he's not. I feel as if there are others, both boys and girls, who would thrive in an environment where they are with other people who feel the same way and have similar goals in the performing arts.

When I studied at Julliard, I was around people of like minds. However, Julliard teaches dance, drama, and music. I want to focus exclusively on dance and be one of Julliard's feeder schools. Later, maybe next summer, after I've fulfilled my current contracts, I want to expand to include figure skating. I'll have to find a facility where I can lease time for classes on the ice."

"That's a perfect idea, and you've racked up a perfect score," Angelique said, taking over the pinball game when Linda stepped aside.

Linda turned to momentarily monitor the children. Dejon, Keaton, and Eugene had Violet standing on a portable stair so they could teach her to play the pinball machine. The little girl's eyes were aglow, and she was catching her tongue in the left side of her mouth as she concentrated on racking up points. Between the bells and whistles and the boys' enthusiastic encouragement, Violet seemed to be having the time of her life. Linda felt Eugene and Violet were progressing well since the death of their parents. She was pleased to be a part of helping them heal.

Then Linda looked over her shoulder at Will. She respected and admired him for taking on the awesome responsibility for raising his nephew and niece. She knew what a selfless act it was to voluntarily take on someone else's responsibility for the long haul. People in his shoes might have opted to give his nephew and niece up for adoption. She witnessed the courageous act of helping others time after time in her own family. Her parents thought nothing of the challenges that bringing a new child into their household would engender. They simply stepped up and did whatever came next for a child in need. She saw those same warm and loving traits in Will Hamilton and wanted that type of man in her life. She wanted babies, too . . . lots of them.

Most of her life she was around children. Hers was not the typical family; larger than the Kardashian-Jenner clan's ten, she mused. Sure, her family was up there in numbers, but not so many that they challenged the record numbers of biological children, like the Vassilhyez family who gave birth to sixty-nine children, including sixteen pairs of twins and seven sets of triplets. One family she read about, Ziona Chana, lives in Baktawng, India with thirty wives and ninety-four children. Daad Mohammed, a Muslim in the United Arab Emirates, has eighty-eight children and seventeen different wives. Her parents actually had five biological siblings but didn't seem to be slowing down.

Linda wanted to do the same thing by emulating her parents; adopt abandoned, health-challenged children who needed a loving home. She wondered whether Will would share her dream and noted he was looking in her direction. Then again, maybe she was projecting more into the relationship with him than he intended. It was true she didn't have a lot of experience with relationships. In fact, she was still a virgin. Yet, everything about him appealed to her on a number of visceral levels. She wondered, with her inexperience, whether they would be compatible in the bedroom. At some point, she wanted to test that theory with him.

The man edged a little closer to Linda, pretending to be interested in the woman who was playing the pinball machine next to where Linda stood. He was very careful today, arriving early at the baseball field ahead of Linda's appearance with her family and friends. Although there was plenty of seating in the bleachers, the woman came and sat next to him, then struck up a conversation. She was very attractive and had a smooth, satin-like voice. The woman, who introduced herself as Natalie Portman, provided good cover for his focus on Linda. Natalie was a friend of one of the player's parents for the opposing team.

By now he knew the routine. After the game ended, the Alexander's team would always walk to a neighborhood restaurant for a celebratory lunch. So, he asked Natalie to have lunch with him and casually and slowly strolled with her behind Linda and the team to someplace called Harry and Mike's Restaurant. There, he was able to get a table near Linda's. When Angelique and Linda got up to play pinball, he got up, too, and brought Natalie to the machine next to Linda's. He was now actually back to back with her, within a foot of Linda and strained to hear her conversation with her friend, Angelique, over the noise of excited voices and the machines' bells and whistles. He caught a whiff of Linda's delicate scent amid the other smells of good food. His plan was to casually bump into Linda and have a reason to actually talk with her. He'd make it very casual and introduce Linda to Natalie. Since their tables were close, he envisioned joining her and her party. His heart was racing, and he struggled to carry on a normal conversation with Natalie while he plotted and planned on the fly.

Then Natalie said, "You're not only tall and handsome, you're the strong, silent type, too."

He was about to make his move when Natalie's comment broke his concentration for a split second. In that time, Gregory Alexander inserted himself between him and Linda to escort her and Angelique back to their table because their food had arrived. He and Natalie eventually returned to their table adjacent to Gregory and his team's, but there were no more opportunities for him to interact with Linda. Still, Natalie, a bank vice president and experienced cougar, invited him to her place a few blocks away. He accepted, not wanting to be spotted tailing Linda from the restaurant and knowing what to expect from Natalie. He wasn't surprised when they arrived at her condo she stripped him bare and had her way with him through lunch the next day.

Chapter 9

Angelique's pal, Emery Arden, another super fashion model who changed careers, looked through the large stack of poster-sized photos taken of Linda throughout her career. Most of them were used on billboards in front of the theatres where she performed. Known as Arden professionally as a high-fashion model, Emery was now pursuing a career as a professional photographer. She had a good eye for color and scale and picked shots of Linda that would enhance her website and advertising copy material for the studio and school.

"I don't know why you think you need me to do a photo shoot with you, Linda. These are really good," Emery said, holding up a picture that caught Linda in full spin on the ice. "Who is the photographer on this one?"

"I haven't a clue. If his or her creds aren't on the back, I'd have to ask Bill Chandler, my agent."

"I know Bill. He's still your agent, too, isn't he, Angelique?"

"He is, yes. He got me and my brother started in the fashion modeling and acting businesses."

"He's your mother's former law partner, isn't he, Linda?" asked Emery.

"Yes, before Mom became a judge. He and Mom were in law school together at Georgetown," mentioned Linda. "He's also a long-time family friend. We call him Uncle Bill."

"He's also a famous fashion model and actor who looks better and better every time I see him. He could be Matt Bomer's better-looking twin," said Emery grinning. "Is he in town?"

"I don't think so," said Linda. "He represents clients all over the globe. I think he was on his way to Europe for the World Cup the last time I spoke with him." She looked at the back of the poster but found no additional information. Pulling her phone from her pocket, she took pictures of the posters Emery liked and then sent a text to Bill with the photo asking whether he knew the photographers. "When he gets back to me, I'll let you know."

"That will work," said Emery, as she casually looked around the bedroom suite level in Linda's residence. "This is an incredible space. I love the skylights and the rooftop garden. You're really bringing the outside in. Is this closet one of those new robotic packages?"

"It is, yes. With a push of a button only the spaces I need to access open up. Everything else stays closed and out of the way. You can't even tell anything is there."

"What happens when or if you lose power?"

"It shouldn't happen because the house is primarily served with the solar panels and a backup propane generator in the basement and on the roof above my bedroom. It's called net zero. The property generates all of the power it needs to function and even stores power in batteries to be used at other times."

"Does it generate . . ." Emery started but was interrupted when someone shouted for Linda.

Linda went to the interior stairs and watched Will as he scaled the steps two at a time. "What's wrong, Will," she asked when he reached her.

"I just got a call from the school. Violet fell and is being taken to the hospital by ambulance. I wanted to ask . . . but I see you're busy . . ." he trailed off taking a breath.

"You want me to go with you?"

He nodded. "Yes, but. . ."

"Emery, Angelique, would you mind if we picked this up later?" Linda asked her friends.

"No, you go ahead, Linda. I'll leave the candid shots I took of you with Angelique. This isn't urgent and I'll be in town all week," said Emery.

"Thanks," Linda said, then pulled her phone from her pocket, pressing one number. "Coming out in two," she announced. Then she grabbed Will's hand starting down the interior stairs of her residence until she got to the service elevator. It was just opening with workers exiting, carrying heavy buckets of paint. She and Will entered, pressing the button for the first floor. As they exited the building, her security car service was pulling to the curb. She and Will got in and away they went, emergency red-and-blue lights flashing.

"Do you know what happened?" she asked Will as they strapped in.

"Not the details. I just got the call that she was seriously hurt and being taken to the hospital."

"Okay, hold one moment." Linda flipped through the numbers on her phone before asking, "Do you have a pediatrician?" with her phone to her ear.

"Oh, hell. No, I don't. I didn't even think about any health concerns. We have an on-call physician and two nurses at Indulgences."

Linda held up her finger when her call connected. "Hi, Dad, don't worry, I'm okay, but my friend's niece has been injured in … okay, yes, we're on our way to the hospital now." She told him which hospital and then asked, "Do you think," she started but stopped talking to listen. "Okay, Dad, thank you. I'll let Will know. Uh, yes, Will Hamilton. His niece is Violet Hamilton. Okay, thanks, again, Dad," she said and disconnected. She turned to Will. "I was speaking with my father. He's an emergency room doctor. He's going to contact the attending physician and find out what he can about Violet's condition and what needs to be done for her. He'll be in touch with us shortly."

"Thank you, Linda," Will said, his gratitude enormous. When she reached for and held his hand in hers, his fears marginally subsided. Gregory was right. She had a good head on her shoulders and didn't panic in the face of an emergency. He appreciated her for not cluttering up his head with inane chatter or offering meaningless platitudes to allay his fears. She just did what came next.

Two and a half hours later, Chuck walked into the hospital waiting room in cowboy boots, attired in his usual Western cowboy garb complete with snug, low-slung jeans, a rodeo belt buckle, Stetson hat, and floor-length duster. The only nod he made to the twenty-first century, was the white T-shirt that hugged his well-toned, muscular body. On his nearly seven-foot frame, he made a picture. All he lacked were holsters and six shooters to make the image complete.

Linda immediately recognized the other man with her father as her former pediatrician, Dr. Curtis Bellingham, a doctor from her first father, Derrick Jackson's, medical practice. She hadn't expected her father to come and knew Violet's injuries had to be serious to get her father and her former pediatrician on a private jet to New York from Washington, DC. Her father immediately came to her as she rose from her seat to greet him.

"Dad?" she asked searching his eyes as he hugged her briefly as did her pediatrician. Dr. Bellingham had taken over her care when her doctor legally became her father.

"It's not as bad as it could be, baby. That's not why we're here, but we want to take a closer look." He turned to Will and shook his hand. "I'm Linda's father, Chuck Montgomery, Mr. Hamilton, and this is Dr. Curtis Bellingham, a pediatrician and pediatric surgeon. My daughter will fill you in on our medical *bona fides*. In the interim, with your permission, we want to take a closer look at your niece."

"I appreciate it, Dr. Montgomery. You and Dr. Bellingham have my permission and gratitude for coming all this way."

"It's not a problem. We'll be back to speak with you momentarily once we've had an opportunity to see Violet." He patted Will's shoulder, caressed Linda's face, and then they were off at a ground-eating pace down the hallway with a couple of interns as their escorts.

Linda and Will sat together preparing for a long wait.

"This can't be good," said Will, his concerns escalating.

"No matter what it is, know that she's getting the best care possible. Dr. Bellingham was my pedestrian after Derrick Jackson became my father. Dad couldn't treat me after that, but he owned the medical practice with other doctors who took over the care of my siblings and me. Believe me, he trusted his partners' skills and abilities and we Jackson kids kept them busy. After Derrick died and before my mother married Chuck, a month didn't go by when one of us was in for some emergency treatment. After Mom and Chuck married, he spent a considerable amount of time running to and from emergency medical appointments," she said smiling at the memory. "Our annual check-ups were like a siege in the medical offices of Goldmahn, Fitch, Bellingham, and Jackson, causing them to have to close to any other patients on those days. So, Dad and Mom started having our medical check-ups done on our birthdays. With so many of us, that, too, wreaked havoc on Dad and Mom's schedules, so they switched to taking those of us who had birthdays in a particular month. That way they could each take alternating months. Of course, it was a given that when we had doctor's appointments, we were treated to lunch or dinner out at a restaurant."

He smiled at her. "You're trying to take my mind off of what's going on." He kissed her forehead and hugged her. "Thanks for that."

"If it's working, you're welcome. If it's not, I'll have to work harder."

"It's working."

"Good. Is Drew picking up Eugene from school?"

"He is, yes. I did have the presence of mind to call him. It's one of his days off from Indulgences because he has classes at City College today. He said he'd pick Eugene up from aftercare. I let Eugene and Violet stay for the after-school programs because they get to play with their friends instead of sitting in the Indulgences' business offices until I can leave to take them home."

"You might want to call Drew and ask him to pick up Eugene early and bring him here. He may have heard what happened to his sister and be worried."

Will smacked his forehead with the heel of his hand. "I didn't even think. Of course, he'll be worried," he said pulling his phone from his pocket. Once he completed his call, he turned back to Linda looking into her eyes.

"What?" she asked when he just continued to stare at her.

Spontaneously, he slowly pulled her to him and kissed her mouth.

"Uh, is this a bad time?" asked a voice.

"Uh, yes, it is, Dad," Linda said, still looking up into Will's eyes as he released her.

They both stood up.

"Oh, hell, I apologize, Dr. Montgomery, but I can't promise I won't do that again."

"Understandable. I kiss her all the time, too, but not like that. Should I be asking you what your intentions are?" he asked, his left eyebrow raised in question.

"Stop, Dad." Linda grinned. "I'll ask that question when I'm ready to hear the answer."

Chuck pointed two fingers at his own eyes and then pointed back and forth to Will's eyes. "I'm watching you, young man."

It made Will smile, and then they sat down to discuss Violet's condition and treatment.

"So," he was saying in conclusion, "she's being admitted, at least, overnight for observation. She lost consciousness when her head hit the steps, but we don't believe she has anything more serious than lacerations and contusions. Head wounds bleed a lot, but we found no blood in her brain or fractures in her skull. She's conscious and her pupils are equal and reactive. She knows who and where she is and her name, address, and phone number. For a little six-year-old girl, she's pretty smart and alert. She told us a boy pushed her down the steps at school and laughed when she cried. There doesn't seem to be any memory loss or eye injury."

"Thank goodness," said Will. "The boy in question is the same one who got into a fight with Eugene. There were witnesses to what he did to her and others. He's being expelled from the school."

"I hope his parents get him the help he obviously needs," said Linda.

Will shook his head. "You really mean that, don't you? You care about what happens to him."

She nodded in the affirmative. "I do, yes. He didn't come into the world as a bully. Something happened to get him to that point and, if his parents aren't conscientious, life won't end well for him."

He understood what she was saying, but he would never have cared one way or the other about the boy. She obviously grew up in a different kind of environment. He had a glimpse of her world when, with one phone call, she was able to get doctors of her father's caliber and Dr. Bellingham's on a plane in the middle of the workday to attend to a child they didn't even know. Yes, he'd say, Linda Lewis Jackson Montgomery was an extraordinary woman . . . regardless of her age.

Linda squeezed Will's hand. She had held it throughout the discussion about Violet's condition and treatment. He appreciated her support and didn't let go of her hand until her father stood.

Chuck shook hands with Will. "We're going to stick around until Violet's released tomorrow." He looked at his watch, a new one, a Christmas gift from Linda. On its face was a cowboy riding a bucking bronco with his arms pointing to the time. Although her father had a multitude of watches to choose from, he hadn't changed this one since she gave it to him. "Curtis and I are going to have dinner at Angelique's. She's holding a reservation for us. Then we're going to Greg's for the night. Will we see you there later?" he asked Linda.

"No, Dad, if it's all right with Will, I'm going to hang around here with him and Violet. I've called Angelique to send meals over for us."

"Okay, babe. I'll see you in the morning before we leave." He kissed her temple and then shook Will's hand again. "Take care of my girl, Will."

"I will do that, Sir, and thank you for everything you're doing."

"You're welcome. *Adios*," he said and met Dr. Bellingham at the elevator to leave.

Will turned to Linda. "Are you sure you want to stay?"

"I'm sure. Where else can I get kissed like that?" she teased.

He took his cue and kissed her again.

"Well, hell," Drew interrupted.

Eugene just giggled looking up at them.

"The next time I kiss you, I'm going do it where no one can interrupt us," he whispered for her ears only. Then he turned to deal with explaining Violet's condition to Drew and Eugene.

Shortly thereafter, a nurse came and admitted them into Violet's private room on the pediatric ward. Her head was bandaged, but her eyes were clear. She talked about the funny doctor who wore a cowboy hat and rodeo buckle on his belt. The doctor told her stories that made her laugh and he said she was going to be all right in a few days.

It warmed Will's heart to hear Violet so upbeat.

Then he looked up as the smell of good food reached him to find the beautiful and talented chef Angelique Menendez-Gaza herself leading a group of people laden down with hot food boxes. A gurney was rolled into the room draped with white tablecloths and, before his eyes, a buffet was spread out complete with fine china, crystal goblets, and silverware. She even had a special light dinner for Violet. Apparently, she had spoken with Chuck or Dr. Bellingham about what she could have to eat.

Linda laughed and shook her head and then hugged her friend. "My sister, my sister," she crooned.

"You better bet it, my sister," replied Angelique. "You may have a lot of nurses and doctors visiting this room tonight, so I decided you might as well get your hostess-with-the-mostess thing going on. *Bon appétit*, babe," Angelique said and breezed out as regally as she'd entered.

The man wasn't sure what to make of the fact that Linda didn't come home this evening. He did see her father come to the house with another man, but Linda wasn't with them. He wondered whether she was with Will Hamilton and his family again, so he drove to the Hamilton place, but the house was dark. He waited until nearly nine o'clock when Hamilton should have been home, as usual, to put his nephew and niece to bed.

He left there and drove to Indulgences. He casually asked one of the desk clerks whether he could speak with Will or Drew Hamilton. He didn't know what he would say if either were available to elicit what they might know about Linda's whereabouts. However, the desk clerk said the owners were unavailable, but offered his assistance if he needed help with something. He told them it wasn't urgent, and he'd check back the next day. Then he walked across the street. Her building's lights were on and workers were coming in and out, but there was someone checking identifications at the door who didn't look like the chatty type. So, the man walked on down the block to his condo.

With his full array of computers at hand, he began to search for any details about Linda or Will on social media sites. He found nothing and began to worry. *Could they have gone away somewhere?* he wondered. *Had he been too conspicuous and caused them to go into hiding? Had something happened to one of them?* He hacked the police blotter and came up empty. He paced the floor trying to figure out where they were or what was going on. It was after two in the morning when he gave up. He was tired and needed rest. He also had projects he had to complete before the deadlines. He couldn't do his best work if he were weary and worried. He went to bed, but he slept fitfully and got up early to work on his project so that he could make time to track down Linda.

Chapter 10

"Whoa!" said Drew expressively when a young woman, wearing what looked like an authentic Western buckskin jacket with strings and tassels, Stetson hat, riding boots, chambray shirt open midway her breastbone, and low slung, snug jeans with a big rodeo buckle, sauntered up to the desk in the lobby of Indulgences. Her impressive hips swung back and forth rhythmically like a metronome with her sexy walk. She wore several long, cascading, silver chains and one gold chain that read **FAMILY** around her neck, an array of musical silver bangles on her wrists, several large, hooped, silver earrings climbing up her earlobes, and silver, intricately designed rings on every finger including her thumbs. Her dark brown hair was loosely contained under the hat in a fat braid curling over her right shoulder and down between her breast with a rawhide tie at the end. What he could see of her gamine face had him salivating over her pouty mouth and straight, narrow nose. She had satin-looking, smooth skin the color of a light, butter-brown biscuit. She tipped up her Stetson with her thumb and forefinger and pulled down her stylish and expensive-looking sunglasses with one finger revealing the most unusual, luminous, crystal-brown eyes he'd ever seen. Her beauty conjured images of the renowned African actress Omotola Jalade-Ekeinde. This woman insolently looked at him.

"Well, howdy, little lady. What can I do you for?" Drew asked affecting what he thought of as a perfect Western accent. He leaned forward with his arms folded on the countertop.

A grin curled her lip and her eyes crawled up his body. "Brotherman, you couldn't do me on a bet and I ain't no lady little or otherwise."

She had him there; her comments setting him back on his heels. Her voice was a husky purr that had Drew's blood warming. "Uh," he said tongue tied and, for the first time, not having a snappy comeback for such a beautiful woman.

She leaned an elbow companionably on the top of the counter, which widened the gap on her shirt revealing the crest of her left breast, cocked her hip, and said, "Look, Slick, is Linda Lewis here?"

"Well, um," he babbled praying she'd have a costume malfunction, "we don't give out information about our clientele."

She fished a phone from her back pocket and thumbed through her call log. Putting the phone to her mouth, she breathed, "Yo, sister woman, where are you?" She didn't wait for a reply but stuffed the phone into her back pocket and leaned both elbows on the counter. "Yo, Brotherman, can you hook a sistah up with some water?"

"Uh," he managed, again, and reached under the counter placing a squat bottle of water with the label Indulgences on it before her. He never took his eyes from her mesmerizing ones. *Please, if there's a God in Heaven let this woman be available and not a client*, he prayed.

"Thanks," she said and smirked. Then she uncapped the water and guzzled it down in one long pull until the bottle was empty while still eyeing him. *Not bad*, she thought appraising him. She licked her lips and handed the empty bottle back.

Watching her lips, Drew gulped, and his member went to half-mast. "Would you like another?"

Before she could answer, Linda rushed into the lobby, her hair still damp from her quick shower.

"Hey, babe," Linda hailed the younger woman giving her a quick hug and kiss on the cheek. "Did you meet Drew?"

"He wasn't very cooperative," said Dena.

Linda shook her head at her sassy sister. "Drew Hamilton, this is my sister, Dena Jackson Montgomery. Play nice, Dena," Linda cautioned.

She insolently sighed. "Mr. Hamilton," Dena acknowledged, nodding while raising her Stetson only to replace it on her head lower on her brows just above her sunglasses. Then she turned to Linda immediately dismissing him. "Can we go now? I'm hungry."

"You're always hungry. I don't know where you put it all."

"I'm a growing girl."

"I'll say," murmured Drew.

Dena gave him another insolent look over her shoulder and then said to Linda, "Let's load 'em up, and move 'em out."

Linda just shook her head. "Drew, I'm going back to the hospital to see Violet and Will before he takes her home. I'll see you later at your place."

"Sure," he said still eyeing Dena. "You're welcome to bring your sister, too."

Linda laughed and with arms slung around each other left amid Drew's audible masculine groan. Linda knew her younger sister had that effect on men. Dena, like their father, had an affinity for Western clothes and wore them well all the time. To look at her, one would immediately think her a model or actress. No one would guess that Dena Jackson Montgomery was a championship rodeo rider since the age of seven and a math genius, currently a Dean's List student at the Massachusetts Institute of Technology in Boston.

"What's with the Walking Gonad?" asked Dena when they were secure in the town car.

Linda laughed. "He's Will Hamilton's brother."

"Hamilton The Hammer, baseball phenom?"

"The same. I've been seeing him socially for a few months now. Uncle G introduced us. Will owns and operates Indulgences."

"Sweet. I didn't know you were dating. Nobody tells me anything."

"You don't make time for family gossip, but, frankly, I'm not sure whether I can call what Will and I do *dating*. He has a young nephew and niece he's recently had to start raising, and he feels a little out of his element with them. I've more or less been helping him acclimate himself to his relatively new situation. We've been out on a handful of 'dates' alone together, but the first time he kissed me was yesterday at the hospital. He did it twice, but I couldn't tell whether they were kisses of gratitude for being there to provide moral support or an indication of interest," Linda said shrugging. "However, he did tell Dad he couldn't say he wouldn't do it again."

"Is your light on in the caution yellow or go green position? You know how single-minded you can be when you're training."

Linda laughed again. "I'm not really in training mode yet. I joined Indulgences so I can stay limber and toned. They also have a great spa I use to relax, keep my skin clear, and my hair healthy. After having to wear heavy stage makeup for so long, my pores get clogged and it takes a while to clean them out."

"Yeah, yeah, like you really need makeup to look fabulous. To me, you still look like the actress Vanessa Williams in her youth," Dena intoned.

"So, you look like Nia Long."

Dena grunted at that comparison. However, others made the same comparison. "Are you interested in him?"

"I'm interested, yes, but he may think I'm too young for him."

"He's what, in his thirties?"

"Yes, I think so. He was in his early twenties right out of college, maybe twenty-one, when he was drafted in the top ten for the majors. I think he was still in his twenties when he retired."

"You know what the Grands say. *Age ain't nothin' but a number.'* Dad is nine years older than Mom and Derrick was even older."

"Mom and the Dads aren't typical of everyone, Dena. Will may feel like the age gap is insurmountable like Uncle G used to feel about Angelique. Like we're in different generations."

"Uncle G got over his misgivings. Men, back in the day, usually married younger women in order to have time to make lots of babies to work the farm. Will needs to get over himself."

"*Whoa, kid!* No one's talking about marriage here," Linda said demonstratively. Then she thought a moment, narrowing her eyes at her sister. "Uh, is something up with you and the Russian?"

"He's German, and no. He's a jerk. Everything with him is a competition. If we work together on projects, he has to be the leader to feel superior. Maybe it's just how he's been raised. Now he wants me to meet his family and he wants to meet ours."

"Uh oh, it sounds like he's seriously interested in taking your relationship to the next level. Why are you holding off?"

"You know what our family tradition is all about. You don't bring anyone home to our Juneteenth family reunion until or unless you're sure the person is *the one*. It's a statement. I'm not there yet with Alfonse and I'm not sure I'll ever be. Besides, I'm too young to make that type of commitment to any man yet. Me and Jill Scott, we're 'living our lives like it's golden.'"

"Yeah," Linda said, hugging her sister cheek-to-cheek. "I know exactly what you mean."

When Linda and Dena walked into Violet's hospital room, Dr. Bellingham was examining the little girl while Will and their father looked on.

"How's she doing?" Linda asked no one in particular as she hugged her father. Dena did the same and both girls received a tight squeeze from Chuck and a kiss.

"She seems to be fine. Dr. Bellingham believes it's probably okay for me to take her home," answered Will. "She has a headache, so he's ordered another CAT scan just to be on the safe side."

"I'm glad he's being thorough," she said and then turned to her sister. "Will, I'd like to introduce you to my sister, Dena Jackson Montgomery. Dena, this is Will Hamilton."

"A pleasure," said Will. "Linda said you were coming into town last night."

"It's a pleasure to meet you, too, Will. Yes, when I called my Mom yesterday, she told me Dad was in New York overnight with Doc B to attend to your niece. I flew in to spend some time with them before they have to leave. Is it all right if I meet Violet?"

"Certainly," Will said and, when Dr. Bellingham finished his examination, made the introductions.

"You're pretty, like your sister, but different," said Violet. "She's a ballerina. Are you a real cowgirl?"

Dena took the rodeo buckle from her belt, handed it to Violet, and then sat on the side of Violet's bed. "Thank you, Violet. I think you're pretty, too. Yes, I'm a real cowgirl and I have horses named Samson,

QuickSilver, and Butterscotch, too. I won this buckle at a rodeo when I was just a little bit older than you are."

She pointed to the buckle in Violet's hands. The little girl's eyes got large as she fingered the heavy, intricately detailed disk of metal.

"Really? You won this?"

"I did, yes. I rode Tapioca, a quick-footed, spotted pony in a barrel race and scored the highest points and fastest time. I was so excited that I cried."

"Do you still race?"

"Sometimes, yes, particularly when I'm at home in Maryland, Pennsylvania or South Carolina. I ride every chance I get."

"Would you teach me to ride a horse?"

Dena laughed. "Sure, if your uncle says it's okay, we'll start with a pony first. I'll come back this summer to teach you. You could also start learning from my big sister, Linda. She's a really good rider, too. Sometimes when we're at home, we like to race. Dad has a quarter-mile track on our farm back home in Maryland. Sometimes we ride through a bridle path to an equestrian park not far from home."

"Indeed they do, and it's a ranch, not a farm," interjected Chuck.

"Dad thinks he's a rancher like they had in the Wild Wild West," Dena whispered *sotto voce* to Violet making the little girl giggle.

Violet had a million-and-one questions Linda, Dena, and Chuck painstakingly answered until the nurses came to take Violet to the radiology lab to have her CAT scan. Then the five of them left to have brunch. When they returned, Dr. Bellingham and Chuck reviewed the results of the CAT scan with the radiologist. There didn't appear to be any indication of serious head trauma except a lump on her head, so Violet was released from the hospital.

Dr. Bellingham and Chuck left for the airport and a flight back to Washington, DC. At Will's request, Linda and Dena accompanied him to his home with Violet who wore herself out with questions. They left her in her bedroom to rest and began making dinner. When Drew and Eugene arrived at half five, dinner was almost ready.

Drew's eyes lit up when he spotted Dena and immediately began to engage her in conversation. It impressed him when she looked unwaveringly into his eyes as he talked, but he couldn't discern from her expression how she was reacting to their conversation. After dinner, while Will and Linda sat talking, the children watched a movie and Drew invited Dena to shoot a game of pool.

"Ladies first," Drew offered, sure he would be able to impress her with his skills. That thought faded and died when Dena racked the balls like a professional, broke the field, started calling out her shots, and then making them quickly with precision. She stalked the table like a gunslinger from the Old West until she cleared it, never giving Drew an opportunity to shoot. After two more games, Drew still had chalk on his fingers from disuse. Dena hadn't missed a shot.

Dena stalked up to Drew, ran her eyes up and down his body, and crooned, "Well, Brotherman, what else can you do with that . . . stick? Show me what you're working with."

"Uh," was all he could manage. However, he had a whole new respect for Dena Jackson Montgomery.

"How did you get started in dance?" Will asked as he and Linda sat comfortably, knees touching, facing each other on a sofa in Will's family room.

"You may remember I told you I was in a serious accident and was immobile in traction for several years. After many surgeries, I learned to walk again. One night we watched this movie *Fame,* and after that, I was determined to dance. Although The Duke Ellington School of the Arts is right there in Washington, DC, in Georgetown, a few blocks from where we lived, I wanted to go to Julliard and train as a dancer. I realized I was too young, and I thought my parents would not let me go. I was afraid to ask for fear they would say no, and my heart would be broken.

"One day, they sat me down and said, *'If you only look out of one window all of your life, you will never see all of the world's wonders.'* They understood me better than I realized and brought me to New York to audition. When I was accepted at Julliard, they arranged for me to live with my Uncle Greg. He was still playing professional basketball at the time, but he made time to take me places like Rockefeller Center to skate, and I was hooked. So, he enrolled me in ice skating programs, and I loved it. Ice skating enhanced my ballet routines and the reverse was true. The rest is history. I've traveled all over the world to dance and ice skate. What inspired your interest in baseball?"

He smiled rather self-deprecatingly. "As I've mentioned, I didn't have the best childhood. In fact, for a while, I was a holy terror. I needed a way to channel my anger because of my parents' drug use. A priest at school put a ball and bat in my hands and said, *'go for it, Slugger'* and I did. Every time I felt angry, I'd go to the batting cages and hit balls until I wore myself out. I did it so often that I really got good at it and could hit balls off the diamond into the school bleachers. I was consistent and could nail a home run the majority of the time."

"That's where the tagline Hamilton the Hammer came from?" Linda asked.

"It is, yes. Although I was compared to him often enough, they couldn't call me Hammering Hank after the legend Hank Aaron, so it became Will *The Hammer* Hamilton. The name clung to me like Crazy Glue all through college and the pros. Every once in a while, if I do an interview or color commentary for a game, the interviewer will resurrect the name. I hoped it would die a natural death."

"Why?" Linda asked, quizzically.

"It's embarrassing, but some women believed the tagline referred to my, uh, prowess in other, uh, venues?"

Linda laughed. "I never even made the connection." Now, she wondered whether he could *nail it* between the sheets.

Later that evening, after dinner and visiting with Will and his family, Linda and Dena lounged alone together at their Uncle Gregory's home. It was late, but their uncle was still at his business office and brokerage house on Wall Street across from the New York Stock Exchange.

"That was fun, wasn't it?" asked Linda of Dena, referring to the evening spent at Will's home.

"It was, yes. I enjoyed Eugene and Violet. They're very close and remind me of the twins Craig and Petra," their preteen twin brother and sister, one of several sets of twins in their family.

"They do, don't they?"

Dena nodded. "I also think Will wants to be very close to you and I don't think it has anything to do with gratitude."

"Maybe," Linda said, uncertainly.

"Really. You two looked good together making dinner for us tonight. He has a nice smile and a twinkle in his eyes when he looks at you."

"How would you know? You spent the whole evening putting Drew in his place and running a clinic on him on the pool table and then throwing darts," Linda said laughing. "I'll bet you didn't mention that you're the best pool player and card shark in our family."

She nodded, shrugging with a grin on her lips. "Brotherman, needed a come-to-Dena experience."

"He seemed off balance all evening."

"He was, but he's easy," Dena said. She leaned back in her chair, lifted her legs to an ottoman, and laced her fingers behind her head. "I have to admit, though, that he's rather cute."

"Do I detect some interest?" Linda asked.

"He hopes so, but I don't know. It might be fun to see what he's working with. He asked for my contact information."

Linda raised a speculative eyebrow. "Did you give it to him?"

"I told him I'd consider it."

"Alfonse?" Linda querried.

Dena nodded. "I'm not sure what I want to do where he's concerned. This whole business about meeting the family has me confused and taking a giant step backward."

Linda suggested, "Remember what Nana Sylvia says."

Dena nodded. "Yeah, *if it don't fit, don't force it.*"

Linda leaned up to high-five her sister. "Exactly. You can't beat Nana's wisdom from the ancestors."

⌒

Outside, the man sat in his car watching the house and the lights as they went on in various rooms. He envisioned what Linda might be doing. He missed her that morning at Indulgences. She was leaving with her sister when he was arriving. Obviously, she had come in much earlier than usual, because it was just past eight when he arrived. He knew her routine. She usually put in a solid three-to-four hours of work before taking a break.

Because he was worried about her, he couldn't sleep the night before and finally got up to finish a number of projects working until the wee hours of the morning. As a result, he overslept, but it was less than a two-minute walk from his condo to Indulgences. There were very few men in the classes she took, so the only place he could get close to her was when she used the exercise equipment and free weights or went to one of the cafés for lunch. However, she was so focused when she worked out, he couldn't risk interrupting her concentration.

Her lunch breaks were often spent with her uncle when he was there to exercise or play in the noontime pro/am basketball tournament and/ or with Will Hamilton. She was never alone.

He recognized Dena Jackson Montgomery, Linda's sister, the minute he saw her. She was quite a character, but a brilliant mathematician. He read a number of articles written by or about her and kept them in his databases on the family and their activities. One of his computer programs was designed to capture any tidbits of information about Linda and her family members.

At an early age, Dena made a name for herself at rodeos. She was a Olympiad in math during elementary and middle school. Still, she had taken a difficult and different route when she entered high school. Now she was at MIT among the best and brightest. She had a guy friend of sorts, Alfonse Jaeger, who was fascinated with her, but in the man's estimation, the guy was a real tool; someone without the star-quality Dena exhibited and deserved.

He wondered whether Linda's disappearance the day before had anything to do with Dena. Apparently, he had worried all night needlessly. Linda was all right he noted when she rushed out of Indulgences with Dena right past him and entered her waiting car service.

Chapter 11

"Yes, come in," Will called out. He had been steadily working all morning and didn't want any interruptions, but when he looked up, he smiled and quickly rose from his seat. "Well, hell, look at what the cat dragged."

"Good to see you, too," Jackson Chase, a Wall Street titan and friend of Will's, said as he entered. He and Will gave each other a brother's handshake and embrace. "You remember my wife, Jackie."

"Of course, I do. How is this big guy treating you?" he asked hugging her.

"Extremely well. We're expecting again."

"Well, hell, congrats. How old are your triplets?"

"They're three now, going on thirty," she joked. "They're happy and healthy at home in Maryland being spoiled by their aunt, uncles, and grandmother. Jackson and I took a little time off to celebrate our anniversary. We have spa appointments and, of course, Jackson wants to get in some time on the hardwood."

"You're in the round robin with your team from CTI?" Will asked.

"I am, yes, but we wanted to stop in to say how sorry we are about your family's loss. Greg Alexander told us about it," Jackson said.

"Thank you, both," Will acknowledged. "It's been hard, but we're making it."

"I understand you have your nephew and niece with you," said Jackie.

"We do, yes. My younger brother, Drew, and I are raising them."

"You'll have to bring them down to Maryland for a visit," Jackie suggested.

"I'll do that and, Jackie, I appreciate all the business you send to me through your travel agency."

"It's good business because my clients, who come to New York, always comment on how well they are treated here."

"Thanks, Jackie, we do our best," Will offered.

"We'll get out of your way," said Jackson. "My games start shortly. Jackie agreed to be my personal cheering section."

"Then you definitely should win. It is good seeing both of you. I hope we'll be able to get together again for a visit before you leave the city."

"We'll do that. I'll call you later today so we can set up a time and place."

"Works for me."

They said their goodbyes and left. Will sat a moment thinking of his friends who had found their soulmates and were happy. He was beginning to feel it was about time he started thinking along the same lines about a wife and an expanded family, too. He didn't have to think hard when Linda came to mind. He wondered whether she would like to get together with Jackson and Jackie Chase. Maybe even include Gregory and Angelique.

Good idea, he thought and made a note to check with Linda when he went home at lunchtime. Because he had a heavy workload today and Drew had classes, Linda volunteered to stay with Violet. She arrived early to have breakfast with them and help get Eugene ready and out the door with him for school. She had plans for creative things she and Violet would do together and promised to have lunch ready for him if he could find the time to come home.

He would make the time no matter what came up. He liked the idea of going home to Linda in his space. She acclimated easily to any environment she was in; comfortable in her own skin, and he liked that about her. Compared to the women he had known, she stood tall above the crowd. She didn't make a fuss if things didn't go her way, the way Jolie would whenever he had to change their plans to deal with a problem at work. Spending time at his home playing chess or shooting pool or just watching a movie wasn't Jolie's idea of fun. She wanted to be out and about to see and be seen at all of the hot clubs and events, but Linda relished the idea of quiet, fun times spent at his home with his family, sharing a big bowl of popcorn and a game of Monopoly. Linda had appearances she was obligated to make, but she usually went alone or with her uncle and Angelique. She didn't need an arm trophy the way Jolie did, and he appreciated Linda's consideration for not using him that way. He had all the bright lights and big city celebrity when he was still playing in the big leagues. He didn't need it then and he certainly didn't want it now. He let his business speak for itself and thoroughly enjoyed his life now, particularly with Linda in it.

When he looked at the clock, he noted that he had about an hour's worth of work to do before he could leave for his lunch date with Linda and Violet, but what the hell. He suddenly had a need to be with her. So, he shut down his computer, left his office, and headed for the garage.

"Anyone home?" Will called out as he came into his home.

Linda rushed out of the kitchen to greet him, putting a finger to her lips to signal his silence. "Violet just went down for a nap," she whispered while leading him toward the kitchen at the back of the house.

Before he reached the kitchen, he caught her hand, pulled her into his arms, and kissed her. After a moment's surprise, she kissed him back...and she kissed him and kissed him some more.

When they came up for air, he placed his forehead against hers; his eyes closed savoring the sweetness of kissing her without any interruptions.

"Hi," she said a little breathless. "You're early. I didn't expect you for about an hour or so."

"I know. I couldn't keep you out of my head."

"Well, that will never do. I want to be in your thoughts."

"You are. I wanted to kiss you like that this morning when you stood at my front door holding Violet's hand and waving goodbye to Eugene and me. I wanted it so much that I was tempted to come back after taking Eugene to school just so I could steal a kiss, but I forced myself to go to work. Then I kept thinking about you and that kiss and gave up to come home a little early." He could feel the smile on her lips before he opened his eyes and looked at her.

"I wanted to kiss you, too, but then Drew, Eugene, and Violet were here." She smiled at him. "May I have another kiss before Violet wakes up?"

"Oh, I think I have some to spare," he said and kissed her again holding her tight to his needful body with his left arm around her small waist and his right hand in her hair.

She could feel his heat and the intriguing contour of his body held intimately against hers. For ponderous, earth-shattering moments she wanted what she felt was as hard as epee between them. She knew she was on the verge, and second by second pulled back from the brink. It was too soon, and they weren't alone in his home. When she went to his bed or invited him into hers, she needed to know that it meant as much to him as it would to her. She wasn't a prude by any stretch of the imagination. Rather, she wanted the real deal; a forever-kind-of-love match.

He felt her restraint and purposely released her enough so that he still held her loosely in his arms. It was neither the time nor the place to go beyond the kisses. Certainly, a relationship only a few months old could burn hot and then fizzle before the season was over. What he wanted with Linda was shaping up to be a woman for all seasons, but she had to want the same from him. She had a career that took her away for months at a time. That and other issues would have to be cleared up before they took the inevitable step toward an exclusive relationship.

"Something smells good," said Will, taking Linda's hand and moving toward the cooking area in the kitchen and adjacent family room.

"I'm experimenting. Violet and I are making Chicken Florentine, I hope. We're following a recipe in Angelique's latest cookbook. If it works out, we'll put them in your freezer, so you'll have a ready-made, home-cooked meal when you don't have time to cook."

"Thanks, Linda. I usually order something from a restaurant on days when I don't make time to cook or there are several good neighborhood restaurants within walking distance. Drew is a real disaster in the kitchen.

He could screw up a bowl of cereal. Beyond breakfast, I'm not very good at it either."

Linda laughed. "Neither am I, and I usually don't make the time to do the grocery shopping needed to put together a meal. Uncle Greg likes to cook and he's really good at it. So, when he's in town, I beg him to cook or, like you, we go out. That's why he keeps a fresh fruit and vegetable garden in his home."

"You're not kidding. He has nearly everything he needs. So, what else is on the menu?"

"Hamburgers and hot dogs with pork and beans," laughed Linda.

He loved to hear her laugh and see the smile on her face. He looked at her askance. "Uh, interesting. I didn't know you ate hot dogs or hamburgers with pork and beans."

"I don't make a habit of it, but I have a high metabolism. I need fuel when I'm in training. Violet picked the lunch menu. She said she hasn't had a hamburger or hot dog and pork and beans or French fries since she came to live with you and Drew."

He shook his head in regret. "She's right. I've spent so much time making sure she and Eugene got wholesome, balanced meals, I didn't think of the fun foods we used to like to eat."

"Don't beat yourself up about this, Will. You're just getting to know them. The estrangement between you will get easier over time and disappear."

He nodded accepting her prediction and guidance. Things *were* getting better between him, Eugene, and Violet, primarily because Linda was in his life. "Don't we get to sample the Chicken Florentine, too?"

"Oh, no, not before I've given it a taste test. If it's any good, we'll have it for dinner."

"Does that mean you'll stay for dinner?"

"Yes, if it's all right with you."

"It is, yes. Even though some friends of mine are in town and I'd like for us to get together with them for a meal."

"Oh," she said, curious. "Who?"

"Jackson and Jackie Chase."

She smiled. "Yes, I know them. Jackson is a partner in CTI with Uncle Gregory. I've met Jackie a few times. They have the most adorable triplets and a niece. They live in Mitchell County, not far from my family's farm. I'd love to have dinner with them."

"Then I'll arrange it and check with Drew to see when he can stay with Eugene and Violet."

During lunch with Violet, the threesome carried on a lively conversation. Then the little girl said, "My mommy used to make the best hamburgers. Can your mommy make good hamburgers?"

Linda laughed. "No, my mommy doesn't do so well in the kitchen."

"She's an important lady, isn't she, but she can't make hamburgers?" Violet asked.

"Yes, she's a very important lady and she's special in a lot of other ways, too. She can play basketball really well and she swims like a fish, but she can't cook."

"What does she do to make her so important?" Violet wanted to know.

"She's the best mommy in the world to me and my sisters and brothers. She's also a Supreme Court judge which means she does everything she can to be the best person to help people."

"What did your biological mother do?" asked Will.

Linda's brows bunched in concentration. "You know, I have no idea. I never thought to find out." Still, her curiosity was piqued. The next time she was home, she'd find out. There was an old trunk full of things saved from her former family's home. It was stored in her room at her family's farm in Maryland. She hadn't gone through it in years. The contents consisted of old pictures of her parents and the people she assumed were either her paternal or maternal grandparents. To the best of her knowledge, her parents had no siblings. That's why she believed she ended up as a ward of the state. Beyond the familial connections, she didn't know anything about the people in her ancestry. She recalled her father died in Iraq and assumed he was in the military, but she didn't have a picture of him in a uniform. He died sometime after her younger brother was conceived or born. She never went to a funeral, so she didn't know where her father, mother, and brother were buried.

Interesting that she hadn't thought of these things before. She was adopted by Derrick and Vivian Alexander Jackson and then again by Charles and Vivian Alexander Montgomery. When Charles married Vivian, he legally adopted all of the children Derrick and Vivian adopted including Derrick Jr. Both Derrick and Charles were wealthy and established trust funds for each child brought into the family.

As the first born and adopted, she was always a part of the Jackson and Montgomery nucleus family unit to the exclusion of all else. It was a view shared by all of the children in the family including those of biological birth. Though they were from different backgrounds and ethnicities, they simply considered themselves siblings and the offspring of Charles Patrick and Vivian Lynn Alexander Jackson Montgomery. They were the grandchildren of Grover and Harriet Minor Jackson, Stephen and Esther Montgomery, and Bernard and Sylvia Benson Alexander. Their uncles, aunts, and cousins on all sides of their extended family were legion. To her knowledge, none of her brothers and sisters felt as if they didn't belong or were not a part of the family. As a result, she and her siblings felt comfortable in their own skins and their places in the family. Nevertheless, curiosity was growing to find out more about her biological heritage.

"Hey, where did you go?"

Will's question brought her out of what must have seemed like a fugue state to him. She definitely was deep in thought. "Oh, sorry. Your question about my biological parents' careers is one I hadn't thought about or looked into. I'm heading home the first weekend of next month for family birthday parties. I have a trunk full of things collected after the death of my biological family."

"I didn't mean to bring up sad memories."

"Really, you didn't. Although I would want to know more about them as an academic exercise, my adoptive family fills all of the spaces in my life."

"Nearly thirty brothers and sisters are more than a notion."

She laughed. "You have no idea. In fact, why don't you come with me for the weekend and bring Eugene and Violet? If you can make the time, I think your nephew and niece would enjoy visiting the farm."

Taken aback, but pleased, Will agreed.

"Then we can get together with Jackson and Jackie Chase on Wednesday or Thursday depending on their schedules?" Will asked.

"That's fine with me," Linda agreed.

"How about we include Greg and Angelique?" suggested Will.

"He's in town, so I'll ask him and Angelique once you confirm the date and time."

"I'll do that today when I get back to the office," he said and looked at his watch. "Regrettably, that's something I need to do right now."

They rose from the sofa and Will took Linda's hand as they slowly strolled to the front vestibule. Will peeked around to make sure Violet wasn't within range when he took Linda into his arms and kissed her. While still in Will's arms, with their foreheads together, they breathed in each other.

"I'll pick up Eugene by five and be home by five-thirty."

She rose on her toes with her arms locking around his neck. "Be sure to bring an extra supply of kisses when you come. I'll be collecting them at various times this evening before I go back to Uncle Greg's." Then she kissed him again, long and slow.

"Maybe I can get here a little earlier, but if you don't stop kissing me, I won't be leaving at all."

She smiled at that and opened the door at his back. With one last kiss, he caressed her face and was gone.

Chapter 12

It was a sunny, bright day when the Adventurer Executive Airline, Cessna Citation Longitude twelve-passenger, business-class jet landed at a small airport in the rural area outside of Washington, DC, in Maryland. The flight originated in Boston where Dena boarded and flew to New York City to pick up Linda, Will, his nephew and niece. In a little over an hour, they landed. A van pulled up to the steps of the jet and identical, male twins got out.

"Hi," Linda hailed her brothers, Ryan and Roger.

"Hey, Sis," they responded in unison as they often did, but their eyes were riveted on Will.

Will's feet barely touched the ground when both young men, who wore gold chains that read **FAMILY,** leaped forward, hands extended.

"Hi, Mr. Hamilton, I'm Ryan Montgomery and this is my brother, Roger. We are your biggest fans."

"Enthusiastic fans are always appreciated," Will said smiling at their eagerness. He introduced his nephew and niece to the tall, gangly twin brothers.

"Can't a sistah get a little love, too?" Dena deadpanned.

"Yeah, but you gotta know you're in the company of Will the Hammer Hamilton, baseball royalty!" Roger joked while giving his sister the hug she demanded. "Everyone at the house is excited to meet him."

Ryan followed suit before helping the ground crew to load the luggage into the van.

"I should have warned you, Will. Everyone in the household is a sports fanatic of one type or the other. Ryan and Roger are baseball extremists. They've infected our little brother, Ronnie, although he's only six years old."

"He's played T-Ball for two years," boasted Ryan. "He's ready to step up to Little League."

Will looked around at the extremely small airport, seemingly plopped down in the middle of nowhere. Yet, there were private planes everywhere on the tarmac. Some, like theirs, bore the name Adventurer Executive Airlines with the AEA logo on the tail and parked near a big hanger bearing the same corporate name. There were a few planes that were larger than the private aircraft they flew here in as well as ones at the airport in New York. There actually was a busy terminal in the city where business men and women were boarding or deplaning the sleek, private jets. However, here he could only see acres upon acres of countryside and hear highway noise in the distance. More curious, the twin boys were allowed to drive an ordinary vehicle right up to the steps of the jet. *How was this possible?* Will wondered.

Linda noticed Will's confusion. "What you hear is US I-50. It begins in Washington, DC, and runs through Annapolis, the state capitol and beyond."

"Okay," he said nodding, "and the jet?"

Linda shrugged. "My first father, Derrick, started a small, private airline, Adventurer Executive, when he was playing professionally. He liked the extra room a private aircraft afforded him because of his height. He needed the extra leg room. My second father, Chuck, agreed, so he invested and eventually other sports figures . . ."

"Like your Uncle Gregory . . .?"

"Yes, like him. He bought into the business and preferred private jet travel versus commercial flight. So, the business grew like wildfire to what it is today."

"Your parents still own it," he surmised.

"My Mom mostly, but because she's a sitting Supreme Court Justice, she doesn't manage the business day to day. Her holdings are managed in a trust . . ."

"Don't tell me. Let me guess, by your Uncle Gregory," he deadpanned.

She grinned at him. "Yes, by my Uncle Greg, Dad, and by the other founding members of Mom's former law firm, Alexander, Carter, Chandler, Charles, Lightfoot, and Towson, PA."

Will nodded his understanding. He knew Vivian Alexander Jackson Montgomery to be one of the wealthiest women in the world, a multibillionaire, but he hadn't really considered what it meant in the big scheme of things. Linda Lewis Jackson Montgomery, the young woman he was coming to care about exclusively, was also a wealthy woman in her own right. Her wealth didn't matter to him. He could deal with that because she was very grounded and didn't flaunt her wealth. However, she was also probably an heiress to her parents' fortune. *Well, in for a penny, in for a pound,* he thought.

He wanted her in his life, and he didn't care whether she came with bags of money or not a penny to her name. He was financially solvent and could take care of himself and his responsibilities. If it came to a point where he wanted to move to the next level in their relationship, he would ask that she put her wealth in a trust fund as her mother had done. That resolved in his head, he helped Linda put the last of their luggage in the van.

They piled into the van and talked baseball for the ten-minute drive to the Montgomery farm on a single-lane road in the spring greening, rural countryside.

"That's Dad's office," Linda pointed out to a quaint, wood-framed, I-shaped mall adjacent to an old-fashion general store and gas station. Old wooden barrels and crates held assortments of fresh-looking produce. A red-and-white barber shop sign hung on a wall spinning slowly on the other side of the space designated as Doctor's Office. Images of the Cracker Barrel chain of restaurants came to Will's mind when he spotted the array of rocking chairs scattered along the boardwalk outside the shops.

"He sees his private practice patients there?" Will asked.

"He does, yes. Otherwise, he goes into the Physicians' Hospital he and some of his pals built and operate," Linda answered. "It's located a couple of miles from here. He likes the idea of being able to walk to work."

"Walk?" he questioned looking around from his left to his right until Roger turned into a long, blacktop driveway through pillars which read "**WELCOME HOME.**" Overhead a wrought-iron sign spelled out **ALEXANDER-JACKSON-MONTGOMERY RANCH.** Tall trees lined each side of the drive like soldiers standing at attention, providing a cathedral-like cover over the roadway. Numerous huge pieces of farm equipment crawled over the expansive landscape, bailing spring wheat and tilling the earth. Cattle and horses grazed lazily inside white, picket-fenced areas.

At the top of the incline stood a three-story, gleaming white, antebellum mansion with tall, thick, round pillars supporting balconies that circled all sides of the massive structure. In front of the mansion was a lake gleaming brightly in the sunshine. Geese and their young goslings paddled across it. As they parked, Will could see acres upon acres of cultivated farmland, outbuildings, bunkhouses, and pristine, forested areas in the distance. It was as iconic as a Norman Rockwell painting. He looked in every direction, but it was hard to take it all in one glance.

"I thought Greg's place needed its own zip code, but this place should become the fifty-first state. This is amazing," Will commented, awed. He turned and could see the country store down at the end of the driveway across the road. "This is where you grew up?"

"It is, yes, after Dad and Mom married. Before that, we lived in the Georgetown area of Washington, DC, and visited here every chance we got. My parents and my Aunt Stacy Greene Alexander accidentally discovered this place the week before Derrick and Mom were to be married. They were trying to avoid the heavy traffic on the I-95 Highway on their way back from a sightseeing trip to Baltimore. Although Aunt Stacy graduated from the Naval Academy in Annapolis, neither she nor Chuck had ever visited Baltimore. Derrick was supposed to go with them, but he had to perform an emergency surgery and couldn't go.

"This property and the shopping area across the road were once owned by the White family, who all died in the Jamestown, Pennsylvania, flood in 1889. Back then it was called The White Mansion even though with all of the nooks and crannies, it's more like a castle. It's a good thing, too, with the size of our family that's still growing. Although the country store and barber shop continued operation after the White family died, the mansion, outbuildings, and farm remained uninhabited for over one hundred and thirty years. According to Mom and Dad, it was in terrible shape, but my parents, who both grew up on farms, saw the potential and Dad purchased it from the state. According to the terms and conditions of the sale, the property has to remain a farm in perpetuity. That was right up Dad's alley. Since he was raised on a farm, he always wanted to be a rancher. My Montgomery uncles and aunts live on farms in Monroe County, Pennsylvania in the Pocono Mountains, but they're all in the construction trades. They came here and literally camped out for many months until the house was put to right again."

"You really know your family history," commented Will as they stood outside in the spring breeze observing the activities underway by the farm hands.

"I do, yes. My family has no secrets. At family gatherings, like this weekend, the oral history is handed down from generation to generation, particularly for the little ones. My parents usually adopt children when they are babies, have been abandoned, and have health challenges, like I did. I was the first one adopted and I'm still the oldest one of the clan, but, although we are legion, we could likely have more of us before the weekend is over," she said laughing. "Last year, Uncle Benny, had a situation where a Marine abandoned a baby in Japan and then the guy died in Afghanistan. The mother, a Japanese national, wanted nothing to do with the newborn because he was born with palatoschisis, a cleft palate, and cheiloschisis, a cleft lip and needed surgery. Sadly, the man's American relatives also rejected the baby boy. Because the baby is the son of an American enlisted man, the Japanese government wasn't willing to pay for the surgery or make the baby a ward of the government. So, Uncle Benny called Mom and Chuck. They got on a plane the same day and flew to Tokyo, Japan. Two days later, they returned with the week-old infant they named Alexander Jackson Montgomery. He's the sweetest little boy and, after his sixteen-hour surgery at Dad's hospital, he smiles and giggles all the time. Come on, I'll show you around the inside and introduce you to the rest of us we call Dad's posse."

"The posse?" Will asked.

"Yes," she said laughing. "Dad says a posse is always the good guys who go after the bad guys and put them in jail."

"I see," Will said nodding his understanding and smiling at the image.

They went in, and Will couldn't wrap his head around the size of the place. The entrance hall was large enough to constitute a master bedroom with cascading stairs leading up on both sides to the upper two levels. Dead center of the home was an open-concept great room which was just that . . . great, massive in fact. Just as on the outside, large round pillars held up what he could see of the wide, open hallway that rimmed the center expanse. It resembled the lobby of a high-end hotel with comfortable-looking furniture throughout. Looking up, Will could see the balconies circumnavigating each level of the interior with greenery draping over the banisters in window boxes under a dome-shaped skylight. Books filled the wall cavities between what were, apparently, bedroom doors along the upper walkways, making it a kind of walkway library.

"Read much?" commented Will.

"My favorite pastime," Linda said smiling at Will's astonished expression.

Hallways led off of the great room in every direction like spokes of a wagon wheel. From one of those hallways came Linda's mother carrying a baby girl.

"Hi, Mom," Linda said.

The joy in her voice was unmistakable, thought Will, and her eyes lit up as she crushed her tall, slim, finely-fit mother to her and noisily kissed the baby causing her to giggle. The little girl reached for Linda and clung to her neck as she took her in her arms. Will noticed the beautiful gold chain that read **FAMILY** around the baby's and Vivian's necks.

"Will Hamilton, this is my Mother, Vivian Alexander Montgomery, and this little cutie is my baby sister, Teresa Angelique Montgomery. She was born over two years ago on Mom's yacht, the ***Vivian Lynn***, as we cruised the Hudson River while celebrating Angelique Menendez-Gaza's twenty-first birthday. Hence the name Teresa Angelique since they share a birth date. Uncle Greg and Angelique are her godparents. Mom, Will is the owner of Indulgences."

"Will Hamilton needs no introduction in this household," Vivian said smiling and reaching to embrace him. "We collect hugs in this family, Will. The more, the better, so be prepared. I've heard so much about you. It's a pleasure to finally meet you. Welcome to our home."

"Thank you, Madam Justice," said Will warmed by her embrace. "Your reputation precedes you as well."

"We don't stand on formalities here, Will. Please, call me Vivian. I hoped to meet your nephew and niece. I understood they would be coming with you."

Will looked around, his brows bunched in confusion. "I could have sworn I had them when we arrived, but I seem to have misplaced them."

Linda and Vivian chuckled. "Dena took them to the barns to meet the horses. Where is everyone else, Mom?"

"Quiet Hour," said Vivian, playfully rolling her eyes to the ceiling. "How soon you forget."

"True that. After we got home from school," Linda explained to Will, "we were subjected to Quiet Hour during which time we were expected to complete all homework assignments and read a book for family discussion. Of course, the word 'hour' was a misnomer. It is more like *hours*. We suspected it gave Dad and Mom some *quiet* time of their own before the hordes were unleashed."

"True that," joked Vivian, and looked at her watch. "Your father should be closing up shop shortly and heading home. I have some calls I need to make. Show Will around while you have a little time. Do you want me to take Teresa?"

"No, you go ahead, Mom. I haven't seen her in a while, so we'll hang out."

"Okay, babe. Make yourself comfortable for now, Will. It will probably be the only sane experience you will have for the duration of your visit," she joked before departing.

Will watched her go, then asked Linda, "Has anyone ever mentioned that your mother and the actress Jada Pinkett Smith could be identical twins? She's taller than I thought from the pictures I've seen of her."

Linda laughed. "Many times people have remarked about the uncanny resemblance between Ms. Pinkett-Smith and my father's resemblance to the actor Johnny Depp."

"Sure, if Johnny was seven feet tall," Will joked.

"Six-eleven and a half barefoot," Chuck joked as he entered the great room wearing blue hospital scrubs, and carrying a toddler, but they also wore an identical gold chain that read **FAMILY**. Little Teresa squealed her delight clapping her hands and reaching for her father and baby brother. "There's my sugar lump," Chuck said noisily, kissing his youngest girl and then his oldest, Linda. "Hello, Will," he said extending his hand. "Welcome to the ranch house."

"Thanks," Will said shaking his hand. "It's the largest *'ranch house'* I've ever seen."

Chuck laughed. "We need every inch for my posse," he said kissing his son and daughter's cheeks. "Don't we, sugar lump?"

The two babies leaned toward each other delivering a noisy kiss and then clapping their little hands.

Linda reached for the baby boy. "Hi there, Alex," Linda cooed to the grinning little boy. For that, she, too, received a kiss from the baby. "Will and I were just talking about you, handsome," she said, then turned to Will. "This is Alexander Jackson Montgomery, my youngest brother."

The boy grinned up at Will and then reached for him. Will took him from Linda's arms. Alex palmed Will's jaw and clearly said, "Kiss," and proceeded to do just that. He kissed Will on the mouth, grinned, and then clapped his little hands.

Will was laughing at the toddler's antics when, "Dad's home," someone yelled from the balcony above.

Will could hear doors opening above and feet clamoring down multiple staircases. Suddenly the great room filled up with the Montgomery offspring. They were like stair steps and every shade from ebony to ivory. Each wore the gold **FAMILY** chain. Each came forward to introduce him or herself, shake Will's hand or collect a hug, barrage him with questions, and chat him up on an array of topics. The noise level grew until Vivian returned causing silence to reign. Chuck kissed his wife salaciously while still holding their daughter, Will noticed.

Witnessing the blatant emotion exchanged between the interracial couple and between them and their horde of children, conjured thoughts of his own parents before drugs and alcohol destroyed their once warm and supportive home. However, watching this family was like nothing he had ever witnessed before. They really seemed to *like* each other, Will thought as he observed their interaction. When Dena returned with her twin brothers, and Eugene, and Violet, they, too, were swept up in the amalgamation of individuals. Because, although they were a tightly-knit group, they were very much individuals with a wide range of interests.

Will wondered how Chuck and Vivian managed to accommodate all of the personalities they were raising. As he continued to talk with various members of the family, learning to put names with faces, he recognized what was central to their household was unquestionable love, support, and deep respect. They talked with each other without arguing and, regardless of the topic under discussion, it never became personal.

Before dinner, Linda took him, Eugene, and Violet on a tour of the mansion, starting with a guest bedroom for him. One of the twins had already placed his luggage in the room. Eugene and Violet would share rooms with children in their age group. Some of the bedrooms had twin or bunk beds with Jack and Jill baths for the toddlers up through preteens, while the teens had bedrooms with single bathrooms to themselves. All of the rooms were spacious and spoke to the creative tastes of the inhabitants living in them. The rest of the mansion was a marvel with salons and even a ballroom on the first floor with a row of ten-foot doors which opened onto a slate-gray terrace on the west wing of the house.

Will and the children were bowled over by the in-home swimming pool in a domed solarium. When Linda led them through, several of the Montgomery children were having a game of water volleyball. They stopped momentarily in the gymnasium to watch Chuck and Vivian wearing T-shirts, shorts, and tennis shoes, playing a full-court game of basketball with eight of their sons and daughters on each team. The referees were another set of twins, Geneviève and Vincent.

The library had bookcases filled floor-to-the-ten-foot ceiling. A number of young people were perched in the comfortable-looking chairs or stretched out on the floor quietly reading or researching something. A ladder anchored and ran along a rail to allow access to books shelved higher up. More chairs and large tables were strategically placed amid large, green potted plants. They moved quietly so as not to disturb the chess games going on in the room.

The trophy room contained mahogany walls and cabinets with glass shelves. Pot lights came on inside the cabinets and shone through the shelves from the top, illuminating awards on three sides of the room.

"Wow, this is real mahogany," commented Will, rubbing a hand up and down the wall.

"It is. My maternal grandfather, Bernard Alexander, and his son, my Uncle Kenneth, are the woodworkers in this family. They salvaged this wood from a place in Pennsylvania days before a wrecking crew took down the building." She rubbed a hand across the fireplace mantle. "Every trophy my dads, mom, me or my sibs ever received are here in this room."

"Your dads, plural?"

"Yes, both Derrick's and Chuck's awards are here. See, this is one of Derrick's Olympic Gold Medals, his championship rings, his diplomas, and certificates." She pointed them out to Will in the cabinets. "Chuck and Mom still receive awards as do all of my siblings. Everything is on display here. We leave space for other awards for the little ones."

"It's a beautiful room," said Will awed.

In yet another large room, family pictures graced every wall. "This is my first father," said Linda showing Will and the children a life-sized portrait of Derrick, Chuck and Vivian posed together. "The dads met as preteens when my uncles were working on the renovation of inner-city homes in Philadelphia. It was summer and Chuck, the youngest boy, was with his brothers living in mobile homes while they worked, but

Chuck, who was only nine at the time, would go to a local playground to watch the kids play basketball. Although he was a big kid for his age who grew up on a working farm, he didn't know how to play. One day, the star basketball player at age twelve tossed a ball to Chuck and asked him if he wanted to learn. The star was Derrick Jelon Jackson who lived in the neighborhood, and from that point on you didn't see one without the other."

"DJ Jackson," said Will. "I was much younger when I first heard about him from my brother Harold who was a basketball fanatic, but I didn't know about Derrick's history. I only knew him to be the most awesome ballplayer ever to live."

Linda smiled. "He was. The news media called him Dunk and Jam Jackson for DJ, but he was just dad to us.

"The families became friends and eventually the Montgomerys, who are primarily farmers, sold land to the Jacksons. They became neighbors," Linda said showing them group portraits of both families as she gave a running commentary. "Two of my Jackson aunts are married to two of my Montgomery uncles," she said again pointing out portraits and putting names to faces.

"*Whoa!*" exclaimed Will pointing to an impossibly long photograph of people sitting on what looked like stadium bleachers.

Linda chuckled. "That's a photograph of last year's Alexander family reunion. See, there I am," she pointed. "It's held for ten days around the Juneteenth holiday in Goodwill, Summer County, South Carolina. We have a home there and one in Monroe County, Pennsylvania, where we usually spend parts of the summer, alternating Thanksgiving, and/or Christmas holidays with our grandparents, uncles, aunts, and cousins. See, here are other photos taken for previous years, dating back to the beginning of flash photography. Easter holidays are usually spent at the Jackson-Montgomery family reunion in Pennsylvania. If we're lucky there's still snow in the Poconos at that time and we can go skiing."

"You have an extraordinary number of twins in each generation I see in these pictures."

"That's true, and triplets, too. Dad and Mom adopted six sets of twins in this family alone. No triplets . . . yet, but who knows what our future holds," she said laughing. "My Uncle Kenneth and Aunt JeNelle have three sets of twins and one set of triplets. Aunt JeNelle's mother is a twin as was her grandfather. My Uncle Benny and Aunt Stacy have two sets of triplets. Aunt Stacy is a twin and her maternal grandmother has two sets of twins. My maternal grandfather, Bernard Alexander, is a twin. His twin sister has a set of twins, Donald and James Dixon. They both are married with twins in their families."

Will laughed and shook his head as they continued to tour the room filled with family pictures and portraits on display. He stopped and looked more closely at a group of sepia-toned pictures.

Linda noticed his interest. "My maternal great, great grands, my Grandmother Sylvia Benson Alexander, from the Benson side of the family. They were a large generational troupe of Vaudeville performers who toured Europe, Asia, and Africa with the great Josephine Baker. In each generation, World War I and II chased them back to the States. However, my grand aunt still lives in Paris, France. Have you heard of the French Mariah?"

"Who hasn't," Will quipped and then just stared. "The French Mariah is your grand aunt?"

Linda nodded.

"Who is she, Uncle Will?" asked Eugene.

"She is one of the most celebrated European singers and actresses. She won all kinds of awards in her career so far, and she's only in her late fifties or early sixties. I have copies of several of her performances I'll show to you when we get back home."

"We have all of her performances on disks. I'll burn a copy for you. She is great. When I have performances in France, I stay with her at a lovely home passed down through the generations of the family since the turn of the century. She still owns and operates a very popular and fashionable nightclub in Paris. The Bensons are originally from the Gullah clans off the southern coast of South Carolina."

"I never heard of them," commented Eugene.

"The Gullah are the descendants of enslaved Africans who lived in the Lowcountry regions of South Carolina, which includes both the coastal plain and the Sea Islands. The Gullah people and their language are also called Geechee. *Gullah* is a term that was originally used to designate the variety of English spoken by Gullah and Geechee people, but over time it has been used by its speakers to formally refer to their creole language and distinctive ethnic identity as a people. They have a very successful cottage industry making beautiful Sweet Water Baskets the same way they were made in Africa before the slave trade destroyed their way of life. When we get back to New York, we'll spend an evening talking more about them and that part of my family ancestry. I have pictures of my relatives and many baskets they've made. I can't wait to display the baskets in my new home."

Will was also looking forward to that experience as much if not more than the children were as they continued their tour of the castle-like mansion.

Amazing, Will thought, again, as they went into a hall that resembled a well-appointed cafeteria for dinner. Beautiful and large chandeliers hung above the round tables which were covered with stunning, spring-colored cloths, flowered centerpieces with lit candles, and gleaming dishes. It looked like fine dining in a five-star restaurant but didn't feel as if this was arranged as a special occasion. For this family, it seemed quite commonplace. After six bells chimed, the room quieted to silence, and one of the children said grace. Again, as if routine, the older ones helped the younger ones serve themselves from the awesome array of buffet stations.

Apparently, the children and teens each had duty work and had dressed the many tables in preparation for the evening meal. Again, Will lost sight of Eugene and Violet who, with smiling faces, were incorporated at tables in the discussions with children in their peer group.

Shortly after she and Will stepped up to one of the buffet stations, in came more family members. Her aunt, US Senator JeNelle Towson Alexander, her husband, former California two-term Governor Kenneth Alexander, and their nine children arrived. Kenneth was the owner and operator of CompuCorrect Global, a telecommunications firm on the cutting edge of technology and an internet and intranet provider. They were accompanied by Linda's cousin, Whitney Ivy Alexander, and her fiancée, physician and Marine Captain, Tucker Cavanaugh. Whitney and Tucker were another interracial couple, both with movie-idol good looks. They entered to welcoming calls and shout-outs from the family in general. All wore the signature **FAMILY** gold chain. After hugs and kisses abound, the new arrivals came and were introduced to Will. Whitney and Tucker stayed with Linda at one of the buffet stations where Linda made introductions.

"Whitney Ivy is the eldest daughter of my uncle and aunt, Benny and Stacy Greene Alexander. You may remember the pictures I showed you in the family room of her and her two sets of triplets siblings."

"*Wait*, what? You don't mean Astronaut Benjamin Alexander, do you? The five-star General?" asked Will stunned. He hadn't made the connection earlier when looking at the pictures. They weren't wearing military uniforms in any of the photos and Linda didn't pump up their celebrity.

"Well, yes, but he's just daddy to me," Whitney joked. "When I heard Linda was bringing you home, I came and brought Tucker with me because we're both big fans of yours."

"It's an honor to meet you, Mr. Hamilton," said Tucker. "I'm a bigger fan of yours than Whitney is," he joked. "She's more of a basketball fanatic."

"Why don't we let Will fill his plate? Then we can sit down and have a little chat about who is his biggest fan," joked Linda.

"I have a feeling Tucker and I would come out on the losing end of that contest," suggested Whitney. She winked at Linda. "You done good, Cousin."

They filled their plates and sat with Chuck, Vivian, Kenneth, and JeNelle. *The conversation around the table was lively and interesting*, thought Will. A great deal of the chat centered on the progress made on Linda's school of dance and new residence. After she brought everyone up to date, the talk shifted from Tucker's progress in his second year of medical residency to Whitney's upcoming exams at the end of her second year of law school. It then dawned on Will that neither Whitney nor Tucker looked old enough to be close to completion of such extraordinarily tough career training. In fact, Whitney looked as if she should still be in high school and Tucker didn't look much older.

"Are you finished?" asked one of the twins, Roger or Ryan, as he assisted with clearing the dishes from the table.

"I am, yes, but I can do that," Will said. He, like others, visited the buffet stations several times and were now finishing coffee and dessert.

"Not this time, Will. Today you're a guest, however, tomorrow, you're just one of the posse," said Chuck, laughing.

"Thank you . . . I think," Will said laughing, too.

"Well, that's my cue," said Linda. "I'm on dish duty, so I'll leave you to fend for yourself, Will," she said rising and patting him on the shoulder when he started to rise. "No, keep your seat."

"My name is on the same list," said Whitney Ivy, as she, too, rose to accompany her cousin and BFF into the kitchen.

Will continued to talk with those left at the table over another cup of coffee and a second dessert.

Once inside the kitchen, Linda and Whitney Ivy joined Dena, Roger, Ryan, and another brother, Preston, and a host of Alexander cousins in an assembly-line effort to scrape the dishes, rinse them, and then place them in the industrial-sized dishwashers. Others took on the task of storing the leftovers while another group attacked the pots and pans, washing them in deep sinks.

"So, what's it like to be dating a man of Will Hamilton's caliber?" asked Whitney Ivy as they worked.

"Yeah, cuz, tell all," commented Kenny Alexander; a twin and the eldest son of Kenneth and JeNelle Alexander, a few years younger than Whitney Ivy and Linda.

"I heard the buzz, too, all the way out in California," commented Marcella Alexander, another twin and daughter of Kenneth and JeNelle.

Linda laughed. "As I told Dena, I'm not sure what Will and I are doing is called 'dating'."

"From what I've seen of them it's exactly what they're doing," commented Dena. "He's very attentive to her."

Linda shrugged. "That's true and we've shared some interesting kisses, but it hasn't gone beyond that."

"It's early days yet," said Whitney Ivy. "What's it been two or three months?"

"Approximately, but he, apparently, dated or is dating Jolie Jance," Linda commented.

"Who is she?" asked Whitney Ivy. "You said her name as if we should know her."

"She's a local television news reporter and personality in the city. You'll probably meet her when you come to the open house for my dance studio. She contacted Uncle Bill to arrange to interview me for her show. He agreed and put her on my schedule for whenever the open house takes place. Some time ago, she made it clear Will escorted her to one of my performances earlier this year. She cornered him at a recent open casting call and audition for The Nutcracker. The way she looked at him," she shared and shrugged, "there was definitely chemistry between them."

"How did he look at her?" asked Kenny.

Linda thought a moment. "You know, I really couldn't tell you. His initial reaction to her was rather bland, but then I was called back onto the stage to resume auditions and didn't notice how they finished their conversation."

"As long as you feel respected, let him deal with any other drama-filled relationships he may have," said Preston. "If this woman is on his case, he seems to be the type of person who will man up and clean the slate."

"I agree with Whitney, Cousin. If or when you feel ready for an exclusive relationship with him, then it will be time to ask the necessary questions. Until then, take it light," Marcella advised and nonchalantly shrugged.

They continued to talk and work. In short order, the remaining food was put away, the counters and floors cleaned, and the trash bagged and taken out to a compost pile. What little garbage there was ended up being bagged for the pigs' trough.

When they returned to the dining hall, everyone was up and moving toward the music salon. The ones who played instruments and/or sang gathered on a raised platform and, after tuning their instruments, ripped off several well-known tunes. JeNelle played the piano like a concert pianist. Shortly, the gathering became a singalong and, for the next hour, the performers took turns soloing. However, when Whitney Ivy and Tucker strummed their guitars and sang a few duets, Will thought he recognized the sound of Whitney's voice. Drew had a favorite group named Ivy and he incessantly played their music. The more they sang, the more Will was convinced Whitney Ivy Alexander was the lead singer and guitarist on the many albums he heard Drew play.

With his right arm stretched across the back of a sofa and Linda snuggled against his side, he was able to turn his head and whispered in Linda's ear, "Is Whitney the voice I've heard from the group known as Ivy?"

Linda turned her head studying Will's face for ponderous moments before she nodded. "Yes, but you have to keep it a secret, Will, please. We all work hard to keep her identity and that of her triplet sisters who perform with her, undisclosed," she whispered back. "I'll explain later," she said as Whitney and Tucker finished their duets and applause filled the room.

"Do you do this often?" asked Will moments later. "Have in-home concerts, I mean."

"All the time when we're here and the little ones can stay up a little later," she said and then pointed out the sound booth where audio and video recording equipment was used to memorialize each occasion. "Then again, we do this especially, during certain holidays when all the uncles, aunts and cousins are at home in Goodwill, South Carolina. We put on shows as part of our Juneteenth entertainment. There's a lot of talent in the family. So far, you've only met some of the Alexander side. Uncle Kenneth is the eldest of five of my mother's siblings. Then there's Uncle Benny, my Mom, Uncle Gregory, and my Aunt Aretha, who you haven't met yet.

"Most of the Alexander and Benson cousins, who are still in school, go home for spring break," Linda concluded.

"You consider South Carolina your home?" asked Will.

"Yes, we do," Linda said nodding. "It's where our family began in this country. We go south for the annual Juneteenth family reunion to renew our connection with our ancestry. Then for Easter and Thanksgiving, we go to the Montgomery and Jackson sides of the family in Monroe County. They all live on farms, so we get to ride horses and all-terrain vehicles or motorcycles. As I mentioned before, if we're lucky we'll get snow. We all love to ski downhill and cross country. We spend Christmas in the north or the south in alternating years, but we come back here to Maryland for New Year's Eve. Dad and Mom always have a New Year's Eve ball for family and friends.

"Just before school opens around Labor Day, all of the young cousins, who are still in any kind of school, trade or profession, college, or grad school, gather at Great-grandaunt Hanna Ivy Benson's home and camp out in tents on the sand in Atlantic Beach, South Carolina. We do that to reinforce our pact to work hard and smart for the greater good for each generation.

"Great-grandaunt Hannah Ivy's place is a big, old, wood-frame home with gingerbread cutouts on the veranda and balconies. It sits right on the shoreline with an unobstructed, panoramic view of the Atlantic Ocean. We're pressed into doing whatever she wants, including painting the place whatever whimsical colors she desires that year. No one complains about the work she has us do because we love her and she's a feisty eighty-something year old. She convinced Uncle Greg to move there with her and place the house in a conservatorship. It's on the National Register for Historic Homes, but she wants the gathering of young family members to continue in perpetuity. We're big on family tradition," she said laughing.

"You're a very supportive group of family members," Will commented.

She nodded, smiling. "We are certainly that. When we have difficulties, we share them and work them out together. It's always been that way and we wouldn't want to change it for anything."

"This seems so idyllic. It's hard to believe this many people can get along with each other all of the time."

"Oh, no, we argue, but the Grands taught us to disagree without being disagreeable. You may not have noticed it, but on the front of every door in every Alexander, Jackson, and Montgomery home, the words 'kindness is spoken here,' appears and reminds us to be civil to each other. Dad and Mom don't allow us to be any other way with each other. Then there are The Alexander Family Principles passed down through the ages from our ancient ancestors we learned along with our A B Cs. The Principles are as sacred to the family as are the Ten Commandments. They are the glue that has held this family together since the beginning. We are not a particularly religious family, but we have studied all forms of religion as an academic endeavor like learning the history of the world and nature. Because we all come from so many backgrounds and ethnicities, our parents don't force us to ascribe to any particular dogma. However, we are free to practice any body of doctrines concerning faith or morals we may choose. I'll tell you more about it later, but it's getting late and we have a big day ahead of us tomorrow.

"I think it's definitely time for the little people to say goodnight," commented Dena.

Will noticed Violet was already asleep in Dena's lap, and Eugene was fighting to stay awake, leaning against Dena's arm. He and Linda rose from their comfortable seats and took the children upstairs to bed. While they were upstairs and passed the open door of room after room, Will noticed the older siblings reading bedtime stories to the younger ones once they were showered and tucked into bed. Then Chuck and Vivian visited each bedroom to kiss and hug their offspring goodnight.

It was such a simple thing that probably meant the world to the children to have stories read to them. Eugene and Violet liked to read, so he ordered books for them. What he hadn't considered was taking time to read to or with them at night. After they showered, they went to bed and he usually went to his in-home office to work. He'd have to rethink his nightly routine with them.

He was learning a great deal about parenting by being around Linda and her family. No wonder she knew so much about what the "little people" needed. It was also good preparation for when he had a wife and children of his own. The more he saw, the more he wanted to have a wife and children. Maybe not as large as the Alexander-Montgomery family, but a noisy crew with a couple of loopy dogs. He wondered whether Eugene and Violet would like to have a dog. He'd have to talk with them about it.

He spent more time with Chuck, Vivian, Kenneth, JeNelle, Linda, Dena, Whitney Ivy, and Tucker until nearing midnight. As he talked with them, he began to see how they were able to cope with so many children. They were operating from a firm set of principles that were central to their existence and an overriding factor . . . family first, last and always. The parents all had busy and challenging careers, but nothing came before their dedication to their children.

As they traversed the halls, on the way to his assigned bedroom suite, Will never would have believed it could be that simple or that quiet with a house full of people and a farm full of workmen and women. Bedroom doors were open, but lights were out, except for those lights in the open hallway overlooking the great room below.

For now, he went to the room Linda had shown him earlier on the third floor to prepare for bed. It was a nice, spacious room with an adjoining bath and standup shower. The bed was king-sized and comfortable with end tables, a desk and chair, and an organized closet system. The furniture looked handmade and sturdy, but the bed and sofa coverings were of a more modern design. Linda had shared that Kenneth and his father were the woodworking hobbyists in the Alexander family and had crafted much of the furniture he saw here and in Gregory's home in New York. When Will crawled beneath the crisp, fresh-smelling covers on the sturdy king-sized bed, his last thoughts were of Linda before he dropped into a deep sleep.

Chapter 13

The next morning, Linda rose early with the sound of the roosters crowing and began her exercise routine in the in-home gym. She then showered and dressed in jeans, a T-shirt, and riding boots. When she entered the kitchen, she found her parents kissing, which was not an unusual sight.

"Uh, is this a bad time?" she teased.

"Yes, go away," said her father before Vivian eased out of his embrace and laughed at her husband's mutinous expression. "To be continued," he told his wife and winked at her.

"You two are worse than newlyweds," teased Linda.

"We *are* newlyweds," Chuck insisted. "We'll always *be* newlyweds."

"What's up with you, Linda? Something on your mind? You've been a little off-center since you arrived."

Linda nodded while pouring a cup of coffee for herself. That Mother Radar was in the On position and always working. She sat at the long trestle table with her parents in the sunny breakfast room. "Recently, I began to wonder about my biological parents. Who they were and what they did. Before I went to sleep last night, Whitney Ivy and I took some time to go through the trunk full of their things, but we didn't learn very much or anything new. Do you remember much about them, Mom?"

"No, babe. I didn't know them at all. You were already Derrick's patient at the orphanage for at least two years before I met you at your eighth birthday party held at the hospital while you were still a patient there. I was twenty-one years old and in my second year of law school.

When Derrick and I agreed to adopt you, as a part of the process, I did a search for any of your living relatives and Derrick had a DNA test done on you, but we didn't find a familial match. I didn't have samples of your parents' DNA to use for a test. What I found through records was that your father died in Iraq during a terrorist attack. He worked for one of the companies which negotiated to buy Arab oil. Your mother was a linguist who also worked for the same company as a translator. I didn't check their passports, but I assumed, because you were born here in the US, your mother returned to the states when she became pregnant with you and your father stayed in Iraq to work. They had a home in Arlington, Virginia. He must have come back to the states periodically. Then your brother was born several years after you. Other than the fact that we wanted you for our own, we didn't search for any other information. The court investigated and then granted permission for the adoption and that was that. Is there something specific you're interested in knowing?"

"I don't have a sense of them, of my biological parents, and that's a little surprising to me. I'm their natural child, but I don't feel as if I belong to anyone except you two. Is that strange?"

"It's normal, babe. You lived with your parents, or at least your mother, until you were about six years old. You've been mine and your dads' since you were eight years old. It's nurture over nature. I believe it's as simple as that. There's nothing unnatural about it."

"Derrick and I were best friends and working at Georgetown Medical Center together during that time," said Chuck, "but I don't remember as much as your mother does. However, if there is something more you need to know, we'll find the answers you're looking for."

"Thanks, Dad. I just wish I knew what it is that I *want* to know. It's like an itch I can't seem to scratch."

"I've got some calamine lotion if it gets to be a problem," Chuck joked and made Linda laugh. "Everything else okay with you?"

"It is, yes. As I said last night, the progress on the school is proceeding nicely thanks to the funds you two gave me and the uncles coming in from Pennsylvania to manage aspects of the project. If all stays on track,

I should be able to move in and open the school on schedule when we return from the family reunion.

"Auditions for my male lead went well. I've narrowed it to two men, both of whom I've worked with before and a third man, who shows incredible promise. I'd like to work with him in the theatre and as an instructor at the school. He's very interested in and enthusiastic about taking on the challenge. Finally, I've agreed to do a week-long Holiday on Ice program just before the start of The Nutcracker, but, beyond that, I'm keeping my options open for the coming year. I've asked Bill not to accept any new contracts."

"What about your relationship with Will? I know you've brought friends home with you before, but I have to wonder whether this time is different. After all, I did find you two kissing at the hospital."

"No new news on that front, Dad. For now, we're still just friends and I'm still a virgin."

"*Whoa!* TMI, babe! There are things your parents don't need to know," said Chuck.

"The heck with that," scoffed Vivian comfortably ensconced in her husband's open arms. "Speak for yourself, pal," she said to Chuck with an elbow in his ribs. Then to Linda, she said, "Your father may be a doctor and squeamish when talking about sex when it comes to his daughter, but I'm not him. I want to know every beautiful and exciting detail. If there are any questions about sex we haven't answered when you were still a little girl and growing up to be a responsible young lady, fire away. However, I believe you know the drill. There ain't no love without the glove. You're old enough, strong enough, and smart enough to know when the time is right for you."

They continued to talk and laugh as the rest of the household came awake and filtered into the breakfast hall.

Will believed he had the best sleep of his life. There was no noise of horns blowing or sirens screaming which contributed to a restless sleep. Just absolute silence and comfort. When he got out of bed, he opened the draperies and a pair of French doors to step out onto the upper terrace overlooking the west side of the property. For as far as his eyes could see in any direction, there were green pastures and woodlands beyond. He looked more closely and spotted deer grazing near the edge and drinking from the stream that contributed to the lake at the front of the mansion. He breathed deep of the fresh air, expanding his lungs and fully stretching his muscles. As he watched the activity underway on the farm, he noticed some of the children coming from a barn carrying what looked like baskets of fresh eggs.

Workmen and women were tending to the farm and raised a hand in acknowledgment as the children passed by. He learned last night Chuck and Vivian hired most of the men, women, and families, who worked on the farm and lived there year-round, from a family homeless shelter in Washington, DC. He met the two men and one woman who cooked the meals for the Alexander-Montgomery family, but according to the cooks, the children did much of the housework keeping the mansion clean. Others came in once a week to do the heavy cleaning of the common areas.

When he left the balcony, he went back into his suite, shaved, showered, and put on a pair of comfortable jeans and a T-shirt. It was shaping up to be another glorious day.

As he came down the back staircase, the scent of breakfast and pastries permeated the air. He followed his nose when he caught the scent of fresh-brewed coffee. Everyone was gathering in a different hall from the one where they had dinner the night before. This one was brighter and airier with live spring flowers and greenery in baskets hanging from the girders supporting the glass ceilings and walls. Soothing music played from hidden speakers.

"This way, Mr. Hamilton," said Brian, the oldest boy, still younger than Linda, but older than Dena. Will also recalled talking with him the night before. He graduated from college and grad school at Penn State with an MBA but chose to come back to the farm as the general manager. He had a sizeable two-bedroom cabin that sat back in the woods near a stream where Will had seen the deer. Brian carried several large fish he apparently caught fresh this morning and was preparing to clean and cook them. Will had never been fishing so he couldn't tell one fish from another outside of a fish market, but these looked fairly meaty.

Brian must have caught him looking at the fish and said, "Aquafarming. These are trout. I brought some other fish up earlier this morning, but this is the last of them for breakfast. We operate the fishery in barn Number 3. If you like, I'll show you around after breakfast."

"Thanks, Brian. I'd like that."

"Okay, help yourself. It's Saturday morning, so everyone operates at their own speed for breakfast."

Again, the array of foods on separate stations was staggering. He never had shrimp and grits or grits with gravy before, but he put a sample of each in small bowls on his plate with a healthy mound of eggs scrambled with cheese, fat, hot sausages, and hot Mexicali home fries. By the time he finished gathering a sample of this and that, with a mug of coffee and a large glass of orange juice, he needed the tray Geneviève Montgomery offered to him. He thanked her, filled the tray, and joined Tucker and someone he didn't recognize at one of the tables. Absently, he noticed that Tucker also wore the gold **FAMILY** chain, but the stranger did not.

"Will Hamilton, this is Wesley Greenfield. Wesley is responsible for the great pastries, cakes, pies, and breads you'll have over this weekend. He and his brother, Isaac, own and operate Greenfield Brothers."

"I've heard of your bakeries and coffee houses from JaiHonnah Baylor, but she mentioned that you head the construction of an inner-city village, Baylor Plaza and Park?"

"I do, yes. Her husband, J Roderick Baylor, and I grew up together. It was his vision for our old neighborhood in a tough part of the city that made Baylor Plaza Park a reality."

"JRock. Yes, of course, like millions of others, I followed his stellar career on the hardwood, but I only met him recently when he and JaiHonnah came to look at the progress on the building Linda purchased. I understand he and JaiHonnah own and operate Baylor and Baylor Design and Developers. They've been back several times to monitor the progress and Linda and I have been out to lunch or dinner with them.

From what I saw, on one of those home show networks, the Baylor Plaza Park is a very innovative and cutting-edge project."

"It is, yes. It's larger in acreage than New York City's Central Park and geared to continue to change and develop with new technologies," said Wesley.

Will nodded, "I'd like to see it when I have more time."

"You're welcome any time," Wesley said rising from his seat and shaking Will's hand. "I wish I could stay and talk more now, but I just had enough time to deliver three of my five children and the pastries, pies, and cakes for the birthday party today. We're breaking ground on another phase of the Baylor Plaza Park project this morning, but my wife, Rosalyn, and I will be back later with our youngest Elizabeth and Hunter. My brother, Isaac and his wife, Carla, plan to come with their sons, too."

"It was a pleasure to meet you. I'll see you later and look forward to meeting your family," said Will as he sat down again to finish eating. "Have Linda and Whitney come down yet?" he asked Tucker.

"They were out early with your nephew and niece for a ride. They've been gone for about an hour so they should be back soon for breakfast."

"Wow, it's not even seven in the morning yet."

Tucker nodded. "Early risers. They're up when the roosters crow," he said laughing. "By the way, Linda mentioned that you recognized Whitney's voice as the lead singer of the group Ivy."

"I did, yes. She has such a distinctive and engaging sound, but Linda asked me not to mention it to anyone, and I won't. Not even to my brother who is a huge fan."

"Good," Tucker said on an exhale of breath. "We're very security conscious, particularly because Whitney's parents are active duty military stationed in Japan and there are factions who would want to take advantage of that situation. Whitney's dad is an Air Force jet fighter pilot, five-star general and astronaut, and her mom is a US Navy Admiral, head of the Pacific Fleet. That's why Ivy only does limited engagements and wears costumes and heavy makeup so they can't be identified.

"A few years ago, Angelique was targeted for abduction by a human trafficking ring. These criminals held silent auctions on a worldwide basis on the dark web and bid on notables they wanted abducted. They operated with impunity for many years, but the authorities, represented in the nations of the G7, sanctioned their capture or demise."

"Yes, I remember the story," Will acknowledged.

"You're probably familiar with Constantina Justice, the talk show host. She is a very close friend of Vivian's. They were in undergrad together. She was also targeted for abduction, but she broke that story during the arrests phase and covered the trials for her Sweet Justice Television Network. There were plans underway to abduct other high-profile people like Vivian and Linda."

A cold chill ran up Will's back causing him to stop eating and stare at Tucker. "Okay, did they get all of the bastards?"

Tucker nodded. "As far as the authorities know they did, but it still means other criminals could target Linda, Angelique, Whitney Ivy, and any number of others. Not only just for their celebrity or familial connections, but also for their wealth. As you probably know Vivian is one of the wealthiest women in the world and a US Supreme Court Judge. Linda and Whitney, as well as all of the siblings, have healthy trust funds. Their Uncle Kenneth is a wealthy industrialist and former, two-term governor of California. His wife, JeNelle, is a US Senator. Their Uncle Gregory is a Wall Street tycoon. Chuck is a former basketball star and now an affluent physician who owns a hospital."

"That's why Linda has armed escorts and private car services. I never even thought of that."

"It's also why she and the rest of her family are very circumspect about getting involved with others outside the family and close friends. They don't want to put anyone in jeopardy by association with them. The criminals thought they kidnapped Angelique for her celebrity and connection to the Alexander family through Gregory when, in actuality, they kidnapped the high-fashion model and cover girl, Arden. Still, a choice person to abduct. Fortunately, the authorities swiftly moved in and rescued Arden before they got her away from the premises in New York City."

"I recall there was an attempt by the Boko Horam to abduct twenty young African girls who were being protected here in the United States," said Will.

"Yes, that was a part of the same criminal organization. Vivian's friends were intimately involved in shielding those girls as was Whitney's mother, Stacy."

"I'll keep my eyes open whenever Linda and I are together, especially when she's in Indulgences."

Tucker nodded. "We all use extreme caution, but I'm a Marine and in love with Whitney. That combination makes me sometimes be overprotective of her, but I don't want to smother her with my concerns for her safety. The security company they use is very respectful of the family members' boundaries and make themselves very unobtrusive and inconspicuous. The system works well, but if you notice anything out of place, go with your first instinct and get her security team involved."

The thought of anyone harming one strand of hair on Linda's head had angry bile rising in Will's gut. He would be extra vigilant with her, but like Tucker, he didn't want to smother her.

Just then, the object of his affection came in with his nephew and niece who were properly attired in cowboy and cowgirl costumes complete with riding boots and Stetson hats. He found himself laughing at the sight as Eugene and Violet rushed to tell him all about their adventures riding the ponies, Smoky Joe and Shiloh.

Linda followed them and added more detail to their exploits. Eventually, Linda sent them off with her siblings to wash before they attacked the breakfast buffets. Then she sat next to him as Tucker got up to replenish his plate of food.

"What's wrong?" she asked, her eyes narrowed on his in concern.

"It amazes me that you can read me like yesterday's news."

"If you think you can divert my question, think again, pal. I'm the daughter of a great lawyer."

He ruefully shook his head in recognition of how transparent he must be to her. "I was talking with Tucker about your family's concerns about security."

She nodded. "I'm glad he talked with you. He's had to deal with it up close and personal where Whitney Ivy is concerned. She had a stalker. It's difficult for some people to understand, but we've had experiences which could have proven catastrophic. So, we are vigilant, and we learn to quickly read dangerous situations. I don't want to put you and your family in harm's way, so if you want to . . ."

"Don't even think it," Will stridently interrupted. "We'll be cautious, but we'll do it together. Agreed?"

She smiled and nodded. "Agreed. Now, how about a fresh plate of food? You've let that one get cold."

"That suits me just fine."

"I'll join you after I wash my hands and face. I'll be back shortly."

"Bring a kiss back when you come," he said smiling.

"I'll see what I can do to accommodate your request."

When she returned to the table with food in hand, the seats were filled with family and friends. However, Will managed to save a space for her next to him. They didn't get to share a kiss at that time, but Will promised to collect later.

Will had never seen so many children and young people in one space darting from one spot to another. They were everywhere in the carnival established on the Alexander-Montgomery south lawn. There were moon bounces, Ferris wheels for little people, merry-go-rounds, bumper cars, shooting galleries, bungee jumps, and row upon row of all manner of rides, games, and crafts being made. Face painters were doing a brisk business. Snow cones and fresh fruit drinks kept several stations busy. The air was redolent with the smell of barbeque, hot dogs, burgers, blooming onions, and something for every palate and taste bud. All this for the eight Montgomery kids and teens who had birthdays that month. As he looked up and around, the adults seemed to be enjoying the carnival as much as, if not more than, the kids.

He spotted Gregory and Angelique when they arrived and were immediately mobbed by his nephews and nieces. Angelique's brother, the actor and new singing sensation, Miguel Menendez-Gaza, was with them and had the young women, and some not so young, squealing. Miguel and his band promised to do a show for the birthday celebrants.

Will lost sight of Linda, Dena, his nephew, and niece down by the corral and track for pony rides. Tucker, Roger, Ryan, and others were in batting cages. He had swung at several balls and helped with the stances of a few but left the field to the next generation. Vivian and Whitney Ivy were teamed and taking on all comers for a three-point basketball shootout contest. It had been thirty minutes and the team was still reigning victorious. It wasn't tough to see how Vivian won Olympic gold playing basketball while she was still in school at Spelman College.

"Welcome to Chaos," joked Gregory as he finally waded through a sea of young family members and made it to where Will was standing near a picnic table.

Will shook Gregory's outstretched hand. "You've got that right. Your family couldn't possibly do this every month. This is insane," he said laughing.

Greg nodded. "The birthday members get their heads together and decide what they want to do for their birthday weekend. The most extreme thing was scuba diving off Vivian's island in Bimini. A month ahead of time, we get the e-mail with the details of what the birthday crew wants to do to celebrate. I've learned just to block off the weekend and expect anything. This is probably one of the tamer events."

Will shook his head looking around. "I can't imagine having to buy gifts for so many children. I'd be lost as to what to give each one of them."

"Uh, no, that's not what happens. They each choose three gifts they want. They know they will get one of the three they asked for. Everyone contributes to it. Then there are big pretzel-sized jars, one for each person, around here somewhere where people can give cash donations instead of individual gifts. Then each birthday person names a place to receive the donation of the jar of money. So, everyone gets a gift and gives a gift on his or her birthday."

"Tradition," said Will.

"Since my great, great, grandfather crawled out of the crib," said Gregory and laughed.

"That's a nice tradition."

Will and Gregory continued to talk, but more people arrived, including Greg's parents, Bernard and Sylvia Benson Alexander. After making the rounds, Gregory brought them to Will for introductions.

"It's a pleasure to meet you, Will," said Bernard shaking his hand.

If he didn't know better, he would have sworn Bernard was a younger version of the Bahamian-American actor Sir Sidney Poitier. His wife, Sylvia, could have been mistaken for the singer-songwriter and actress Phyllis Hyman. The photos in the family salon were engaging, but now he could see where the strong resemblances between the siblings, Kenneth, Benny, Vivian, Gregory, and Aretha originated. They were all perfect blends of their parents.

After introductions, Bernard and Sylvia sat with him for a while talking and laughing about stories in the annals of the family history.

"Really?" asked Will still laughing about a story Bernard and Sylvia told concerning their grandchildren, particularly about Linda, Whitney Ivy, and others.

"I kid you not!" declared Bernard. "They put lipstick on those pigs, tied ribbons around their necks, and proceeded to take them for a walk."

Will was laughing so hard tears were leaking out of his eyes.

"I didn't have the heart to tell them those pigs were going to be barbeque in a few days," said Sylvia, laughing.

Will laughed harder.

"Uh-oh, which story did you tell this time?" Linda asked when she came to the table where Will sat with her grandparents. She kissed and hugged them before she sat down next to Will.

"The one where you slapped lipstick on the pig and called it pretty," Bernard said, barely controlling his laughter. Tears were leaking out of his eyes, too.

"Oh, no," Linda said shaking her head.

"That was the most hilarious story I have ever heard," said Will.

"Oh, hang around my grands long enough and your sides would be splitting open because they've got jokes," declared Whitney Ivy as she joined the table with Tucker after hugging and kissing her grandparents.

"All of it is the gospel," said Sylvia holding up her right hand in witness. "When the grandchildren come for visits, I have to break out a pack of Depends!"

"Nana!" both Linda and Whitney said in unison, scandalized.

"Oh, Nana Sylvia speaks the truth," agreed Tucker. "I've seen the video versions of some of their antics. I've also been on the receiving end of their tricks. Last Juneteenth, they. . ." he started, but Whitney Ivy's hand quickly clamped down over his mouth.

That caused everyone at the table to laugh, but nothing could stop Bernard and Sylvia from telling other family stories with a great deal of animation contributing to the hilarity. During that time, plates heaping with food with bottles of beer were served by the children and teens. It surprised Will to see Bernard and Sylvia turn the beer bottles up to their lips and eat the barbeque ribs and ears of corn with their fingertips. They had such style, class, and sophistication about them that their grounded behavior seemed somehow out of character.

"So, that's how the Alexanders came to the shores of what is now South Carolina," Bernard was saying.

"So, your family originated in Alexandria, Egypt?"

Bernard nodded. "My ancestors, a father an six sons, were privateers who hunted the oceans in packs. If they hadn't attacked a British Man of War that was attacking a Bahamian ship, we wouldn't be here today. Caleb Alexander, the youngest son of only nineteen, boarded the Bahamian ship and saw the pretty fourteen or fifteen-year-old Bahamian maiden who was being sent into matrimony in exchange for horses. As the story goes, he was instantly in love. He lost his ship in the battle and when what must have been a hurricane blew in, he and his father's ship and his brothers' ships were separted. However, he saved the Bahamian ship although it was severely damaged. They had to sink her off the coast of South Carolina and, with the aid of the Indigenous people, hid in the swamp from the British and pirates. Over time, the Egyptians, Bahamians, and natives intermarried and set up a village which remained undetected throughout the period of slavery. They were one of the routes for the Underground Railroad. Some of the escaped enslaved stayed in the village, married, and raised families. That village became Summer County, South Carolina," finished Bernard.

"What about your family history, Will?" asked Sylvia.

He shrugged. "I vaguely remember grandparents, but I was very young, maybe five or six at the time. I do remember my father had a brother who moved to somewhere in Canada, never to be heard from again, but my mother was estranged from whatever family she had. They didn't visit and neither did we. I imagine there are family members, distant cousins, out there somewhere, but I have no idea who or where they may be. For the most part, it was the three Hamilton brothers. Now, there's just me, Drew, Eugene and Violet."

"Delightful children, they are," commented Sylvia, smiling.

"Thank you, Mrs. Alexander. Thanks to Linda's guidance, I'm learning ways of parenting."

"She's had a great deal of experience, caring for her siblings. You can't go wrong following her advice."

"Thanks, Nana," said Linda smiling at the grandparents of her heart.

Later that evening, the air chilled, and the birthday party was moved indoors to the ballroom. Miguel and his band set up at one end of the room on a stage a few feet above the dance floor. Tables and chairs were set up around the perimeter and the buffet was continuously replenished in an adjoining salon. The doors to the terrace were open, allowing people to flow back and forth. Will and Linda snuggled on a settee outside while watching the activities of the family and friends dancing to the music that never seemed to stop. They were near one of the outside fire pits that was putting off an impressive amount of heat from some strange looking logs.

"Are those real logs?" asked Will.

Linda laughed. "They were at one time. You see, nothing goes to waste on this farm. A lot of paper is generated around here and the barns are cleaned of the old hay. It is one or two of my sibs jobs this month to take old hay, paper, and paper bags, wet it down and twist them into the shape of logs. They usually have to help muck out the stalls to get the old hay and stack 'cow pies' for reuse as fertilizer."

"Oh, yuck," Will complained.

"Oh, yeah. You learn quickly in this family that if you do something wrong or exhibit unacceptable behavior, you're likely to draw cleaning out the stalls as your duty work for a month. It certainly cures the behavior problem never to be repeated. Dad and Mom tolerate a lot and turn nearly everything into a teachable experience. So, we really have to do something incredibly stupid to get the job of cleaning out the stalls."

"Have you ever had to clean out the stalls?" Will asked.

"I refuse to answer on the grounds there is no statute of limitations on crimes and punishments in this family. If I were found to be guilty, even today, I'd be sent to the barns and given a rake and hose," she said laughing. "However, we swear Dad and Mom have eyes in the back of their heads and parent radar that's always in the On position. We never got away with much. Even if we did, we felt so guilty about it, we'd tell on ourselves, just to have a clear conscience. None of us could withstand the little heart-to-heart conversations Dad and Mom would hold over infractions of the behavior rules. Many times we'd rather take a beating, than have them hold a family pow-wow, because everyone, and, I do mean everyone, got called into the discussion. We would be in the media room with a split screen with all of the aunts, uncles, cousins, and the grands watching as we explained what we did and why we thought it was a good idea at the time. It's the most painful experience to have to share your stupidity with the family like that and that is the rule in each family. Because we're spread out all over the globe, we video conference though Uncle Kenneth's company for hours during set times on Sundays. No matter when an infraction occurred, we knew we were going to have to face the family on Sunday."

"I imagine your cousins were as vigilant as you were in keeping down the crimes because of the punishments."

"Oh, yes, they were, but my parents didn't always stand us up before the firing squad. For example, we were giving our lunches to some kids we knew were hungry, but we didn't tell our parents about it because the kids' father was brutal and threatened them. We were afraid if we told Dad and Mom they would get involved and maybe it would make things worse for the kids we were trying to help."

"Did your parents find out?" Will asked.

She nodded. "They did, yes. You see, in this family, the worst thing you can do is tell a lie. We learned early to always tell the truth. We don't know how Dad and Mom knew we were giving away our lunches at summer camp, but they asked us point blank one day, and no one could lie about it. As we expected they got involved and we were afraid we made the situation worse."

"What happened?"

"Dad and Mom hired a private investigator to find out why the children weren't being fed. The investigator learned that the father was abusive and drank away the money his wife made as a grocery store clerk. He didn't have a job and he beat his wife and children all the time. When the investigator had enough evidence, Dad, Mom, and the investigator took the matter to the police and the county attorney. The man was arrested, later incarcerated, and killed in prison. My parents helped the woman and her children get back on their feet, and now she's an assistant manager of the grocery store where she worked for years. We kept in touch with the family and they're doing fine now."

"So, you didn't have to face the firing squad for that infraction?"

"Oh, we got a good talking to by our parents, all right. They made it clear they expected us to tell them whenever we discovered anyone in jeopardy like that and not to let it go on or try to handle it ourselves. We learned the lesson to trust our parents without question. They have never let us down."

Will squeezed her to him and kissed the top of her head. "I want you to be able to trust me the same way," he said holding her.

"You're earning my trust, Will, believe me."

They sat quietly listening to the music coming from the ballroom until Will noticed Chuck dance past one of the open doors.

"What's that your father is doing?" he asked sitting up straighter, craning his neck to follow Chuck's movements.

"The Down N Dirty," said Linda rising and grabbing Will's hand to lead him into the ballroom.

Will stood with Linda just inside the ballroom doors watching a complicated line dance being led by nearly seven-foot former basketball great *cum* medical doctor Chuck Montgomery. He was smooth with his moves even though he was wearing cowboy boots, his Stetson pulled down on his head with his thumbs stuck down in his jean pockets. The steps were so quick and intricate; Will couldn't quite get the pattern of the moves in his head.

Linda grabbed his hand. "Come on, I'll show you," and she did.

He thought it was a cross between the line dance Foot Loose and Can't Touch This, but regardless everyone was in sync including his nephew and niece. Then the music changed up and there was another line dance to master. After a while, Will was glad to just stand on the sidelines clapping and watching Chuck, Vivian, their parents, and offspring, along with friends, and the rest of their family in synchronized movements. He expected Linda to move with the flow, but he never expected his pal Gregory to have the slick moves down pat at six-foot-ten inches tall. Vivian and Gregory's parents didn't miss a step or sit down either.

At about nine o'clock the little ones started dropping off in someone's lap in sugarplum land. However, once the children were abed, the party continued with the teens until well after midnight.

Chapter 14

When Sunday morning dawned sunny and bright, a large contingent of the Alexander and Montgomery family members with Will, Eugene, and Violet, made the best of what time they had left in the Maryland countryside. They saddled horses and took a ride through a well-established bridle path in the woods to a private, gated golf course community, Havenhurst Estates. The Baylor and Baylor Design and Developers project had large homes, lakes, and an equestrian park. Other people, families, and young children were out on horseback riding the quarter-mile track or traversing the different bridle paths surrounding the golf course and lakes.

Linda, Dena, Kenny, Whitney, and Brian rode chaperone for the younger ones, including Eugene and Violet as they rode on the ponies several times around the track while Will, Tucker, and Bernard Alexander looked on. Again, the older children and young adults rode with the little ones in front of them on horseback. Vivian and her mother, Sylvia Alexander, rode as if born in the saddle as did Chuck and his father, Stephen Montgomery.

Later, a starting gate was brought onto the track and eight horses and riders lined up in the stalls. Right out of the gate, Dena was in the lead and won by a full horse length with Kenny on her heels. Linda made a decent showing at fourth. As that race finished, another group of eight lined up and off they went flying around the track.

After the races, they rode up to the back of the Foxes Lair Restaurant at the Havenhurst Country Club where they dismounted, and stable hands took the horses and ponies for a cool-down session. The riders spread out at tables and chairs on a restaurant's terrace overlooking tennis courts and an outdoor pool. After the food was ordered, Will excused himself from the table on the pretense of going to the men's room. Instead, he detoured to track down the restaurant manager and pick up the tab for the lunch swearing the manager to secrecy. Then he went to the men's room to wash his hands and found the Montgomery males there already.

The spring breeze across the terrace carried the scent of pine and early spring flowers. Will watched golfers lining up to tee off on the seventy-two-hole championship golf course.

"Have you ever played golf?" Will asked Linda.

She shook her head. "I know *how* to play, but it's never held much interest for me, although I do occasionally enjoy a little putt-putt golf."

Will laughed. "That's not exactly the same thing."

"I presume you play?"

"I used to every Wednesday."

"You don't now?"

"No, time's short. I used to play with a group who would fly down to Myrtle Beach, South Carolina, a couple of times a month during the winter the night before and then get in a full couple of days of golf before flying back to the city."

"Why don't you still do that?"

"It wasn't fair to Drew. He had to manage Indulgences, attend his classes, and then take care of Eugene and Violet while I was away. As a result, to ensure that Drew and I weren't overworked, I brought in two assistant managers who report to Drew so that he and I can take a breather now and again and be with the kids. I sometimes have obligations outside of Indulgences and things going on in Eugene and Violet's school he and/or I need to attend to. So, the extra hands come in handy when we're stretched to the limit."

"Look, if you enjoyed golfing that much, you should keep it up. You deserve to have outside indulgences," she joked. "I would be happy to take care of Eugene and Violet if you want to get away to play golf. In fact, you should talk with Uncle Greg. He plays, particularly when he goes to Great-grandaunt Hannah Ivy's home in Atlantic Beach. It's just north of Myrtle Beach."

"Thanks, Linda, but that's too much to ask you to do. You've got the school and your preparation for your performance to contend with."

"It's not a problem for me. I think Eugene and Violet would like to be in my dance school over the summer anyway. If you give me a few days' heads up, I'm sure Drew and I can work out something to cover the children while you enjoy some time relaxing and doing something you enjoy."

"I still think it's too much for you to take on, but I'll talk with Gregory. I didn't know he played."

"He does, yes, and he's good at it. So be sure to bring your A game."

After such a wonderful weekend at home in Maryland, Linda was back at her uncle's home. Gregory flew back to South Carolina with his parents and Angelique came back to New York with her. After checking on her restaurant, having dinner there with Will and the children, she and Angelique spent the rest of the evening lounging.

Will took Eugene and Violet home to get them ready for school the next day, but they were chatterboxes about all of the exciting things they got to do and the people they met. Before they went to bed, they called her again to thank her for taking them along on the trip to her family's farm in Maryland.

"They're really so excited," said Will as he lounged on a sofa in his in-home office. "It was hard for them to settle down."

"Did you read with them?" Linda asked.

"At least five stories from the books you gave them from your family's collection. The problem was they only wanted to talk about the fun time they had again as if I hadn't experienced it with them. Then they wanted to see the hundreds of pictures taken. It was a great idea to give them each cameras so they could each record what they enjoyed most."

"I'm glad they had a good time. My family enjoyed having all of you visit with them. We'll have to go shopping for more books."

"I agree with that. Considering all the kisses Violet gave me for reading with her, I felt ten feet tall instead of six-six."

"That's real progress, Will. Both children need affection and they're beginning to show it."

"I know, but right now, I wish we were together so I could kiss you goodnight."

"Well, is Drew home for the night?"

"No, he wasn't here when we got home, but I think he worked pretty late at Indulgences and then went out with his friends. Why?"

"Well," she hedged, "If he were home for the night, you might be free to come by and deliver the goodnight kiss in person."

"The problem is I wouldn't stop at one goodnight kiss, so it's a good thing Drew isn't here. At some point, in the near future, I'd like to sit and have a conversation with you."

"You sound serious, Will. Is this something we should address sooner rather than later?"

"It's not urgent, but it is important."

"Okay. You let me know when you're ready to talk and I'll make myself available."

"I'll let you know. For now, I'll say goodnight."

"Goodnight, Will," she said and disconnected.

Moments later, Angelique entered Linda's bedroom suite carrying two bowls of frozen yogurt with fresh fruit toppings. "Why do you look so perplexed?" she asked handing one bowl to Linda and then curling up on the bed against the pillows.

"I was just talking with Will. He wants to have an important conversation with me sometime soon."

"Did he say what it's about?"

She spooned a mouthful of the black cherry and chocolate yogurt from the bowl and shook her head. "He sounds serious, but he didn't say what he wanted to discuss."

"Well, that's interesting."

"I'll say." She shook her head again and sighed. "I wonder whether he's overwhelmed by how close our relationship has grown in such a short period of time. I mean, the whole idea of taking them with us for the birthday party may have been a bit too much too soon. I did it to help ease Eugene and Violet's sadness because of the loss of their parents. I wasn't trying to make a statement, but I'm the worst when it comes to reading men's intentions."

"I really don't think he's shying away or putting on the brakes, Linda. I wasn't there when he met Chuck and Vivian in their home environment or the rest of the immediate family, but what I saw of Will on Saturday and Sunday tells me he enjoyed the experience. I think you're reading this 'let's talk' suggestion of his all wrong."

"Whatever," Linda said changing the subject. "I need to focus on these three dancers," she said spreading the promo photos out on the bed for Angelique to see, then picked up her bowl of frozen yogurt and began to eat again.

"*Whoa!* Talk about handsome and built, too. I can't imagine why you don't fall in love with your dance partners on a regular basis. I think I remember seeing this guy in Paris when you danced the lead in *Giselle* last spring."

"I did, yes. His name is Carlo Bettini and he's a fabulous dancer."

"Didn't you date for a while?"

Linda shrugged. "For a few months, yes, but I didn't plan to stay in Paris, so I ended it with him. Since then, he's moved to New York. He contacted me over a month ago to go out to dinner. I said no and the next thing I know, he shows up for the open casting call for The Nutcracker. He's a man who doesn't need to do auditions and he doesn't take no for an answer. Nevertheless, no one can deny his talent. We mesh on pointe because he's a natural dancer. His movements are instinctive. We have this incredible ability to synchronize our movements exactly. There are only a few men I trust completely to balance me over their head and carry me around with one hand. He has never dropped me, not even in rehearsals after working together for hours."

"So, what's the problem? He's as handsome as sin, built like a Greek god, and you have chemistry."

Linda laughed. "He *is* a Greek god and he expects every woman in his sphere to bow down in reverence. The only reason for his constant pursuit is because I wouldn't prostrate myself at his feet . . . outside the theatre. Besides, sometimes the way he watches me, raises my creep index."

"Oh," said Angelique, nodding her understanding. "What about this one?" she asked lifting another photo to study.

"Petrov. He's German, not that it matters, and a real technician when it comes to dance. He's very exacting and a perfectionist. He says, '*Linda, we must marry to have perfect dancers*'," she said in a perfect German accent and then laughed. "We had just completed a performance of *Don Quixote* in Rome, Italy, and we're still on stage before a couple of thousand people taking our fifth curtain call when he made that statement. I thought he was joking, so I laughed. Only the orchestra in the pit heard me because I was bowing with my forehead nearly touching the floor at the time. Still, Petrov stormed off the stage leaving me alone. The audience thought it was a part of the show and showered me with roses."

Angelique laughed and picked up the last picture. "You've danced with this guy, too?"

"Ah, Augustino," she breathed the sound, swooning. "He's from Bolivia and absolutely beautiful inside and out. He's an incredible flamenco dancer as well as a classical ballet artist. Believe me, if he hadn't just divorced his husband, I'd consider him a love match in a heartbeat. Regrettably, he loves me only as a friend and dance partner."

"Oh, well, you certainly can't tell a book by reading the cover," exclaimed Angelique laughing. "There's nothing wrong with being gay, except when you look like this and have a body to die for, women feel cheated."

"Yep, he's got a great personality, he's gorgeous, and he's gay. The last performance we shared was *Firebird*. The costuming does him no justice there. Still, seeing him in a full-body leotard when we danced Swan Lake several years ago in Bonn, Germany, is an absolute gift to humankind."

"So why are you focusing on these three dancers?"

"I'm thinking of writing a script and designing the choreography and costumes for a new ballet. I'd like to do it in concert with one or more of these three men and the school. I want the new ballet to be our signature piece as representative of what the school has to offer.

Each one of these men has multiple talents and qualities to contribute to scoring a new, unique ballet."

"*Wow!* Has this ever been done before?"

"I really don't know for sure, but not to the best of my knowledge, no. Most ballets are repeats of classical movements. Maybe Katherine Dunham or Arthur Mitchel, but they were not famous for classical ballet. Even the Alvin Ailey Dance Theatre of Harlem's repertory is made up of modern dance. The closest I've come is to mom's friend, Kristine Catherine Bryant."

"Oh, yeah, I've met her. She and Vivian were in undergrad at Spelman College together," said Angelique. "Now she's married to Thomas Ashton Marshall."

"Yes, KC Bryant Marshall. She's also the lawyer Mom asked to step into her position as a judge on the US Court of Appeals while Mom took an extended leave of absence when she was pregnant with Eden Ann."

"Wasn't KC Bryant's mother the great Canadian prima ballerina Lydia Martine Booth?" Angelique asked.

"She was, yes, and she trained KC. After Mom returned to the court bench, KC took a leave of absence from the law to start a dance troupe on a Polynesian Island. They successfully combined native dances, classical ballet, and modern dance. I performed with them a few seasons when I was still in my late teens, early twenties. If I can pull this off as one of the offerings of the New York Academy of Dance, it would open doors for the students of the school just as KC's troupe has done and is still doing even though she's back to being a judge now that Mom is on the Supreme Court. I'm scheduled to talk with KC about her experiences of starting a dance troupe. If she's interested, I'd like for her to work on the choreography with me.

"I'd also like to talk with Matthew Kennedy about scoring the music for the ballet."

Angelique's jaw dropped. "*Whoa!* You really are going top-shelf for this plan of yours. He's just won a slew of Grammy Awards for his work with the singing sensation Loretta. I know he's one of the top male vocalist and songwriters, but I didn't know he wrote music for the stage."

"Yes, I know, he hasn't, but he's very versatile. However, there may be a little hiccup there."

"Oh? What?"

"Well, Uncle Greg once dated Capri McAllister . . ."

"Ah, and she's now married to Matt Kennedy's brother, Tate."

"You know about this?" Linda asked her friend, her Uncle Greg's fiancée.

"Of course. Gregory told me about all of his serious relationships, but you know the rule. He didn't take any of them home with him to meet the family during the Juneteenth family reunion. We don't keep secrets from each other. Otherwise, we won't have a strong, trusting marriage. I don't think you're going to have a problem with introducing your ideas to Matt. He and Gregory are good friends. We've even been to Matt's home here in New York and in DC for dinner with Matt, his wife, Audra, and Tate and Capri. Capri is a lovely woman and she and Tate are crazy in love with each other. The last time we got together with them, they told us they were expecting again. They already have the most adorable twins; a boy and a girl."

"That's good to know. Since I don't know Matt, I'll ask Uncle Greg to introduce us."

"Good, now are there any other potential bombshell pieces to this plan of yours?"

"Well," she hedged. "I'd like to talk with Maxwell Kennard, III about directing and producing. He's had a lot of experience with big productions and full orchestras."

"Trey Kennard?"

"Yes."

Angelique laughed. "Then say no more. Trey is one of my steady customers. He lives and has his studio in the building next door to my restaurant."

"You live in a condo above your restaurant and you're telling me that he actually lives next door to you?"

"He does, yes. I've catered luncheons and dinner parties for him. If I don't have a seat available in the restaurant or the nightclub, Trey makes himself comfortable in my kitchen. He's very informal, spontaneous, and rolls with the punches. I'm sure he'd be amenable to meeting with you. He's a great guy, too."

"Have you ever dated him?"

She laughed. "No. He said he wanted to ask me out, but he was afraid he'd lose a good friend and his favorite chef if things went south between us. He didn't want to take the risk. If it's okay with you, I'll give him your contact information and ask him to call you."

"You're the best, Angelique!" Linda said, hugging her BFF, the woman who would also become her aunt.

"Anything else?"

Linda laughed. "Not now, but stay tuned," she joked.

"Then with that, I'm going to my room and call your uncle, the love of my life, to say goodnight. I'll see you in the morning?"

"Yes, I'm up early tomorrow, too. Security will be here at five."

"Okay, sleep fast," said Angelique with a quick squeeze before she picked up the empty bowls to take to the dishwasher. Then she went to one of the other bedroom suites.

Watching surreptitiously as the various lights went out in the converted fire station, the man didn't want to be too conspicuous or predictable. Parking a few blocks away, he walked the neighborhood and noticed several police cars pass by and slow but didn't stop him. He carried a couple of grocery bags after shopping at midnight at a neighborhood bodega; one of the better ones in SoHo that actually stayed open late. Gregory Alexander shopped there, but he never caught Linda there. He chatted up the clerks in the store, gathering bits and pieces of information. Since the clerks knew his face in there, it would have been the perfect place to engage Linda, but Gregory or his housekeeper did the household shopping.

Spotting another police car cruising the neighborhood, he slowed so he'd look like any other person heading home with groceries late at night. Maybe he had better hack the police blotter again to determine whether someone filed a report about a suspicious character in the neighborhood. Keeping up with certain police routines in or around Linda was necessary to his plan.

It was a quiet, relatively safe area, so he wasn't particularly concerned about his own safety. Besides he trained religiously in hand-to-hand combat. It served him well, too. He knew how to subdue a person quickly, efficiently, and quietly. Protecting himself in any situation was a necessary skill. He never knew when it would come in handy and it had from time to time.

After passing slowly by Gregory Alexander's home again, he headed for his car. Her family had birthday celebrations on the first weekend of each month. This was one of the tidbits of information he learned from one of the pretty female clerks, Maria, in the Bodega. It had cost him a lunch with the woman, but it was worth it. So, he had a good idea about where Linda had been over the weekend. Actually, he traveled to Maryland on a few occasions and stayed in a quaint little bed and breakfast within half a mile of her parents' farm during one of those weekend birthday festivities. He couldn't get away this time because of his heavy caseload. He promised himself not to take on new clients so that he could spend more time keeping up with Linda. Now that he knew Linda was back from her trip to Maryland, he breathed a sigh of relief.

She'd be following her routine again and at Indulgences early in the morning. That opened more opportunities for him to connect with her. He made himself available in areas he knew she would be, so she'd be accustomed to seeing him around. It would then be a simple task of finding a way of casually engaging her in conversation.

After getting into his car, he pulled a crisp, Granny Smith apple from his grocery bag and took a healthy bite. When he and Linda were finally together, he wanted to be sure he had everything she enjoyed available to her. He wanted to be able to spend a considerable amount of time with her. As he started the engine, he dreamed that day wasn't too far in the future. Still, time was running out.

Chapter 15

It was the beginning of the Easter holiday. Drew volunteered to take Eugene and Violet to visit their great-grandparents in Portland, Oregon, so Will agreed to accompany Linda to visit the other halves of her family, the Jacksons and Montgomerys in the Pocono Mountains of Pennsylvania, north and west of New York City. Since she wanted to be there early, they left at two o'clock in the morning driving Linda's vintage 1965 Pontiac GTO.

Will thought the convertible purred like a contented cat and roared like a lion northwest on I-80 and I-380. They put the top down and drank hot, black coffee while they talked, cruised leisurely, and listened to jazz on the XM satellite radio channel. The car, a pumpkin-orange color with white top and white leather interior was Linda's choice for her sixteenth birthday gift. Her Uncle Gregory reconditioned the car, putting in all of the modern conveniences and delivered it to her in pristine, showroom condition. She rarely had an opportunity to drive it, so when Will agreed to accompany her for Easter in the Pocono Mountains, she brought her car out of her Uncle Gregory's storage garage.

By the time they reached I-280, the last leg of the journey to Monroe County, Pennsylvania, the sun was beginning to peek over the mountains to the east.

"This is beautiful country," commented Will sitting in the driver's seat. They had changed drivers at the last rest stop. He hadn't been on a road trip since he couldn't remember when. He owned a car and enjoyed driving on the open road, but he didn't make time to take long road trips into the countryside. After all, he was a city boy born and bred. Yet, he was thoroughly enjoying being on the road with Linda by his side. She was a great companion and conversationalist.

For long stretches of time, they could sit beside each other just holding hands in companionable silence. He liked that she didn't mind if he opened doors for her and she teased him when she would open doors for him. He liked holding her hand when they were out somewhere in public, like to see a show or a movie. They went to basketball games when her Uncle Gregory was doing the color commentary from the sidelines in the arena and she accompanied Will sometimes when he did studio work about the upcoming baseball season. They were being picked up on social media as a couple, but she didn't flaunt their relationship when questions were asked about them. She simply ignored the reporters as did he. However, he liked it best when they were able to spend quality time together with nothing planned on their agenda. He no longer looked at her as being too young for him. She was mature beyond her chronological age and always conducted herself as a lady. Although they had only known each other for a matter of months, he liked everything he was learning about her.

"Only a few more miles before we get to my Grandmother Harriet Jackson's farm."

"Okay, so refresh my memory. Harriet is Derrick's mother, right? His father was Grover Jackson who died a few years after Derrick?"

"Yes, that's right. Harriet Minor Jackson was a native of Philadelphia and a beautician with her own beauty shop in the city. She still has a shop now in Monroe County, although she has other people working there and managing it for her. She goes in to work there occasionally, but Derrick left her financially secure, so she really doesn't have to work to make ends meet. She's in her late fifties and doesn't work as hard as she used to.

"Grover, her husband, was former military and was born and raised in Alpharetta, Mississippi. His family members were farmers and still are. He wanted to get back to farming, too, so when the Montgomerys offered him a parcel of land, he retired after thirty plus years from the post office and moved his family to Monroe County.

Grover and Harriet had seven children, four girls and three boys. My father was their fourth child. Sheila is the oldest and she is married to Bob Montgomery, who, by the way, is one of Chuck's older brothers. They have six children," she said and continued down the list. "Kadijah Jackson married Martin Montgomery a few years ago, but they don't have children yet. Finally, there's Troy Jackson, the youngest, you already know. He and Uncle Greg are founding members and business partners at CTI."

"That's quite a list. What about the other side, the Montgomerys?"

"You've met most of my Montgomery uncles, aunts and Granddad Stephen between those working on my studio and the birthday party you attended with me. We lost Dad's mother, Esther Hardyston Montgomery five years or more ago, but, as you saw, Granddad Stephen is still hale and hardy. By profession, he's a mechanic who can fix any piece of farm equipment ever produced, but he loves working his farm. He grows winter wheat for animal feed and hay for use in making glass.

"We wish he would slow down, but I don't think that's going to happen anytime soon. He likes to keep busy and, since he lost Grandma Esther, he's never home and always on the go. He and Grandma Harriet come to stay with Dad and Mom whenever they are needed, but they don't stay long anymore. They're always in a hurry to get back to their homes."

"With that many children and grandchildren between them, they have already paid some heavy dues," Will said laughing.

"You're right, but I hate to think of them alone on their farms in the mountains. Their nearest neighbors are miles away. I know they have family living nearby, but it has to be hard after spending most of your life living with someone and then losing them. I know it was hard for Mom when she lost Derrick so soon after they were married. "

"He died on April Fool's Day, right?" Will asked.

"Yes, the same day Derrick Junior was born. In fact, Chuck found him in the nursery at the hospital holding DJ in his arms. Chuck, for over an hour, tried to resuscitate him and had to be restrained, but it was too late. Derrick and Chuck were best friends for so long it nearly killed

Dad to lose him. Then Mom was angry with Chuck because he knew Dad had hypertrophic cardiomyopathy, a serious heart condition, and didn't tell her."

"Yes, I've heard of it. For some reason, a number of athletes have had the condition. I didn't know that was why Derrick left the game."

"It was. However, Derrick had sworn Chuck to secrecy. Derrick didn't want Mom to treat him like an invalid because of his condition or to suffer because he knew he wouldn't live a long life. What he didn't expect was that Mom would be so angry about the secret he forced Chuck to keep, she wouldn't even speak to Chuck for five years. You see, Chuck and Mom were good friends even before he introduced her to Derrick one night at a dance club."

"It's hard to imagine your parents ever being angry with each other."

"Believe me, it was tough on those of us Mom and Derrick adopted before he died. Mom wouldn't even let us visit with Chuck," she said laughing. "Still, everyone knew we loved Chuck and missed him, so there were conspiracies afoot to let us see and be with Chuck behind Mom's back. Everyone was in on it, the Jacksons, the Montgomerys, the Alexanders, and even Mom's law firm partners."

"Whoa, I can't imagine anyone putting something over on your Mom."

"It worked for those five years because Mom was busy building her and her partners' law firm, until DJ Junior was upset because Mom forgot about his birthday party. She was away in Chicago trying this big case before the US Court of Appeals for the Seventh Circuit. We thought we had several days before the Court's opinion would be rendered, but the Court issued the opinion in Mom's favor in two days. She immediately came home the same day and we were out of time and out of luck.

"We were trying to keep it a secret from Mom, but Chuck bought a pony for DJ's birthday and planned the party for him to celebrate. When Mom came home early, it nixed the planned party. DJ was upset, let it slip about the pony, and the gig was up.

"Still, Mom realized she wasn't being fair to Chuck or to us by keeping us away from him. So, she buried the hatchet and then one thing led to another and Mom and Chuck married that same year in Goodwill. You see, they were in love with each other, but Chuck never told her how he felt about her before she started dating Derrick. He kept it a secret and didn't admit the truth until DJ spilled the beans. So, that's why secrets will never be tolerated in our family's household. Mom admitted she would never have taken up with Derrick because she was falling for Chuck, but never told him how she felt."

"They wasted years of not being together because of their secrets," said Will in summary.

"Yep, that's exactly what happened. Now, they don't waste time. They go out on date nights, take short trips to somewhere no one knows them, and spend quality time together talking with each other every day. They are truly each other's soul mate and best friend."

"That is clear to see. They seem very much in love and protective of each other."

"You've got it, and now if you'll turn thru those gates up ahead on your right, we'll be at Grandma's house," she joked.

Will did as instructed and turned into a long, blacktopped, driveway leading to a traditional two-story farmhouse with acres and acres of spring grass, gardens of flowers, and blooming trees dotting the picturesque landscape. She instructed him to drive around to the rear of the house where a covered porch led off of the kitchen door. They parked beside one of those big, black, muscle trucks Will didn't know the name of other than it was a Ford and was polished to a fine sheen.

"Huh, I wonder why Grandpa Stephen is here so early in the morning. He's an early riser, but it's barely six," she said, absently feeling the truck hood, finding it cold and hustled into the kitchen door only to be brought up short. Her grandfather, Stephen Montgomery, had her grandmother, Harriett Jackson, pinned up against the refrigerator door with his barely clad body in a lip lock that must have been going on for some time. They were both barefoot. Grandma Harriet's thigh was hiked up and being held in Grandpa Stephen's firm grip. He was wearing pajama bottoms low on his hips which matched the pajama shirt her grandmother wore half unbuttoned down the front. One shoulder was free from the garment and a fairly large breast with a pointed nipple was clearly visible. Linda's eyes widened and her jaw dropped. "Oops!" she said flabbergasted.

The lovers disentangled themselves and began to laugh, their foreheads together.

"Busted," said Harriet and then quickly kissed Stephen again.

"Well, hell, you knew we couldn't keep this a secret forever, Harriet," he groused good-naturedly. "I told you we should have announced that we're a couple and let the chips fall where they may."

"Yes, but I didn't think we'd get caught literally with our pants down by one of our grandchildren. It would help my level of embarrassment, Stephen, if you would let me put my leg down from around your hip."

He kissed her again and said, "If you must," before letting her leg go.

"Well, this is awkward. Close your mouth, Linda," said Harriet as she buttoned a few more buttons on her shirt and approached Will to shake his hand.

"Hey, don't mind me, Mrs. Jackson," he grinned shaking her hand.

"I was looking forward to meeting you, but not quite in this state of undress," Harriet said laughing. Then she turned to Linda and crossed her arms over her impressive unbound breasts in the pajama top. "Well?"

Linda shrugged. "I'm impressed that you have the dexterity to, uh," she faltered trying to suppress a giggle and failed.

Harriet smirked, and she and Linda caught each other up in a tight embrace with kisses on both cheeks.

"Are you sufficiently recovered to give our granddaughter a hug yet, Stephen?"

Stephen rolled his eyes, but Linda couldn't hold back the giggle any longer when she went laughing into her grandfather's arms.

"Make yourselves at home while we get some clothes on," said Harriet. "We should be back in thirty minutes or less unless Studly has other ideas.

"I've got other ideas, woman," he groused and swatted her affectionately on her high, still tight bottom as they went through the kitchen door headed to a master bedroom on the first floor.

Linda watched them go and then turned with both hands clamped over her mouth. Tears rimmed her dancing eyes and merriment was in her voice when she said, "Well, I certainly didn't see *that* coming. I wonder whether or not anyone else in the family knows?"

"Hey, they seemed to be comfortable with each other. That looks like the type of intimate relationship that takes a long time to build. When did you say your grandmother Esther died?"

"Five, no, six years ago, I think. I wonder how long this has been going on."

"I wonder whether this is one of those times you're going to have risk cleaning out the barn stalls for keeping a secret? I've got your back, babe, but I draw the line at picking up cow pies."

Linda's jaw dropped again before she broke out in laughter. Will joined her holding his sides as they laughed with tears leaking from their eyes.

An hour later, the foursome sat in the warm kitchen finishing a big country breakfast and talking.

"I tell you, Ms. Harriet, I'm beginning to like these grits things. Especially the way you cook them with fat, hot sausages, red, yellow and green peppers, and gravy."

"Thanks, Will," said Harriet. "Stephen slaughtered that hog, when? Last week?"

"Yeah," said Stephen finishing up his third cup of coffee with a freshly made cinnamon sweet roll. "He was a good ole hog, Porky was, too."

Linda laughed at the expression on Will's face. "Grampa, this is one of those times when Will doesn't need to know how the sausages were made."

"Sorry, son," said Stephen grinning, his voice a deep resonance with a slow Western drawl. "Hang around us farm folk long enough and we'll wipe the city right off of you." He rose effortlessly from the table, his tall raw-bone physique lean, but sturdy with long, ropy muscles that flexed and bulged noticeably under his dark blue T-shirt that matched the color of his vibrantly striking blue eyes. Will thought he resembled the actor Sam Elliott with his horse-shoe shaped mustache, his long, thick pelt of iron-grey hair that waved, curved, and curled around his head and around the collar of the plaid shirt he wore open over the T-shirt. His low-cut blue jeans had white stress points in interesting places. Given what he and Linda witnessed upon arrival, the phrase, *hung like a horse*, came unbidden to mind as Stephen took his dishes to the sink where Harriet stood. "Good grub," he said, palming her waist, pulling her to him, and kissing her deeply on her waiting mouth. "I've got to go into town. I need you to give me a haircut later before the kids come. You need anything?"

"Dry ice. I'm going to make ice cream, but I'm low on dry ice and sea salt."

"Okay, anything else?"

"Not that I can think of right now. I'll call you if I do. I've got the hams and ribs smoking out by the barn. I checked on them last night before we went to bed. The children are bringing everything else we need for supper. I expect they'll all be here about noon." She kissed him this time and grabbed his cowboy hat from a peg on the wall fitting it low on his head.

"I'll see you kids later," Stephen said, winked at Harriett, and then was gone. They heard the big engine fire up before settling down and moving away.

When Harriet came back to the table, sat down with a fresh cup of coffee and her pad and a pen, Will studied her features more carefully. She wasn't a particularly tall woman, standing only about five-foot-six and pleasingly plump still with an hour-glass figure of sorts. The type of body a man like Stephen Montgomery could really get his hands on. Her rear was high, meaty and wide, attesting to the fact she bore seven children in her youth. She had a rather round, brown face, with dark features about the dark-brown eyes and brows, but plump, cherry-colored lips as if she were wearing gloss. Her hair was thick, shoulder length, mostly dark brown, with lighter highlights and nicely styled to fit her gamine features.

"What do you need for me to do, Granma?" asked Linda.

"I think everything is covered except the ice cream. I've got jars of fruit in the pantry your mama and daddy brought up after canning season last fall. I've already got some of the makings chilling in the refrigerator. You remember how to make the ice cream?"

"I do, yes, Granma. How many do you want?"

"Let's see, I know you're partial to anything with black cherries, chocolate chips, and nuts, so make up a batch of that. You can take some home with you. Then there are pineapple, peaches …" she went on naming different combinations of ice cream for Linda to make.

"Okay, that looks like seven different types. Anything else?" Linda asked.

"No, the rest will bring the cakes, pies, and other desserts. They have the lists. For now, get Will situated in your daddy's old bedroom while I figure out whether I need anything else."

"Okay," Linda said as she and Will went out to her car to get their luggage and bring it into the house. She hadn't planned to, but apparently, she and Will were expected to stay with her grandmother, instead of at her parents' home five miles away. She took him upstairs to the second floor to Derrick's old bedroom which had been left pretty much as it had been when he was a boy and lived there. They had updated his bed to a king size and adult furniture, but the pictures and posters on the walls were nicely framed to preserve them and the memories that went with them.

Will looked at the photos of a young Derrick Jelon Jackson Senior from the days when he was born through the time he left to go away to Boston College. Linda explained how his career skyrocketed from there and Will began to see the talented, inner-city Philadelphia street kid who later grew up on a rural farm to become an icon. She went on to explain he came home from time to time for visits, rarely missing a holiday, but he never lived there again after he left. When he retired from basketball at the top of his game because of his heart condition, he initially told no one except Chuck. Not one to sit and brood about his misfortune, he subsequently was accepted into medical school at

Georgetown. He did his residency there and started a private medical practice in pediatric medicine with his med-school friends.

Derrick was already a multimillionaire, but, as a pediatric surgeon, developed a webbing system and other medical software and hardware devices which revolutionized pediatric medicine. As a result, he became a multi-billionaire about the time he met a young law school student who scored Olympic gold in basketball while in college. She was a farm girl, too, though twelve years his junior. Yet he fell in love with her.

"Chuck never said, but we believe he knew Derrick knew he was also in love with Mom. We think Derrick had a premonition he wouldn't live a long life. He wanted to live his life fast and to the fullest, before it was too late. So he and Mom married in September the year she graduated from law school and passed the bar exam. They lived at the Watergate condo complex in Washington, DC, but bought a farm in the rural Virginia countryside. Mom always worked while she was in college and law school. After becoming an attorney, she went to work on Capitol Hill as an aide on the US Senate's Ethic's Committee.

"They had already adopted me, Brian, Geneviève, Vincent, and Andrew, and started adoption proceedings on Dena, Ryan, Roger, Darren, Spencer, and Samantha. We were all Derrick's patients at the orphanage, and Mom, knowing how Derrick felt about us, suggested they adopt us. The farm was being renovated to accommodate all of us when Derrick died on April 1st of the following year. Mom went through with all of the adoptions as she and Derrick planned, but we never moved to the farm. We lived in a big, four-story brownstone townhouse Uncle Benny bought from Aunt Hannah Ivy in the Georgetown section of Washington, DC, on the edge of Rock Creek Park. It's where Mom lived with her law school classmates before she married Derrick.

"The year before, when they graduated from law school, Derrick arranged to finance the creation of a law firm for her and her pals as a surprise Christmas gift for Mom. The founding partners are still in the law firm, except, of course, Mom. In her fifth year practicing law, the President picked Mom for a judgeship on the US Circuit Court of Appeals. She was confirmed and served five years with distinction. Mom is apoliticall, but a different President picked Mom when a seat became available on the US Supreme Court. She's the youngest judge ever to be seated on the High Court because she's still in her thirties."

"She looks even younger than that and the way she still plays basketball, she's amazing."

"She regularly plays with a female team of lawyers, law school students, and judges called Final Justice." Linda laughed. "The Dads played on a team of medical personnel, doctors, nurses, technicians, etc., called The Body Snatchers and Chuck still does. I would have taken you to see them play, but they didn't play the weekend we were there because of the birthday party. Otherwise, they rarely miss playing year-round," Linda finished.

"Just as Gregory and Troy play several times a week at Indulgences. Because of Gregory, the facilities are always packed with different leagues," said Will.

"Basketball is in the family DNA, except, of all the aunts, uncles, and cousins in the family who play or played through high school and college, only Uncle Greg made a career out of it and he only did it for a short time."

"Did you play?" Will asked.

"Not seriously, no. Knees take a pounding in basketball and I would have to have developed different muscle groups. Sometimes I'll shoot around at family gatherings, but the grands always cautioned us to seek our own levels and interests, to explore careers and life outside of the norm or our own comfort zone. It's another example of the wisdom passed down from our ancestry. In the entire family among my siblings, I don't think we have one person who is a natural basketball player, much to Dad's dismay," she said laughing.

"What does your dad say about that?" Will asked.

"He's going to keep having babies or adopting them until he gets a ball player. He doesn't care whether it's a boy or a girl," she said still laughing.

Will joined her in laughter.

"Stop dawdling, you two," called Harriet up the stairs.

"Coming, Gram," Linda shouted back.

She and Will went down the stairs to find Harriet wearing her gardening gear. "I'll bet my Linda was regaling you with stories about my Chucky Pie and DJ," Harriette said smiling at Will.

"She did mention them a time or two," Will teased.

"Ha!" Harriet barked. "They were a caution, those two, our salt-and-pepper team. They couldn't have been closer if they shared womb space in my belly or Esther's," she said laughing, but a tear welled in her eyes. She batted it away, drew herself up, pulled her ice cream ingredients from the big side-by-side refrigerator and freezer, and then led the way to the spacious pantry.

The shelves were filled to capacity with huge, glass Mason Jars of fresh, canned fruits and vegetables. She had corn, lima beans, okra with red peppers, pickled pigs feet, and all manner of other vegetables and fruits lined up with military precision.

"I put some of these by from my garden last harvest. I don't think the ground is going to freeze again this season. So, I need to start tilling my soil and plant my seeds for this year. You youngsters, grab what you need and get to making that ice cream before it gets too late."

"Yes, ma'am," said Linda as she and Will each hefted two heavy jars of canned fruits and followed Harriett out of the combination mud room and pantry door toward the barn.

Three, large, steel barrels stood on makeshift legs with fragrant smoke escaping from the sides and filling the air with enticing aromas. Harriet lifted the heavy lid of one of the barrels to find huge, whole hams slowly turning over on skewers with a fire burning some type of fragrant wood. Juices chased around the turning meat, sizzling and coating it as it cooked. She took what looked like a string mop head inserted through the lid of a jar from something red and spicy and generously slathered it over the three-foot-long, two-foot-wide pieces of browning meat.

Will's eyes widened when Linda opened the other two barrel lids which held racks of pork ribs in one container and lamb in the other. As her grandmother had done, she ladled on some type of sticky, gooey brown sauce as the meat continued to turn on the spits and added more wood to the fire.

"Those are doing nicely," said Harriett standing behind Linda looking over her shoulder. "A few more hours and they'll be done." She nodded her satisfaction. "You haven't forgotten what your Grandpa Grover taught you," she said giving Linda a quick squeeze before going into a shed and gathering her gardening equipment.

"When I finish setting up the ice cream, I'll come give you a hand."

"No, child, put up the ice cream and then I suspect you'll want to go visit with your father."

"Yes, ma'am," Linda said obediently before hefting the jars and ingredients from an old wooden table and leading Will into the barn.

Okay, Will thought, when he entered to find rows upon rows of big, bulky, black and white cows chomping on hay while some type of gizmos sucked fluid from fat teats and udders. It took a moment for Will to get used to the smells, but he was surprised about how clean and warm the place was. "Your grandmother runs a dairy farm with all of these cattle?"

"Uh, yes, but this isn't the entire herd. These are just the ones brought in so far this morning by the ranch hands. She's thinned her herd somewhat since Grandpa Grover died. It's still a lot of work for her and she still has her beauty shop in town."

"Why are the cows making that noise?" Will asked.

"It's painful for the cows if the milk isn't drained from their udders early in the morning. These are the older ones that can't hold their milk as long as the younger ones still nursing the spring calves. Let's get the cream and start the churns before we head out."

She led him to one of the large, stainless steel vats collecting milk from the cows and turned off a lever before lifting a lid. She beckoned Will to take a look inside. "This is where the cream and butter are separated from the milk before it's homogenized," she explained as she tipped the canister forward to pour off the cream through a screen that captured the butter. It was surprisingly white, Will commented. Linda went on to explain the process as she diverted the cream into various vats and added fruits, nuts, grated vanilla beans, and/or bits of white or brown chocolate. They talked while returning to the house to gather more jars of fruits and repeat the process in the barn. On their second trip, they could see Harriet working in her garden with several other people as the sun at a certain angle made the ice droplets shine and sparkle off the greening grass, shrubs, and trees.

Will took a moment to look at the wondrous sight Mother Nature provided to those lucky enough to see it. He had to arc one hand over his eyes to see the mountains surrounding them. Some snow still clung to the upper mountain range, but it was clear winter was losing its grip and spring was taking over.

"What are you looking at?" Linda asked.

"These mountains are spectacular."

Linda laughed. "Will, these are more like foothills, not mountains."

He looked at her skeptically. "Hills? You call these hills?"

"Sure. Come on. I've finished setting up the ice cream in the electric churns. Once Grandad adds more dry ice, we should be good to go." She walked away toward another barn. This one filled with farm equipment. She pulled the tarp off of an ATV.

"Look out, Linda!" Will shouted. "There's a snake over there!"

Linda casually looked beyond Will who was trying to shield her. She shrugged. "It's only Mr. Slithers, Will. He's an old black snake; not poisonous. I'm surprised he's still alive. Grampa Jackson used to threaten to cut him up and make snake burgers of him."

"You name the snakes?" he incredulously asked.

"Sure. He's harmless, but he still keeps the mice population down along with the barn cats. They learned to live in peaceful co-existence. Come on, climb in," she said after unplugging, then getting into the ATV, and firing up the engine. They drove out of the barn onto a barely-there dirt road, waving as they passed Harriet and her helpers. "This is all Montgomery land for beyond as far as the eye can see. They've been in this area on this land for at least seven generations. Dad's DNA indicates that he's about twenty-five percent Native American on his father's side, along with English and a little French Canadian and Scottish thrown in for good measure.

"There were a lot of sons born into the Montgomery family and fewer women. Many, if not most, still live here in and around Monroe County, but in different towns, townships, burgs and other small municipalities. I haven't met all of them and, frankly, I don't think Dad has either. You see, there was a bit of an uproar when the grands sold Montgomery land to the Jacksons. It mostly died down after a time, but there are still certain resentments. Some family members felt the land should never be sold outside the family, but then again, two Jackson women married into the Montgomery family, so that argument died a natural death."

"Do you believe that any of the discourse had anything to do with the fact the Jacksons aren't white?"

"Not so much, no. It bothered some of the mavens in county society that three handsome, well-to-do men chose three women of African descent to marry when they had eligible daughters at the ready. Granma Ester was a real pistol though. She didn't take no guff off anyone about who her sons or daughters chose to marry. However, the Dads put Monroe County on the map when their high school consistently won state, regional, and national basketball tournaments. Dad said he couldn't believe the flags and banners displayed when and wherever they played. Nearly the whole county turned out for those games. The high school never won anything before the Dads teamed up for their years in high school. Then they went off to colleges a couple of years apart continuing to break records, and reporters beat a path to the county again. Uncle Troy had stellar years playing basketball here in high school and college in Florida, too, but not to the extent the Dads did. There are still pictures of those gravy years posted in the high school gym here and the championship flags for the years they won."

Linda carried on a running commentary as she drove past hills where cattle grazed languidly in grassy fields, forested areas, and through tall pines so thick they blocked out the sky. In another field they passed, sheep grazed, their bodies sheared of its wool. At one point, they came out of a forest into a field of tall grasses and wildflowers surrounding them and swaying in the frisky breeze that made the flowers appear like waves in the sea. Will took out his phone to take pictures and videos of the spectacular sights. Birds he had never seen or heard before sent up a cacophony of sounds while other woodland creatures went about their daily tasks.

The trail wasn't much wider than a goat path, but the changing landscape was beautiful and intriguing. Will mentioned that his ears began to pop the higher they seemed to climb. Eventually, Linda pulled the ATV up onto a single-lane, blacktop road and around a bend where the view was awe inspiring. Off in the distance was a spectacular waterfall. However, as they got closer, Will noticed cars parked on the roadside and a group of people standing up on top of a steep incline. Linda parked the ATV, got out and she and Will began to make the climb.

About halfway up where patches of snow still clung to life in the morning sunshine, he could now hear the waterfall in the distance. He began to recognize Chuck, Vivian, and their offspring reverently standing at the top of the hill. He and Linda were quiet as Chuck spoke out loud to the large white headstones they surrounded.

"You'd be astonished at what Brian is doing at the ranch," Chuck said as he continued to have a conversation with the graves of Derrick Jelon Jackson, Senior, and Derrick's father, Grover Jackson.

It seemed so natural as Will watched and listened to the Montgomery children carrying on a conversation as if they were sitting in a comfortable room having a chat. Linda eased her way into the crowd, holding hands with her siblings and bringing her deceased father and grandfather up to date on her activities since she last visited the graves. As they were wrapping up, everyone searched the ground for a pebble or stone and, one-by-one, placed the small offering on the top of the headstone. Will turned away from the heart-wrenching sight and realized they were standing on a plateau that offered an unobstructed, panoramic view of truly tall, snow-covered mountains. He took a deep cleansing breath of the fresh, clean, pine-scented air and tried to capture the enormous natural beauty surrounding them. It was so splendid, yet humbling, his mind couldn't capture it all.

"The Appalachians," said Linda, as she slipped her hand into Will's to take in the view. "There's Gram's house over there," she said pointing to the east. "Grampa's farm is on the other side of that ridge. I've often wondered why no one built a place on that ridge. It has such a great view of the Poconos and the Appalachians. To wake up to that every morning would be astounding."

"Tell me why you placed stones on the graves."

She looked at him quizzically, and then said, "Oh, that. I place a stone or pebble, sometime a coin or a stone from a different country on a headstone to indicate I've visited the grave and to show respect for the deceased."

"Still, it's a nice tradition. I haven't been to either of my parent's graves since we buried them."

"Maybe we'll go do that sometime."

Will didn't respond to that, but instead, pointed off into the distance. "It didn't seem like we came that far to get here, but your grandmother's farmhouse looks far away."

"I took a shortcut through the woods to get here. There are other routes, but longer because of the switchbacks needed to climb these hills. To me, it's just easier to go cross-country. When we come up here and the snow is on the ground, it's a great ski area for both downhill and cross-country. Derrick loved to ski and, after he left basketball, he traveled to as many ski resort areas as he could manage while in med school and after he started his medical practice."

"Yes, I saw some of the pictures of him skiing with Chuck and/or Vivian on the walls in your Maryland home."

Linda nodded. "He didn't learn to ski until he moved here. He taught Dad how to play basketball, but skiing was one of the things Chuck taught him. Some days they had to use skis to get to school when the school buses couldn't make the trip. They used to joke about having to go ten miles from home to school uphill both ways," she said smiling at the memory. "Then there were the stories about the bears, mountain lions, cougars, and pumas. The tales kept getting bigger and bigger."

They had started moving down the hill when Linda stopped and turned to look back at her parents still holding on to each other at the foot of Derrick's grave. Will turned, too, and saw Vivian bury her face in Chuck's chest, her body shaking, gripping him fiercely as he wrapped his long arms around her and pressed his tear-stained face into her hair at the top of her head. Faintly, they could hear Chuck and Vivian share their grief aloud over the loss of a man they both obviously loved very much. He took Linda's hand in his as she wiped away her tears and continued down the incline toward the cars.

Eventually, Chuck and Vivian joined them at the cars. Will was in a circle of guys talking about the baseball season.

"I figured you must have gone to one of your grands' places when you weren't at home when we arrived."

"Will and I didn't fly up. We left New York at two in the morning and drove up. We had breakfast with the grands, set up the ice cream churns, and then brought an ATV up to visit with . . ." she trailed off, as her eyes filled.

"You're okay," said Chuck, embracing Linda, and kissing the top of her head. "What time does Mama Harriet expect us there?"

"I think around noon or so."

"Good, that will give us some time to saddle horses and ride over. We'll see you and Will a little later," said Chuck.

On the way back, Linda took a different route taking Will on a sightseeing tour of a multifaceted waterfall and mountain lake where a large herd of deer, some with huge antlers, drank peacefully at the water's edge. They didn't stop to talk but waved to farmers tending their fields on picturesque plots of land, with fat, happy children playing in the yard. Stephen Montgomery's truck wasn't in the yard of his pretty farmhouse with a wide veranda and brightly painted rocking chairs across the front. A couple of dogs barked, but their tails were wagging, and no angst was heard in their voices when Linda stopped the ATV to get out and greet her grandfather's dogs. "That's Butch Cassidy and the Sundance Kid," explained Linda as the dogs pranced and wiggled around her begging for her attention. They lay in the grass legs up and bellies exposed for a rub that had them blissful.

"I hate to break it to you, Linda, but I think the Sundance Kid is a bitch."

Linda laughed. "Don't worry, Will, we've known all along about her gender. Butch Cassidy gave us a clue when he was found humping her. They've had numerous litters through the years."

After about fifteen minutes of playing with the dogs, she sent them back to their spots on the sunny veranda and then drove away.

By the time they reached Harriet's farm, more cars had arrived. They returned the ATV to the barn and hooked up the electric power to the machine before covering it and leaving it in Mr. Slither's care. As they crossed toward the house, a woman with dark blond hair came out of the kitchen door with a rolling pin in hand and a wide grin on her face.

"Thought you were here when I saw that pumpkin orange beauty," called out Joyce Montgomery Calloway, a much shorter, but still big-boned replica of her older brother, Chuck. She had dancing blue eyes, like her father, Stephen, and a pleasant, ingratiating smile that grew to be pretty on her otherwise ordinary face.

Several years ago, she joined Gregory in founding CTI. Holding a Ph.D. in both finance and economics, she managed much of the trading portfolio handled through the CTI institution. The man she married was Peter Calloway, from some small community in the Tennessee Ozarks who went to UVA on a full-ride football scholarship and shared Gregory's house on campus with two other sports figures. Linda explained to Will that "Peter often tells the story of how it was love at first sight when Gregory introduced him to Joyce Montgomery, Chuck's baby sister. Peter put an engagement ring on Joyce's finger before they were in their third year in school, but then, with her agreement, he took his engineering degree and left the states for the next ten years to travel the world designing sails for boats and ships racing in regattas."

Joyce laughed and picked up the story. "When Gregory called Peter in Australia to warn him that I was about to kick him to the curb for being away so long, he dropped everything, moved heaven and earth to return to New York City to save our relationship. Within a month of Peter's return, he and I were married at the Montgomery's homestead farm and in less than a year our first child, Alexander Calloway, named for Gregory, was born. Now we have a little girl, Joy, who is still a toddler.

Peter no longer roamed the world. Instead, he set up a ship-building business on the Hudson where he and I and our little family live in a two-story space above the business. You should bring Will by for a visit."

"They owned a thirty-foot sailboat, *The Lucky Duck*," Linda continued. "They often take us boating on extended trips with friends and family including me when I'm in the city."

Following Joyce onto the porch was Kadijah Jackson Montgomery, the youngest daughter of Grover and Harriet Jackson; a fairly new newlywed married to Martin Montgomery, the fourth son of Stephen and Esther. She was a pretty woman and a former Air Force pilot. After two tours in Afghanistan, she resigned her commission and now flew helicopters and private planes out of Monroe County to places like New York City, Syracuse, Boston, Philadelphia, Washington, DC, Pittsburgh, and as far west as Chicago, Illinois. She routinely flew her brothers-in-law to New York early on Monday mornings and returned them to Monroe County, on Friday afternoons.

Martin, her husband, a seasoned electrician, was the one wiring Linda's new studio, school and home in New York City. Will met Chuck's brothers on Linda's job site on many occasions. All of the Montgomery men were tall and slim like their father, but none were as tall or as thickly muscular as Chuck.

Although they had their specialty trades, a carpenter, brick mason, plumber, electrician, welder, painter, and plasterer, they also operated different types of produce farms in the county. They were better known for building homes, schools, and businesses in and around the area, but would drop everything to take on a project for members of the family. They invested eight months of time and effort rehabilitating and renovating Chuck's farm in Maryland. They virtually moved there living in mobile homes until one of the reconditioned bunkhouses was ready for occupancy. Then they brought in skilled and unskilled labor to work on the rest of the farm until the project was completed and Chuck moved in.

"Hi, Aunt Kadijah, when did you get here?"

"Just after you and Will went up to visit your father," said Kadijah. "I heard the jet and figured we were starting earlier than planned. So, I came to see what Mama needed doing."

"I didn't fly in. Will and I drove up. We got here at just about dawn."

"You should have let me know, babe. I would have picked up you and Will," said Kadijah to her niece.

"I actually wanted to drive because I don't get to do it that much. It was an easy trip that time of the night. Not much traffic on the roads."

"He's a cutie, Linda," Joyce said, winking. "I can see why you wanted to be alone with him."

Linda turned her head and looked over her shoulder to where Will was standing talking with Peter Calloway and Martin Montgomery by the still smoking grills. Little Alexander was chasing butterflies around them.

"Did you make your pumpkin squash, Aunt Joyce?" asked Linda.

"I did and I even put some aside for you to take back to the city with you."

The three of them slung their arms around each other and went back into the kitchen to see what else needed doing.

Later, on her way to wash her hands in the first-floor powder room, Linda happened to spy her grandmother giving her grandfather a haircut on the side porch. He palmed her rear cheek giving it a squeeze before she looked around and swatted his hand away. Linda ducked into the powder room before they caught her watching them. She surely didn't know what she was going to do with the knowledge of her grandparents carrying on an affair.

It was really none of her business what two grown, consenting adults did in the privacy of their bedroom, but *mercy* this was a conundrum. *Would this scandalize the family members?* She wondered. *She really didn't want to be the one to break the news. What if their relationship caused a rift in the family? After all, Granma Ester had only been dead for six years. Was it too soon for Grandpa Stephen to start seeing other women . . . his in-law by marriage at that? They shared grandchildren, for pity's sake! What if it didn't work out between them? What then?* She worried.

A soft knock on the door took her attention away from her thoughts. She turned on the water and began to lather and rinse her hands. "Just a moment," she called out as she dried her hands on a paper towel and then tossed it into the trash.

When she opened the door, Will was leaning against the opposite wall, his arms folded across his broad chest and his long legs crossed at the ankles. He looked up at her and began to smile before his face clouded.

"Is something wrong?" he asked.

Quickly, Linda pulled him into the powder room with her and firmly closed the door. He blankly stared at her, his eyes narrowed and roamed her face.

"Is everything all right with you?" he asked.

"No, it's not. What am I supposed to do, Will?"

"About what?" he asked, genuinely confused.

"About my grandparents?" she said as if it was a major issue.

Will's face relaxed into a rueful smile. "I have one word for you."

"What word?"

"Cowpies."

She pursed her lips and rolled her impressive, dark-green eyes at him.

Raising an eyebrow, he grinned at her. Then leaning forward to within a breath of her mouth, he opened the door at his back and shoved her out into the hallway.

There were oblong, sturdy, hand-built, wooden, picnic tables all over Harriet Jackson's yard covered with Easter-colored paper, tablecloths and bums hip-to-hip along each bench. Cups were filled with ice and lemonade or iced sun tea while others drank beer straight from the bottle between bites of ribs, succulent slices of ham, melt-in-your-mouth lamb, chicken barbeque, potato salad, mac and cheese, green beans, buttered corn-on-the-cob, oven rolls and an assortment of other vegetables and casseroles. Two, fat rolls of paper towels and a container of moist towelets stood sentry on each end of every table and were being liberally used to wipe away the evidence of barbeque sauce on faces and hands. However, somehow before long, more sauce magically appeared causing more paper towel disasters.

Butch Cassidy and the Sundance Kid didn't have to use paper towels to remove the tell-tale sauce from around their mouths as they gnawed on the generous amount of bones tossed in their direction. Regrettably, they had little, if any, of the delectable meat still clinging to the bones. Yet, they were content to stay in the shade of trees out of the way of foot traffic.

Children dashed from here to there playing tag or hide-and-go-seek among the bushes, trees, and shrubbery. However, no little people dared to run up and down the rows of Grandma Harriet's freshly tilled garden. Oh, no, that would likely get a firm hand to a little bottom and no amount of tears would save them.

Those young and old, who gave up the battle to see who could eat the most, sat sprawling like shipwreck victims in lawn chairs, chaise lounges, or on blankets spread out on the grass in little conversation spaces from which to dose, watch clouds or birds soar in the sky or watch the world go by. More than a few released another notch or two in their belt buckles.

Chuck, face covered with his Stetson, reclined on a blanket snoring with baby Teresa curled comfortably cuddled on his broad chest sleeping, his arms securing her to him as they visited dreamlands. The noise from the rambunctious children didn't disturb them one bit. Several snapshots were taken by numerous family members to share on social media sites and for family history annals.

A band was gearing up for a little hoedown. This led to the introduction of jugs, spoons, guitars, and washboards to provide the rhythm. Upside down, round wash tubs were pressed into service as drum sets for an original Zydeco-like sound. By the addition of wood blocks, cowbells and cymbals, people were tapping out the beat on table tops, hand claps, and voice calls. These home-made instruments and ordinary objects, like the washtub bass, washboards, spoons, bones, stovepipe, and comb and tissue paper, adapted to or modified for the making of sound could have been a full orchestra concert in Carnegie Hall.

Will, his flat stomach filled to capacity, found himself picking up the beat using silverware against beer bottles abandoned over the tables in favor of other, colder ones. As he accompanied the band, arranging the bottles to provide the best sounds, he rocked his head on his broad neck and shoulders.

Men, women, and children began to get up and into the swing of things dancing freestyle to the music. Even the youngsters abandoned their modern moves to swish and sway Old School. The tunes that accompanied the music would never appear on any top one-hundred hits list, but the words were as familiar to all as if they were Grammy-nominated hits.

As the sun began to sink behind the mountains in the western sky, the party moved inside. Remnants of the supper were set up buffet style on the big trestle table in the country kitchen and kept warm over water heated by Sterno fuel cans. Cakes, pies, cookies, and other treats were brought to the dining table and displayed for perusal and selection. The coffee urn was set up on the buffet with cups and condiments surrounding it. The homemade ice cream was scooped directly out of the ice cold vats they were made in.

It was a relatively tight fit in Harriet Jackson's house, but people snuggled in wherever space was available, including the floor. They began to have dessert and talk and reminisce about times gone by and people who were no longer around. Still, the mood never dipped to a maudlin level.

Martin Montgomery cleared his throat three times, his face flushed, and said, "Well, I guess it's time for you all to know there will be another Montgomery coming this fall. Kadijah and I are expecting."

Cheers accompanied his announcement and several more followed around the room, including Linda's update on the opening of her school and studio. Finally, the announcements got around to Stephen who, standing beside Harriet's side said, "I guess it's time to say I've found someone I want to live with for the rest of my born days." A pin dropping in the Alaskan tundra would have sounded like a bomb blast in the silent room. However, undaunted, Stephen pressed on. "I've asked this lady to be my wife, but she's a mind to say no because of how you may feel about it. Now, I don't mix in none of y'alls business unless asked, but ..."

"Oh, for cryin' out loud, Stephen," said Thomas Montgomery, Stephen's oldest brother, and the oldest family member in the room. "Go on and tell us you want to marry Harriet like that's some secret to the lot of us," he groused good-naturedly.

"Yeah, Pop, it's about time you stop trying to keep this under your hat," said Bob, Stephen's firstborn. "We've known about this for years."

"Go for it, Mama," Bob's wife, Sheila, Harriet's oldest daughter added.

"Well, gosh dang it! Can't keep nothin' a secret no more," grumbled Stephen.

As encouragement continued around the room, Linda looked up over her shoulder at Will and sighed. "Thank goodness, no cow pies in your immediate future."

Chapter 16

"You're serious?" asked Linda of Roderick and JaiHonnah Baylor, perplexed. "You're that far ahead of schedule?" It was two weeks later after her and Will's return from the Easter Holiday visit in Monroe County, Pennsylvania.

"We are, yes," said Roderick, smiling. "My foreman reported after the walls are painted, they only need to sand the floors and apply several coats of polyurethane before you'll be able to move in. During that time, the windows will be boarded up so that the exterior walls can be sandblasted. He estimates two weeks, tops."

"I can't believe this," Linda said enthusiastically.

"Believe it. We want to schedule your final walk-through on this date," Roderick said pulling up a calendar on an iPad. "Do you think this is a convenient date for you?"

"Wow, just wow! Yes, my head is spinning, but yes, I'll make that date work."

"Good, then feel free to walk the spaces as often as you like and note anything you see needing attention. Once we have a confirmed punch list completed, we'll be out of your hair."

"I can't thank you enough for taking on this project and handling it so quickly. To be finished a full six weeks before the deadline is just unbelievable. Now I have to step up my plans for the staging company to come in and gear up for the open house."

"Don't forget, after the stagers leave and the open house is over, you'll have to change the date for the moving company to transfer your things here from your storage facilities," said Gregory. "You'll also need to give Angelique a heads up about the change for her catering schedule."

"Oh, my, that means the invitations to the open house need to go out next week and I've barely put together a list of people I want to invite!"

"I can loan a couple of people, interns really, to you from my office to help with the administrative work for a few weeks. However, you're going to have to step up your task of hiring administrative staff for the school and have them vetted."

"Okay, okay, I can do this. I know I can. I just need to get organized."

"If there's nothing more, Roderick and I have to get back to DC," said JaiHonnah smiling.

"Yes, I mean, no, there's nothing more. I'll see you in a couple of weeks," she smiled hugging them both.

The next week, Linda worked like a demon completing her to-do list. She was up early and at Indulgences by half five, but she had to cut back on her schedule there to only half days. After lunch, she spent the rest of the afternoons and evenings attending to details, interviewing administrative staff and dancers who would work for her either full or part-time as instructors. She worked closely with Angelique on the food services for the school and the plans for catering the open-house event.

As the date for the open house grew closer, her tasks seemed to increase rather than decrease. She didn't even have time for dinner or outings with Will, Eugene, and Violet. They said they understood, but she still felt badly about not being around for them.

Linda was finishing up with her temporary administrative staff when Will came into the school. She was pleasantly surprised to see him, but he didn't look particularly happy. She excused herself from her temps and met him near the front of the first floor. "Well, hello, stranger," she said smiling.

"Uh, is there somewhere we can talk?" Will asked.

Her brows drew together in confusion. "Sure, uh, come with me," she said moving toward the elevator. "I'll be back shortly," she called out to her temps. They acknowledged her with a wave.

She and Will boarded the private elevator and, since it was a nice day, she went to the rooftop deck which would be her bedroom suite in another few weeks. When they stepped off the elevator, Will stood and stared momentarily stunned by the beauty of the surroundings.

Linda noticed his awestruck expression. "You like?" she asked.

"No, I love. This is beautiful, Linda. You've succeeded in making this an indoor-outdoor solarium. Trees, grass, flowers and a pool?"

"Yep, and the Murphy bed will go here," she said motioning to a space. "Everything else will go into the closet over here," she said showing him to a wall. Then with a flick of the several switches, the boxes that constituted her closet started moving apart allowing her to walk through the spaces.

"Moving closet walls?" Will asked.

"Yes. Closets take up a lot of space especially when I only need it to store clothes, shoes, and lingerie. Otherwise, it just sits there. This way the walls close up and I gain two-thirds of the space that traditional closets utilize. The same thing is true of the bed. For me, robotic walls and a Murphy bed are a perfect solution. It also aides with cleaning." She walked into the shower room with a water closet. The roof was open to the sky and water would drench her from several different directions. A double, free-standing sink area was back-to-back minimizing the amount of space to accommodate the countertops.

"I see you're right, but as much as I would love to talk with you about the innovations you've included, I need to discuss something else with you."

She nodded. "Okay, shoot."

"Look, I don't know any other way to approach this except straightforward."

Her curiosity grew even more. "Okay?" she said uncertainly."

"Linda, are you dumping me?"

For a humming moment, she just stared. "Dumping you?"

"Yes, you know, pumping the brakes on our relationship?"

She slowly shook her head while looking into his eyes. "No, I'm not dumping you. What gave you that crazy idea?"

"Are you sure? I mean, if your feelings for me, for us, have changed…"

"*Whoa! Whoa! Wait!*" she said, putting up her hands to forestall his next words. "My feelings have not changed toward you."

"Then maybe I've been reading more into our relationship than you intended. If I've gotten signals mixed or crossed or if you're interested in someone else, perhaps a younger man. I mean, I've seen how some men look at you, younger men and I know I'm older than you . . ."

"Will, stop talking. When you're digging a hole and you have no way of getting out of it, my best suggestion is to stop digging." She stepped to him, her arms going up to encircle his neck. Then she went up on pointe and kissed him long and deep.

It didn't take long for him to crush her to him and devour her mouth. When they came up for air, he breathed a sigh of relief fitting his forehead to hers. "Okay, maybe I'm an idiot, but it's been weeks since I've seen you to hold you like this. Ever since we got back from Easter in Pennsylvania. Eugene and Violet think I did something to make you stay away after they came back from visiting their great-grandparents in Oregon. I really didn't know what to tell them."

"Tell them I'll be there tonight for dinner, a movie, hot buttered popcorn, fresh fruit drinks, and a few goodnight bedtime stories. Then, pal, you're all mine for the rest of the evening." She had a ton of stuff to do, but she wouldn't let it interfere with her relationship with Will and his family. He was becoming very important to her.

"That's good to hear. I've missed you, Linda."

"I've missed you, too, Will. Believe me, my absence has nothing to do with you and everything to do with getting geared up for the open house. I've been a little preoccupied and crazy. I go to Uncle Greg's and he or Mrs. Conway feeds me. Then I start working on one task or the other. When I look up again, it's too late to call to say goodnight to you and the children. In the morning, I've compressed my schedule at Indulgences, so I don't get an opportunity to stop by and say hello to you. So, let's make a standing date. Wednesdays we'll have dinner and fun night at your place and Saturdays we'll spend at my place. How does that sound?"

"Like a plan I can work with." He kissed her again, long and deep. "I'll see you later tonight."

They walked to the elevator hand-in-hand until Will turned back to look at her spacious garden bedroom suite. He nodded in appreciation of what she'd done to create a sanctuary for herself . . . and he hoped she'd want to share time in it with him.

On the day of her Open House for the New York Academy of Dance, it was raining like a monsoon hit. Because of the forecasted rain, at the last moment, Linda had the red-carpeted entrance tented from the street where, under the canopy, guests would unload and uniformed parking attendants would take the cars away to store in Will's multilevel garage across the street. Many guests would arrive in cabs or chauffeured cars which would help the ebb and flow of the traffic.

The press and media reporters, for Arts and Entertainment elements of local, regional, and national newspapers and magazines, were the first to arrive. They were on time at an earlier hour allotted for interviews. Before the guests were expected to arrive, private, escorted tours were conducted for the press by the instructors she hired. After the tour, they were shown to an office space where Linda, with Bill Chandler at her side, allowed interviews.

Although the press release went to all outlets, she hadn't expected the television stations and networks to cover the opening, but they were there, too, in full force, causing the office to be crowded with camera equipment and on-camera reporters with their crews. However, thanks to the magic of robotics, the desk, chairs, and walls were folded into the wall cavities and out of the way. A blizzard of photos covered that little trick and then, with the room enlarged, the barrage of questions began.

Standing at a mic on the podium with her business and foundation logos designed by Arden on wall-sized billboards at her back, she gave it thirty minutes to appease the questioners and photographers. When the inquisition became repetitive or strayed into areas unrelated to the school or studio, such as the questions about her relationship with Will posed by Jolie Jance, it was time to shut it down and she did so efficiently. With

Bill Chandler, her theatrical attorney and agent in attendance, she was able to pass her more aggressive paparazzi off to him. Actually, he was far more photogenic than she. He had years of experience as an actor, movie star, and high fashion model. It made him imminently qualified when he became a much sought-after sports and entertainment attorney. He and her Mom were law school chums and founding members of their law firm. So, she left him handling a barrage of questions while she attended to other matters like forming a receiving line to welcome her guests.

She allowed camera crews to film her guests' arrival just inside the front double doors rather than out on the street in the pouring rain. She hadn't thought of the possibility of having to store wet umbrellas and raincoats for over three hundred people, not including her family, on her guest list.

Thankfully, her family arrived earlier than the press and news media and pitched in to help save the day. From somewhere they unearthed Rubbermaid trashcans to store wet umbrellas and ticket stubs to be used to reclaim wet raincoats. So, at the front entrance, after showing the invitation with the embedded security strip and proper identification, one after another of her siblings stepped up to collect wet raincoats and umbrellas and hand out a ticket stub before disappearing into the locker room with the wet garments. A few of her cousins, with mops in hand, immediately dried up any water trails. She hired a company to provide amenities; waitstaff and restroom attendants. Added to them were plenty of hands of her uncles, aunts, cousins and more taking on tasks of whatever needed doing.

She hired four administrative staff and an office manager to oversee the day-to-day operations of the business while she and her eight instructors concentrated on those young, and some not so young, people who were going to be there to learn the new skills, techniques, and abilities. The day her business website, designed and managed by her Uncle Kenneth and his communications company, CompuCorrect Global, went live it was flooded to near capacity with applications to lease studio space or from across the country and around the globe to audition for admittance to the academic and dance school. She didn't want to have to turn anyone away, so she resolved to hire more instructors, if necessary, to accommodate the number of applicants. The first group of auditions was scheduled to be held starting on Monday of next week. She would be able to evaluate skill levels and align them with the right instructor. However, that was next week's task. Today she had to deal with the number of acceptance cards and the potential arrival of every single person who was on her guest list.

Linda was pleased with the staging company's work on each level of the building and the cafeteria and theatre in the basement. Tall, green plants and trees on each level were draped with twinkling fairy lights and strategically placed to provide the illusion of intimacy in the otherwise large, cavernous room on each level of the building. Poster-sized, black-framed photos depicting various ballets, dance moves, and dancers hung proud of the wall as if hung in an art gallery. Again, Arden's photographic artistry at work. Tall tables, some with tall chairs or stools, provided respites for individuals or groups to gather and hold conversations around the ballroom-sized spaces. Little venue groupings of sofas, chairs, and tables were spotted here and there. Her studio lights added accented ambiance, yet the spaces seemed enormous and uncluttered even with the building crowd roaming about from floor to floor. Turbo-sized but decorative ceiling fans kept the air moving and the spaces comfortable.

As those guests started to arrive, Angelique's hot and cold food buffets and bars festooned with colorful cloths and bunting were revealed on each level. Her staff, and the ones hired for the event to float among the guests with hot and cold hors d'oeuvres and crystal flutes of champagne kept each buffet replenished and the open bars were well-stocked and very popular. Angelique was cornered and subjected to impromptu interviews and photo ops. As a supermodel, she was accustomed to having photo flashes going off in her face as did Gregory when he was voted the top athlete in professional basketball. Together Gregory and Angelique were a stunning couple.

So were Linda's parents, Chuck and Vivian, as they were stopped several times for spontaneous interviews. Their attire alone garnered more than a few rave reviews. Linda's dad in his Western duds and her mother wearing a birthday gift Linda gave her designed for her by Carlos Ortega. Her sibs also came dressed in fashionable attire.

More and more notables and stars arrived, including Angelique's mega movie star brother, Miguel Menendez-Gaza. He was launching a singing career and helped Linda by having his band play for the occasion with Tucker Cavanaugh on his electric guitar and some of the other Montgomery offspring joining in on voice and different instruments. The music was piped through the speaker system to every level, including the basement. They played a wide range of music to suit everyone's taste.

Tina Justice, the head of the Sweet Justice Network arrived with her industrialist husband, Nico Collins, a New Yorker who Linda learned was a long-time friend of Will's. Her parents' friends Judge KC Bryant and her husband, international attorney Thomas Ashton Marshal arrived with another power couple, attorneys Peter and Cheryl Lawrence Brock. More surprising was the arrival of Cheryl's internationally well-known parents, columnists, investigative reporters, and television commentators Farrow and Helen Kendall Lawrence. They were followed shortly by Roderick and JaiHonnah Hawkins Baylor and unexpectedly by members of JaiHonnah's family, her father, US Ambassador Jake Hawkins and his wife, Roderick's sister, Kelley Baylor Hawkins. Moments later JaiHonnah's sister, LaiLoni Skai Hawkins and her husband, US Ambassador Jefferson Logan, came with her brother, business mogul and Formula One race car driver, Adam Hawkins. *Better eye candy was not to be found in the Lower 48*, thought Linda of Adam, and planned to introduce him to her architect Fiona Lowry.

No one escaped scrutiny by the insatiable press and news media, including notables from the theatre world both domestically and from abroad. Music sensation Matt Kennedy and his wife, Audra, drew a crowd as did his brother, Tate Kennedy, the science phenom and astronaut, and his wife, professional lobbyist and attorney, Capri McAllister, Gregory's former romantic interest.

At one point, Linda noticed the donations jar for the not-for-profit arm of her operation, the Linda Lewis Foundation, was filling up to capacity with checks and cash. Some of the donors stood posing while dropping checks or cash into the square glass container while a blizzard of photos was taken, but others waved off the press and made their donations unobtrusively. Members of Gregory's staff were distributing receipts for the cash donations at an impressive rate.

Linda's eyes moved from the pictures being taken over the burgeoning crowd to where Will stood, having just been approached by the television reporter, Jolie Jance and a young, very handsome man. The plus-one with Jolie looked somewhat familiar. Initially, Linda thought he was the actor Augustus Prew from the popular television show Pure Genius. She didn't have time to observe the interaction between them as she needed to stay on the move greeting guests and garnering support for her students.

She moved as quickly as possible from one group to another and from one floor to the next without being rude but constantly acknowledging the presence of her security team. They were ever vigilant and unobtrusive, so she didn't make their job harder by disappearing on them, but it was hard to stay in their line-of-sight when there were so many people everywhere in the building except her private residence. There, only her family was permitted along with Eugene and Violet. She checked in on them periodically, but a few of her under-eighteen-year-old siblings had everything under control.

By hour three of the planned four-hour open house, Linda had been up and down the stairs of the twelve story building several times. The event morphed into a party with people of various age groups dancing on each two-thousand square foot level to the music Miguel and his band provided. People were enjoying themselves, singles from different backgrounds and interests were hooking up, and no one seemed inclined to leave.

"Great party," Will said snagging Linda's hand as she tried to squeeze through dancers on the fifth floor. "How are you holding up, Legs," he teased.

Linda grinned at him and went willingly into Will's arms. "Oh, I think I'm good for a few more hours." She snaked her arms up around his neck and easily followed his dance moves across the ballroom floor. "You're good at this. Have you ever taken lessons?"

Will threw back his head and laughed. "Oh, I've had a few hot and sweaty experiences on a dance floor in high school, college, and when I was a randy young ballplayer."

"Ah, yes, my brother, show me what you're working with," she teased back, swinging out of his arms and executing popular dance moves.

"Can't touch this, my sister," Will said as he showed off his smooth robotic moves. "I was The Hammer before Hammer knew his left foot from his right."

"Ah, *sukki, sukki*, now," Dena called out and danced around Will.

She was joined by Angelique, Emery Arden, and Whitney Ivy.

Will found himself the center of the women's attention, but he was loving it. He expanded and exaggerated his repertoire of dance moves to the delight of Linda, the women who joined in, and the crowd who were cheering them on.

Applause rose and high-fives abound at the end of the dance marathon. The next piece to play was of a slower tempo. Will turned a grinning Linda into his arms.

"You can really bring it on the dance floor," Linda enthused, her arms again up around his neck. "I had no idea."

"Old school, baby," he joked while his hands on her impossibly narrow waist guided her movements against his body. "I could rock it back in the day. Now," he shrugged. "Not so much. I haven't danced like that in quite a while."

"It didn't look like it. You're very limber."

"I happen to have access to a place where I can work out. It's called Indulgences. Ever heard of it?"

"Oh, yes! Great place. Is that where you got this great body?" she said rubbing suggestively against him.

"Uh, Linda," he warned. "Be good."

"Oh, I intend to be," she said and kissed him as the music ended.

Oh, yeah, thought Will as he watched Linda walk away leaving him hard and in need. She looked at him again over her shoulder and winked before disappearing into the crowd. Lately, she'd been doing and saying some fairly provocative things to him. Yet, she confided, during one of the evenings together after Eugene and Violet were in bed, she was still a virgin. That had set him back on his heels. Still, they participated in some heaving petting, but with children in the house and Drew likely to come in at any moment, they let it go no further.

Linda had to fan herself with one of the decorative ones she provided as gifts for her guests. Her hand rested on one depicting a scene from the ballet *Don Quixote*. Wouldn't she just know it? After dancing with Will, she was so aroused that the ceiling fans weren't enough to cool her down. Everything about him captivated her. She knew many men, dated a few in her twenty-plus years, but never met a man she was more intrigued with than Will. She loved Will's scent, easygoing personality, sense of humor, his willingness to open himself to her and new experiences, and the care he showed to his nephew and niece and even to his brother, Drew. Nothing about him sent up cautionary signals for her or from any branch of her family. Everyone—her parents, grands, sibs, aunts, uncles, and cousins—thought him to be an honorable and trustworthy man. Uncle Gregory considered him a close, personal friend and she implicitly trusted her uncle's judgment. When she talked with her parents about Will, despite the age difference, they had no misgivings. He got along with her extended family and fit right in with the controlled chaos which was prevalent in her current situation. She hoped he was ready for the next steps and stages of her life.

"Linda," someone called out as she was about to head down another flight of stairs.

She turned and observed Jolie Jance approach. "Yes?"

"Lovely party," Jolie said, but Linda felt a little undercurrent of something.

"Thank you. I'm glad you're enjoying yourself."

"I saw you and Will Hamilton dancing upstairs."

Linda raised an eyebrow. "Yes, he's a very good dancer, wouldn't you agree?"

"I would. We danced quite a bit when we were lovers. Most often we did the horizontal mambo."

O-kay, now Linda knew what the impetus was for this undercurrent she felt around Jolie Jance and the likely purpose for this little tête-à-tête. "In order for him to be as proficient as he is, he must have danced with quite a few of his lovers and other women, too," said Linda. "After all, I've learned in my career, practice makes perfect in preparation for the person who won't just be relegated to 'lover' or understudy status."

"You think you're going to be that woman?" Jolie snidely asked.

Linda shrugged. "You've questioned me about my relationship with Will in the interview gaggle. I didn't answer your questions then, so I'm curious to know what makes you think I'll answer them now?"

"You're a cool one, aren't you, Linda?"

"Perhaps, but I have enough self-respect to not put myself in the face of the next woman Will chooses to befriend. Enjoy the rest of the party," Linda said, smiling before continuing down the stairs to the second floor. She was immediately brought into another group conversation and didn't give Jolie Jance another thought.

Hours later, when all of the guests, her family, her staff, and the cleaning service were gone, Linda kicked off her shoes and collapsed on one of the sofas in her living area. With her eyes closed, she propped her interlaced fingers behind her head and sighed.

"Tired?" Will asked.

"Not, too, no. You?"

"Pleasantly exhausted."

"I guess so with all the women who lined up to dance with you," Linda said laughing.

He gave her an ironic grunt. "You should have warned me that your Nana Sylvia could dance like a teenager. She was smokin' the moves."

Linda laughed again. "I thought I told you her ancestors were entertainers. Nana still has great legs."

"Oh, yeah, you did tell me, but not that she could move like *that!* Your mother is no slouch either! However, when your Dad broke out with the *Down N Dirty* line dance, I was done!" Will said shaking his head. "You may need to open a different type of dance school just so your father can teach us to do what he does. Even your little seven-year-old brother had the steps down pat while the rest of us just looked on trying and failing to get the complicated steps right."

"I'll give you a private lesson," she said, still laughing.

Will sat and lifted her legs and feet into his lap and then began to give her a massage.

"Ummm, that feels soooo good," Linda moaned pleasurably.

"You were on your feet quite a bit. Did you ever sit down?"

She shook her head. "I didn't, no, and I didn't get anything to eat either. I'm starving."

"Ah, that's what I thought." Will put her feet on an ottoman and rose to go across the space to her kitchen area. He washed his hands, grabbed a couple of mittens to take hot plates out of the warming drawers and set them on wooden trays. After grabbing a bottle of chilled white wine from her tall beverage cooler, he carried the trays and placed them on a table beside the sofa.

The aroma of good food caused Linda to raise her head and open her eyes. When she sat up straighter, Will placed a napkin across her lap, before he sat down across from her and handed a fork, knife, and spoon to her.

"Wow, this is nice. How did you arrange this?" Linda asked as they began to eat from the different serving bowls.

"I asked Angelique to set aside these samples of everything she had on the buffets."

Linda bit into a stuffed mushroom and moaned with pleasure. Will put a sample of everything on her plate and then on his. They fed each other and drank the wine while talking about their observations during the event until they were stuffed.

"I can't eat another bite," Will exclaimed.

"I can't either," Linda said rising to clear away their debris. "I'll have to save the desserts to have later with coffee." Once the space was put to right, and the dishwasher started, she grabbed another bottle of Pouilly-Fuissé and two wine glasses.

Will was sitting on the sofa with his head resting back against a cushion and his eyes closed when Linda took his hand. He opened his eyes and looked up at her.

"Come on," she said tugging him to a standing position and then leading him to the elevator.

"Where are you taking me?" Will asked sleepily.

"Somewhere we can get comfortable and relax."

When she pressed the up button on the elevator, he warily looked at her. They came off the elevator on the rooftop, bedroom suite level. The rain was still pouring off the glass-top solarium pooling in her rain-barrel system. It made a pleasant sound and the changing colors of lighting in motion in the room resembled an aurora borealis.

Will pondered the romantic effect as Linda continued to guide him from the area where her massive bed was located through the open doors into the grassy garden area to a double-wide chaise. Her exercise pool churned and gurgled adding to the musical sounds the rain made and her lights enhanced. After setting the wine and glasses down, she relieved him of his sport's jacket to hang up and sitting him down on the chaise, she took off his shoes.

He got the message and poured two glasses of wine while Linda made herself comfortable beside him. He handed one glass to her as they lay back against the thick cushion and headrest with their feet up and stretched out before them. She snuggled close to his body and rested her head on his shoulder.

"This is nice," Will said taking a sip of wine.

"I found it on a trip to Mâconnais, a sub-region of Burgundy, France. Uncle Gregory couldn't get away to come to see an old winery that was being sold, so he asked me to go in his place and I did. When I told him what I found, he told me what and how much to buy and have shipped. I liked the taste so much I purchased some for myself. I had it stored at Uncle Greg's home with my other eclectic finds from my travels." She looked up and around at her decorative things displayed in niches in the wall cavities. "Now that I have my own space, I was excited to unearth all of my things."

"You've done a great job, Linda, but when I said this was nice, I wasn't referring to the wine."

"Oh," she said, chuckling. "I wish I could take credit for it, but JaiHonnah, Fiona Lizette, and JRock really pulled this place together."

"No matter who did what it was your vision that made it happen, but you still didn't get it. When I said this is nice, I was talking about being here like this, relaxing with you."

"Braindead, Will," she said and laughed.

"Nevertheless, I especially like the way you used robotics to maximize your space and tucked all of those books into the wall cavities. I've never seen that done before I saw it at your home in Maryland."

"We are a family of readers."

"So, I noticed. Dena took an armload of books when she left with Eugene and Violet."

"She was going to take them with her to Uncle Gregory's house, but somehow Drew convinced her to go to your home with him. I found it particularly curious, didn't you?"

"Oh, maybe you didn't know Drew's been to Boston several times to visit Dena?"

Linda looked at him skeptically. "No, I didn't know that. She never mentioned it to me. Do you think something is up between them?"

Will shrugged. "I know my brother has stepped up his game since he met Dena. Every time he comes back from visiting with her, he's a happy camper. He's working harder and being more conscientious at Indulgences so he can have more time off and he seems more serious about his classes, too. He's racking up frequent flier miles between New York and Boston. All of this began to occur after he met your sister. He doesn't talk about any women to me particularly, except for Dena. It's 'Dena did this or Dena said that' all of the time now. I think your sister has him wrapped. Just like you have me wrapped. Was that statement clear enough this time?"

She looked up at him then, her eyes going to his mouth.

He couldn't resist the look in her eyes or her pretty mouth, so he kissed her and kissed her some more. Blindly, he took her empty wine glass from her hand and sat it on the end table beside him while he continued to kiss her. Linda shifted to her side reaching up to curve her left hand behind his neck while with his right hand he brought her leg to rest across his lap. She could feel his heat and taste his need and what she wanted. So, she did what she needed to do to cure the desire building inside her. Moving her hand from his neck, she reached for him intimately.

She felt him moan deep in his chest before he clamped his hand over hers and held it still. He broke the kiss and placed his forehead against her.

"It's time for me to go. It's getting late, we've had two bottles of wine, and you probably need your rest," said Will.

He was still breathing hard, Linda noted. He was also rock hard under her palm. She squeezed him, flexing her fingers up and down him before he stopped her again.

"Stay," she whispered. "Spend the rest of the night with me."

He shook his head in agonizing need and groaned, "You don't know what you're asking, Linda."

"I do know, Will, but if you're not into me in that way, you don't have to tell me twice."

"You have to be crazy to think that I don't want you. I want you physically, but more importantly, I want and need you emotionally. No half measures, Linda. No experimentation. This is not going to be a one-and-done for me. Can you handle that?"

Linda shifted until she was under him and then brought his mouth to hers. "Show me what I've been missing," she said, and he did.

Will was quick and nimble in divesting her of her clothes and his own while causing her breath to catch when his mouth followed in the wake of the removal of each garment. He feasted on her breast and then the little indented navel. His thumb pressed back and forth over her clit causing her to thrash about and moan long and deep until she lost her breath. His fingers slipped between her thighs until he could insert two inside her hot, moist portal and continue to play her clitoris with his thumb.

She was like a fire flashing into an inferno in his arms, thought Will when he could think at all. Yet, her hands on his body could make him tremble with a greedy need to taste her and mate for an eternity. Her thighs quivered while he ravished her core with his mouth and tongue with his heart hammering in his chest. The thrill of her, the hunger for her, and the unadulterated need rushed over him while he savored her scent and the long, lean, but strong muscles under his hands.

The first of successive orgasms rushed through and over Linda so rapidly that she wasn't prepared for how they swamped her. She called out Will's name and somehow found her voice. *"Now! Now! Now!"*

On her demand, an oath rang out from him as he filled her, kissed her like a man on a mission. Hands intertwined, their hips were like out of control pistons. They breathed each other in and cried out when they flew free of their mutual madness into a peace never before experienced by either of them.

On a shaky breath, Linda said, "I'm sorry," just as Will also said, "I'm sorry."

Will lifted his head and frowned down at Linda. "Sorry? What have you got to be sorry about?"

"Oh, Will, I lost control. I was trying to give you as much pleasure as you were giving me, but … I don't know how to explain it. Everything was out of my hands."

Will rolled off of Linda and then brought her into his left side. With his right hand he palmed his face removing the moisture. "Christ, Linda. You tell me I caused you to lose control and you think I need an apology for that?" He was beginning to get his breath back when he laughed. "I'm the one who needs to apologize. I wasn't wearing a condom. That's never happened to me before. I shouldn't have done that, especially since this was your first time. I was so far gone that I wasn't thinking at all."

Linda turned into him and ran her hand down his body until she could touch him intimately. "We should be okay. I'm wearing an IUD." She felt him harden in her hand.

"Don't tell me that, Linda, or I may not ever let you out of here," Will groaned.

"My, what recuperative abilities you have," she said enjoying the feel of him. Climbing on top of him, she began to rock her hips until he filled her again.

Moments later, they were off on another adventure of the intimate kind.

He rolled off of her in the dark of her bedroom suite. He didn't have the stamina he once had and he was tired, but still exhilarated. He had met Linda up close, shaken her hand if only briefly, but he had been in her presence and that of her family and friends. He knew so much about them and their interests, it hadn't been difficult to engage each one in conversation. He moved from floor to floor extremely pleased with what Linda accomplished in her space. He could see her creativity at work in each public area, but only family was permitted into the private elevator that went to her residential level. Disappointed, he had to satisfy himself with what he had seen before the space was completed and tight security installed.

Still, the basement level didn't resemble a basement at all with the open and breezy cafeteria beside the theatre where students would perform. Even there, the robotic walls opened to create a much larger space; large enough to put in an ice skating rink.

He gave a large, anonymous donation toward the perpetuation of the next generation of artists she would train. He wanted to be by her side when that occurred and hoped it would be soon. For now, he basked in the glow of having finally met her and touched her.

As the woman's hand reached across his sweat-laden body to reignite his passion, he thought of Linda and what she was doing now. Instead of responding to her, he went to the bathroom, took off the used condom and flushed it before cleaning himself up and putting on another one. He thought he had another session in him with the woman before he had to leave. Now that he had met Linda, he had more work to do.

Chapter 17

It was seven-fifteen on Monday morning in mid-May and the first audition of the first classes began at seven sharp. Those classes were underway on several levels of the school. Classes began at six for professional ballet dancers who worked in other jobs while waiting for open casting calls and keeping their skills sharp. By eight, Linda expected scouts for certain repertory companies to come in to evaluate the existing professionals and the budding crop of new dancers.

Some of the experienced dancers approached her about the availability of positions as instructors for her school, and she was seriously considering three of them. The risk was they were talented dancers who might drop their duties as instructors the moment opportunities for them to perform opened up. That would leave her shorthanded for students who would have become accustomed to a certain style of instruction. A new instructor would have to be brought in and the class would have to be acclimated to start all over again. She didn't want her students frustrated and confused by the changes in their routines. So, she was going to have to think carefully about who she hired especially because all instructors were required to successfully undergo the vetting process before they were offered a contract.

Linda walked among this group of youngsters, both boys and girls, watching them go through the routine she outlined for them using the balance barre. Their parents anxiously stood outside the glass partition and watched. Across the hall was another group of youngsters being evaluated by two of her instructors; one man and one woman. The scenario repeated on each level with successive age groups and skill levels. She would shortly cross the hall to observe and coach the other group as she had done with this one.

"Heads up!" she sharply called out to the group in general and loudly clapped her hands to give them the tempo she expected. "Up on one, balance, balance, on two, and down on three. No bending. Keep your backs straight. Four. Yes, yes, very good! Now switch. Plié! Chin up slightly," she said touching a young boy's chin who was trying to watch himself in the wall-to-wall mirror. "Shoulders down, rib cage pulled up, and back straight. Tuck in your behind tightly, and on one down, and gently rest your hand on the barre, but don't grip too tightly or you'll rely too much on the barre for balance. Find your center," she said while demonstrating the movement she expected them to perform. "Now turn your feet out from the hip, keeping your legs straight. Eyes on me. Yes, yes! Very good!"

Her instructors were making notes on the novice dancers during the auditions and would then switch and go to another studio to repeat the tasks. Another set of instructors would come in here to record their evaluation. By the end of the day, they would be able to rank the students on the list. School was out for the summer and there were seven-year-olds up to those who were in their early teens in attendance on this first day. She slipped Violet in with one group and Eugene in with another.

Will stood outside the moveable glass partition and watched Linda in a full-body, pink leotard move through the group and the routine. Her lustrously thick hair he had his hands in on Saturday night and Sunday morning was pinned up out of her way. She wore pink ballet slippers with the wide pink ribbon tied gracefully around her incredibly long, strong, shapely legs. She was a sculptured masterpiece, he thought as he watched her movements rather than the students.

The other instructors also wore full-body leotards of various colors and ballet slippers or shoes. One man in particular at the Open House and again here this morning, couldn't seem to keep his hands off of Linda. Also, if Will hadn't noticed before on Saturday, the same man was clearly sporting a boner whenever he was around Linda. What the...

"That's some body on that babe, ain't it?" commented a man standing next to Will. "The wife sent me down here on my day off to bring the kids to this audition. I'll tell you I wasn't happy the wife sent me to handle this nonsense until I saw this walking wet dream! She won't have to ask me twice again! No, sir, buddy. I'll be here early with bells on the whole class just to watch this pretty, young, sweet thing move. Oh, hell, did you see the ass on her? *Man!* I'll bet she could crack walnuts with thighs like that. Look at her abs, man! When she spread her legs to . . ."

Will turned his head and stared at the man. The expression on Will's face had the smile slipping from the other man's face in mid-rant. He moved away from Will to watch the audition going on through the glass on the other side of the hallway. It wasn't that the man didn't have a point. Linda was most men's fantasy under any circumstances. However, when it came to Linda, he didn't want anyone disrespecting her. He'd found nirvana in her arms and was more than ready for the next step in their relationship.

While he watched Linda in full instructor mode, his thoughts returned to the discussion they had early on Sunday morning. She explained that, for ten days around the Juneteenth holiday, her family held a reunion in Summer County, South Carolina. He saw pictures of the large crowds who attended and the number of weddings held during the event. They were preparing for five weddings this coming June; one of which was Gregory's and Angelique's.

He was curious about how Gregory and Angelique met. She went on to explain that, back when Vivian was still in law school at Georgetown Law Center, she by happenstance met Chuck Montgomery, a young physician doing his residency at Georgetown Medical Center. Vivian, who volunteered at a family homeless shelter, was the one who discovered Angelique, her mother, and younger brother living in the DC shelter. They were from Peru and came to America to search for Anna's husband who had disappeared. Chuck sought Vivian out to return her wallet when one of her housemates told him he could find her volunteering at the shelter. When he arrived, he was the one who noticed Angelique was a gravely-ill eight-year-old. Chuck took the little girl out of the shelter and arranged to have her seen immediately by his best friend since puberty and a pediatrician, Derrick Jackson.

Vivian went with the Menendez-Gaza family to the doctors' office and met the handsome, former basketball icon. That's where the saga of the threesomes', Derrick, Chuck, and Vivian's relationships, began. Vivian took Angelique's mother, Anna Menendez-Gaza and younger brother, Miguel, out of the shelter to live at a huge brownstone with her and five of her law school friends and housemates. Anna took care of the law school students as if they were her own children while Angelique was hospitalized and her care and expenses covered by Chuck. For the next several years, the housemates and Chuck saw to every aspect of Anna and her family's needs.

As a result, Angelique credits Vivian and Chuck with saving her life and the lives of her mother and brother. Through Vivian, when Angelique was nine years old, she met Vivian's younger brother and sister, Gregory and Aretha Alexander. He was in his teens, yet Angelique was infatuated with Gregory; an emotion that grew into love. Aretha became Angelique's first BFF.

So, since her father was deceased, Angelique asked Chuck to walk her down the aisle and for Vivian to be her matron of honor. Linda, Arden, Whitney Ivy, and Aretha were slated to be the bridesmaids. Will was surprised when Gregory asked him to be one of his groomsmen along with one of his business partners, Troy Jackson, Angelique's brother; Miguel, Stacy's brother; Russel Greene; and Tucker Cavanaugh, Whitney Ivy's fiancée. Gregory's best "men" would be his older brothers Kenneth and Benjamin Alexander.

Will felt honored, but also now understood what showing up at the reunion would portend. It was a statement of epic proportions for Linda to make to her family and friends. An unmarried Alexander family member only brought to the annual reunion someone who was expected to be a permanent fixture. He wanted that with Linda but wasn't confident she wanted it as much as he did. Of course, he would be there for Gregory even if Linda's feelings for him were ambiguous at best.

Fortunately, Gregory expected him to bring Drew and the children, too. Drew was in the same quandary with Dena Montgomery as Will was with Linda. It was only mid-June, and he hoped by June, Linda would have made her feelings clear. Although it had only been five months since they met, he could envision her as a permanent fixture in *his* life. He was ready to make that statement to her family and friends. He was staking his claim, loud and clear. So, he continued to watch her work with the youngsters and wondered whether next year around the Juneteenth holiday, he would be looking forward to his own wedding in Summer County, South Carolina.

"We really have to stop meeting like this," said Jolie coming to stand next to Will. Her cameraman was shooting B roll film through the glass as the auditions continued.

"Hello, Jolie." He hadn't tried to ignore her presence on Saturday during the Open House, but he certainly was trying now. Her constant text messages and phone calls were annoying, but he hadn't responded to any of them. He only talked with her when she caught him off guard like this. He had seen her with a date on Saturday; a younger man, true. He hadn't thought of her as a cougar at age thirty considering she was still fairly young. However, it wasn't any of his business whom she dated or his place to judge her behavior. After all, he was definitely interested in a woman a lot younger than thirty years old.

"Why haven't you returned my messages?"

"Didn't we say all that needed to be said nearly six months ago, Jolie? This dog don't hunt no more. I can wish you and the new man you brought to the Open House the best of everything."

"Didn't seeing me with another man make you feel jealous?"

"Is that the reaction you were looking for from me?" Will asked.

"You're good at answering a question with a question."

"Isn't that what you reporters do professionally?" Will asked.

"You can honestly stand there and tell me you had no reaction to knowing I would be taking another man to my bed, the same bed I had you in nearly every night for six months? You've forgotten how you called out my name when you came hard and long inside me?"

Will shook his head and sighed. "Where is this line of questioning going, Jolie?"

"Didn't your little Linda tell you we had a girl talk on Saturday?"

"Why would you think she'd tell me something she obviously felt was insignificant?"

"You're in denial, Will. You couldn't have made love to me like that for six months and not feel anything when you see me with another man. Would it spark your interest if I told you he was excellent between the sheets, but couldn't hold a candle to you? I did things with him you and I used to do together just so I could visualize it was you I still had between my thighs."

"Don't you think you're the one in denial, Jolie? Yes, I feel something for you. I feel gratitude that you moved on and found someone who deserved your time and attention. Or do you have a short-term memory loss problem? In any event, listen carefully while I make a declarative statement. I've told you before to catch a clue and to stick a fork in it because it's done. Is that clear enough for you?" Without waiting for an answer, he walked away to watch Violet in her beginners' audition on a different floor.

Linda had her back to the glass partition while moving along the rows watching the class go through their routine. Yet, she couldn't help but see through the mirror in front of her an agitated Jolie Jance arguing or pleading with Will while her cameraman recorded scenes of the class at work. Given the disinterested expression on Will's face and his nonchalant stance, clearly, whatever Jolie was saying wasn't having her expected effect on him. She hadn't thought to mention to Will about Jolie buttonholing her at the Open House. This was one of those situations she wanted to stay far away from.

Besides she was having enough trouble keeping Carlo Bettini at arm's length. From the moment he entered her school, he was trying to insinuate himself into everything she did. He was like an octopus, always touching her. She had to keep on the move to stay out of his clutches. When he arrived at six this morning, Security stopped him from trying to access her residence. She wanted, and, indeed, needed his help with the new ballet she wanted to create, but wondered, given his behavior, whether it was wise to work so closely with him. Although it would be a headache to constantly be on his radar, she knew, in the long run, she could handle him.

Still, she had Will to think about and his clear mandate that their relationship have a direction and a purpose; not something they just fell into because of their close proximity to each other or because she was helping him with his nephew and niece. She had to give his proposition some serious thought. That was the advice her mother gave her when Linda called her to talk about what had transpired between her and Will after the Open House. Vivian assured her that she would be there should she need to talk more about her feelings.

"Tendu," Linda called out to the group as she watched Will in the mirror walk away from Jolie. She agreed to let Jolie and her television station record actual auditions. Stories about the school and studio ran on Sunday magazine television shows and news reports. Newspaper stories about the academy were on the front page of every Arts and Entertainment Section of major outlets. Although, in her opinion in each instance, the reporters focused too much attention on her and recounted her career achievements, it was, nevertheless, good press. Still, all of the stories received favorable responses and that was a very good thing, particularly for the Foundation. As a result, the show Face to Face, a Tina Justice production asked to feature her and her school as a highlighted segment of an upcoming show. Bill Chandler, her agent and theatrical attorney, tentatively agreed.

In addition to the inordinate amount of funds raised during the Open House, an impressive amount came in on Sunday through her website. Because of the amount of the donations received, she wouldn't have to turn away promising, indigent students. That factor put a smile on her face.

"Use the feet a bit more, by slowly sliding them along the floor until you are fully pointing your toe. Yes, that's it, but not so fast. Slowly. Repeat and give it a count of five for the full extension. Again," Linda demanded. "This is quite slow. While you're learning to pointe, the exercise is warming up your feet and legs, which is crucial if you're going to dance well and take care of your body at the same time. Remember your posture and your checklist. Think about where your weight is and maintain a nice straight back throughout your movement. Very good, very good. Now we will do these two moves to music." She nodded to the pianist and joined the exercise.

Chapter 18

Linda stood looking out of Dena's living room double French doors at the Charles River in Cambridge, Massachusetts. It was a beautiful sight. She and Dena had just returned from a one-block walk from the Massachusetts Institute of Technology's campus, where she was a student, to her three-bedroom condo on Memorial Drive. Because the restaurants were crowded, they picked up lunches to go and were settling in to spend quality time together.

"I saw the Face to Face piece on screen. How has the first month at the school gone?" Dena called out from her kitchen.

"I'm pleased with both. Frankly, I didn't expect it to go this smoothly, but so far, so good. However, I didn't come to see you to talk about me. What's up with you? Will tells me Drew comes up to visit you several times a month."

Dena came out of the kitchen carrying a tray with soups and salads they picked up from a local, whole-foods store. She carried it to a table near the balcony doors and distributed the napkins and spoons. "He tries to come as often as possible, but, between his job, classes, and helping to take care of Eugene and Violet, it's difficult. The last time he came, he brought the children with him. We did a lot of sightseeing."

"Yes, I know. They missed their dance classes to come with him."

"That's what he had to do since you were tied up and Will was at a convention in Denver, Colorado."

"You're still not telling me what's up between the two of you."

Dena shrugged. "He's different from the guys I usually date. He's real people; not nerdy or a Brainiac. We go out to places just to have fun."

"What about the Russian?"

"German, and his nose is out of joint. The first time he saw me with Drew, you would have thought I was his property. I've called it off with him. He shows too many traits of . . ."

"Your father," Linda finished for her. Reaching across the table, she held one of Dena's hands.

"He wasn't my father, remember? He was the man who married my mother and then killed her when she finally caught him in my room one night. Then he brutalized me."

Linda squeezed Dena's hand. "He's dead now, Dena."

"Yes, he is, but he molested me for three years before my mother caught him when she came home early one night from turning tricks."

"I'm listening if you want to talk it through again."

Dena shook her head as if to clear away the memory. "Drew asked me about my history before . . . before my life turned around and I told him. I didn't expect it, but he cried. I told him I didn't need or want his pity, but he said it had nothing to do with pity and everything to do with his memories of his own childhood. His older brother caught one of the priests touching him when he was six and beat him up. The priest was transferred out of the parish."

"Oh, I didn't know. Will never mentioned it."

"I don't expect he will talk about it. Drew said Will gets emotional when the subject comes up, so he may not share it with you."

"You and Drew seem to be getting pretty close."

"He shares things with me because he says he wants to get me into his bed," she said and laughed. "When I told him about my stepfather and what he did to me, he stopped joking about me and sex. Still, he calls almost nightly to talk about how our day went. Sometimes we talk for hours. He even asked me when were you going to put Will out of his misery?"

The soup spoon was halfway to Linda's lips when she looked up at her sister. "How would Drew know that I haven't already done the deed with Will?"

"Oh, please, Linda. You're as transparent as glass. If you had been intimate with Will, everyone would know it. You'd be glowing like a neon sign. Obviously, Drew would know if his brother was gettin' some," she said laughing.

Linda ruefully shook her head and continued eating her lunch. Ordinarily, she would tell Dena her secret, that she and Will were "getting' some" often and continuously, but not yet. She wasn't sure she was ready to come out to her family, other than to her mother, unless or until she decided where she wanted the relationship to go with Will. If this was just a short-term affair, she didn't want everyone speculating on where it would end up.

Dena peeked up at her sister. "Are you going to invite Will to come home with us for the family reunion?"

"I suppose the news that he's been invited to be in Uncle Gregory's wedding as a groomsman has made the rounds through the family?"

"Well," Dena hedged. "Grand Aunt Olivia did call me to get the 411 on the situation. Apparently, Nana Sylvia is being tight-lipped about it and so is Granddad Bernie."

"Yea, Nana! Yea, Granddad!" Linda said enthusiastically.

"They may not be nosey, but I am, so what's it going to be? Are you going to invite him to be your guest or is he going as Uncle Greg's guest and groomsman?"

Linda sighed. "I don't want to put any pressure on Will, Dena. You know if he comes home as my guest, then everyone will assume he's my man. They'll start talking wedding bells next year."

"So, what's wrong with that? Aren't you in love with him?"

"How would I know? What does being in love with him look like? I know I care deeply for him, enough to want to sleep with him. However, what if we sleep together and it doesn't work out? Maybe we won't be compatible between the sheets. I don't want to lose his friendship because we took the leap too soon or at all. It's only been about five months since we met. Actually, he turned down an opportunity to sleep with me a month ago after the Open House. What's that about?" What she didn't say was that she coerced him into making love after all.

"Respect," said Dena succinctly as she polished off her soup and started in on her salad. "He's met Dad, Mom, and the sibs. You know how intimidating that can be. He knows he'd better come correct if he wants to survive in this family. He's not about to hit it and quit it."

Linda nodded in agreement. "That's what he said. I thought maybe he was involved with someone else."

"You mean Jolie Jance, don't you?"

"I do, yes."

"Scratch that. According to Drew, Will shut that down earlier this year. She wanted him to put Eugene and Violet in some exclusive boarding school in Switzerland she attended. He refused even to consider it and called it off with her. Since then, she's been trying to get back into Will's good graces, particularly back into his bed. Apparently, he's a powerhouse between the sheets," Dena said laughing.

Amused, Linda just shook her head. She could attest to the fact that Jolie wasn't wrong about Will's prowess between the sheets. "So, what are you going to do about Drew? Are you going to invite him as your guest to the family reunion?"

"Oh, yeah, indeed I am."

Surprised, Linda looked up into Dena's eyes. "You really do like him a lot."

Dena shrugged. "It's the wisdom of the ancestors: nothing beats a try but a failure. I'm willing to try having a friendship with Drew to see where it goes. Surprisingly, we're rather simpatico. We were both molested as children and we can talk about it with each other in ways I haven't been able to express to any other guy friend I've had. The way I see it, you're afraid to even try with Will because of Jolie Jance. What's *that* about?"

"I'm not particularly concerned about Jolie Jance and Will. I've shared my history with him. At least the part I know about. This is such a huge step for me. I don't want to get it wrong."

"Other than helping him with Eugene and Violet, have you let him into your world?"

Linda laughed. "My *world* is an open book. I'm covered 24/7 by security and paparazzi. In spite of that, I was even willing to share my body with him."

"If you were willing to do that, then there's no reason not to take him home as your guest. Yes, it's a statement to the rest of the family, but he's going to be there any way for Uncle Greg. Besides, when you start rehearsals for your winter performance in The Nutcracker, you close everyone and everything out. This might be your last opportunity to get to know him better in a different environment before you go into the deep freeze."

"A different environment? Ha! That's putting it mildly, kid. He saw pictures of the previous reunions, but as you well know, it has to be experienced. He was overwhelmed with the number of people in our immediate family while visiting for the birthday weekend and when we drove to Pennsylvania for Easter. Everyone wasn't even there at either event. Imagine what he'll feel at the reunion."

"Flabbergasted," Dena said laughing. "I've warned Drew to be prepared for ten days of insanity. Brotherman says he's up for the challenge. I'm willing to see if he's right. Are you willing to see whether Will can handle the tough stuff?"

There was a question, thought Linda.

Chapter 19

Surprisingly, Will didn't feel half as nervous as he thought he should be as he approached the study in the Montgomery-Alexander home in Goodwill, Summer County, South Carolina. He asked for this meeting and Chuck and Vivian agreed to the time. Even though he got lost twice in this home, one of Linda's siblings, a six-year-old, finally showed him the way. The door was open when he approached, but since Vivian was sitting on Chuck's lap kissing her husband, he thought it only polite to knock.

They didn't jump apart, but Chuck broke the kiss long enough to say, "Come in," to him before stealing another quick kiss from Vivian. Will noticed they kissed each other quite a lot and it didn't really matter where or when it occurred. They were rather spontaneous that way. Linda told him her parents still had date nights several times a week where they went out to dinner and may not come home until the next day.

The look in their eyes as they gazed at each other always seemed to promise more intimacy at an opportune time and place. Will didn't doubt it since Vivian seemed to be carrying a child for every year she and Chuck were married. He wanted that type of closeness with Linda and it all depended on whether her parents agreed.

"I know you just got here early this morning, Will, but how are you and your family enjoying the reunion so far?" asked Chuck as he stood to shake Will's hand.

"I've never experienced anything like it and neither has my brother. When we arrived, I never expected to see so many people already here setting up for the arrival of more of your family members. It's hard to imagine this number of people all related to each other coming together for ten days. The tent for the meals and entertainment is the size of a football field and, apparently, you're going to need it. Food stations are being set up all around it. Linda introduced me to so many people while we were helping cover the tables with cloths and set up the chairs, I lost count, but I want to get to know each and every one of them. That's why I asked to speak with you privately before the day got away from us. I want to ask your permission to propose marriage to Linda." He stopped to take a deep breath before he continued. "I know you may have reservations because Linda and I haven't known each other that long and she's on the sunny side of twenty-five while I'm over thirty, but she is the most special woman I have ever met. I'm hopelessly in love with her."

Vivian looked up at her husband smiling and then held out her hand. Chuck pulled a dollar bill from his pocket and placed it on Vivian's palm. "Yes," Vivian said, "you have our permission because you've said the magic words, Will. We believe Linda is in love with you, too. I knew it when she brought you to our home in Maryland. My husband knew it, too, but hoped it would take longer before he had to give his daughter over to another man's care," she said smiling, "but we couldn't be more pleased to welcome you into the family." She approached and hugged him.

Chuck reached out and hugged him, too. Will released a breath he didn't know he was holding.

"When do you plan to pop the question?" asked Chuck.

"Soon," Will said and reached into his pocket to extract a small royal blue box. He flipped it open and Vivian caught her breath.

"It's beautiful, Will, and exactly the right one for our Linda," Vivian said holding the box in her hand for Chuck to see. "If you want to do this soon and you're not shy about public displays of intimacy, may I suggest you do it tonight at the meet and greet? Everyone should be here by then and, as Linda's guest, she will be the one to invite you on stage and introduce you to the family."

"Wouldn't it embarrass her if she rejects my proposal?"

Chuck shook his head. "I know my daughter, Will. She won't reject you. If she weren't seriously in love with you, she would not have invited you to come to the family reunion."

"Actually, it was Gregory who originally asked me to be one of his groomsmen."

Vivian nodded. "My brother wouldn't have done that without first discussing it with me, Chuck, and our immediate family. We all agreed to your selection before Gregory asked you to participate in his and Angelique's wedding. The decision was made after you met some of our family members at the birthday weekend, particularly my parents, Chuck's father and Derrick's mother, and my older brother, Kenneth. We all recognized that Linda has never brought any male friend who was special to her home to any event."

"For reasons we need not discuss now, you've been vetted," Chuck confirmed.

Will nodded. "I understand. Linda told me some of it. About the threat to Angelique, the assistance you lent to shield the twenty young African girls from terrorists, the danger to your friends from your days in undergrad who are now very prominent individuals, and your concerns for your children's safety from those who might want to abduct any of them."

Chuck nodded. "There's more, but Linda's told you some of the important parts."

"It has something to do with the gold chains all of you wear, doesn't it?" Will asked. "It's not just a piece of pretty jewelry, is it?"

"You're right and, as Linda's husband, you and your family will be asked to wear a family chain, too," said Vivian. "You see, if you ever fear being harmed or abducted, you only need to break the chain. It will automatically send a distress signal to the closest cell tower anywhere in the world about your location. My brother, Kenneth's company, CompuCorrect, will receive that signal and trace your last known location within seconds and signal the appropriate authorities. A geostationary satellite will have the person on camera in less than one minute and be capable of following the signal wherever it goes. Our family is extremely large," she continued, "and we can't keep every one of them under constant guard. However, for the younger ones, like Linda, who is a world renowned celebrity, we take extra precautions. You and your family will need to be protected, too."

What neither Vivian nor Chuck said to Will was it would likely be members of the super-secret organization created by the G7 and known only to a few as The Nursery who would likely be the ones responding to any threat to a family member. They also didn't mention the home base of the covert security organization was headed by a member of the family, Code Name: Delta Dawn, and was located in the most inconspicuous location of Summer County, South Carolina. Richardson Investigations and Security, based in Portland, Oregon, was one of the public faces the organization used to provide protection, but Slade Richardson, Code Name: Cobra Kahn, was a member of the Nursery's elite force and was still now, as an outlier, performing as an agent when called upon to do so. It was his operatives and agents who provided security for Linda and others in her generation.

"Thank you, both," said Will. "I will feel better knowing my family will be included in the ring of protection. Also, I appreciate you for accepting me into your family and your confidence."

"Where did Uncle Will go?" asked Violet as she sat at a table by the swimming pool in Bernard and Sylvia Benson Alexander's rear yard.

Sylvia hugged the sweet girl to her side. "I think he went to the house for a moment. He should be back soon. Are you having fun?"

"There are so many people to meet," Violet enthused, her pretty smile a mile wide. "They just seem to be more and more coming all the time."

"You're right. Every time I look up there are more and more mobile homes pulling up the lane and parking around the farm," said Sylvia.

"My Uncle Drew and Dena went to help hook up the campers and mobile homes to the water, sewer, and electric," offered Eugene. "Some of the campers look like real homes inside with televisions and everything."

"I like the ones where you can sleep up top," piped up Violet. "They are soooo cool."

"They are, yes," said Sylvia laughing.

"I like the ones that are flat like a pancake and then you push a button and the top pops up so high you can walk inside. It even has walls to close up if it rains and sofa beds, too."

"Also screens to keep the bugs out," added Sylvia. She was so taken by these precious children who she hoped would be raised by her granddaughter, Linda, and the man who Sylvia believed loved her, Will Hamilton. She looked at her husband, Bernard, the love of her life, as he played in the pool with some of their grandchildren.

He gave her five wonderful children and made her life something dreams were made of. She smiled when Whitney Ivy, their first biological grandchild, poured water over Bernard's head and then Linda, the granddaughter of their hearts, did the same thing. She believed the men her grandgirls chose would be very good husbands and wonderful additions to the family.

"Look, Nana Sylvia," Violet piped up, laughing. "Poppy Bernie caught Linda and Whitney Ivy! Angelique is trying to get away, too!"

Just then it looked like all of her grandchildren decided to join in the pool free-for-all. Eugene and Violet deserted her and dove into the pool, too. She marveled at the family she and her Bernard managed to make in their nearly fifty years of marriage. Kenneth and JeNelle had nine children, Benny and Stacy with seven, and Chuck and Vivian had twenty-seven. She wasn't sure any of them were finished adding to the Alexander clan. Soon, she knew her son, Gregory and Angelique would add to the family. Then, she scanned the yard for her youngest daughter, Aretha Grace, her wanderlust child and her male friend, Stacy's brother, Russell Greene. She sighed wondering what it would take to get her last child happily married to the man she loved. Russell and Aretha loved each other fiercely but were so busy with their lives they didn't take time to make plans to be together.

"Oh," Sylvia yelped when Linda and Angelique sat down at the table on each side of her shaking their heads while drops of water poured out of their hair, wetting her skin. "You two are no better behaved than you were as preteens," she protested without heat.

They squeezed her between them, further drenching her with water from their wet hair and skin. It didn't really matter as she squeezed them in return. She wanted a happy life for all of her progeny, the nostalgia of yesteryear bringing a smile to her lips. Whitney Ivy joined her at the umbrella-covered table, too, with large plastic containers of home-made sun tea over ice.

That night at the first event of the family reunion, the Meet and Greet, Linda was next in line to take the stage and introduce her guests to her family. Her grandaunt, Olivia Alexander Dixon, the twin sister of her grandfather, Bernard Alexander, performed the duties of the Mistress of Ceremonies. She was well accustomed to taking charge of that evenings' event since for the past thirty-plus years she was also the Mayor of the Town of Goodwill.

"All right everyone, simmer down," Olivia instructed. "Next, we have our Linda, Chuck and Vivian's daughter, and her guests from the Big Apple, New York City."

Linda climbed the stairs to the sound of whistles, catcalls, and loud applause. She grinned at her audience and on pointe, danced to the podium amid raucous calls for more. "Stop it," she called out joyously when the applause didn't die down but instead elevated another level. "I'mma tell my mama on you, if you don't stop that," she joked. Finally, the crowd simmered down enough for her to speak. "First, originally from Portland, Oregon, now making their home in New York City, are brother and sister, Eugene and Violet Hamilton." Again, applause and whistles rose as the children walked across the stage hand-in-hand, their faces wreathed in smiles, and waving with their free hands until they stood next to Linda. She gave them each a shopping bag that contained the families' survival kit: T-shirts with their names on the front and the family reunion tree and years in operation on the back, a matching ball cap, other goodies, the program for the events, and the gold chain which Linda placed around their necks.

"Next, we welcome, the one, the only Will 'The Hammer' Hamilton," her voice lifting over the roar of the crowd and more than a few bawdy calls and remarks from the female members of the audience. "Will is a native New Yorker and the owner and operator of Indulgences, and yes, ladies, he is a bachelor," she teased as he strode across the stage toward her waving. "In this year's family survival kit, you will find coupons to visit Indulgences at a *steep* discount," she teased. "Ladies and gentlemen, Will Hamilton." However, when he reached her, he took the microphone from her, and said "I hope to be a bachelor only for a short time more." He then went down on bended knee in front of Linda and spoke into the microphone in one hand and flipped open the ring box with the other.

The audience hushed to the point of absolute silence. Linda's eyes widened in shock, her hands palming her mouth.

"Linda Lewis Jackson Montgomery, I'm in love with you. You're it for me; the one woman I want for the rest of my life. Would you do me the honor of becoming my wife?"

"*Girrrrrlllll*, if you don't say yes, I will!" called out someone from the audience.

"Get in line!" someone else hollered.

"Oh, no, sister woman!" Linda shouted back smiling into Will's eyes, "I'm taking him up on his proposal quick, fast and in a hurry, before he has time to get a look at all the beautiful, available women in this family!" Sticking out her left hand, Will fit the ring on the third finger. It fit perfectly and, as he stood up grinning at her, she launched herself into his arms for a long, salacious kiss, amid clamorous cheers, whistles, and applause.

Next up was Dena who introduced Drew and received a number of shouted comments about how good-looking and virile he is. Jokingly, she warned he was off the market for the foreseeable future. He nodded his agreement but took the opportunity to kiss her mouth in front of her family.

At the conclusion of all of the introductions, people crowded around Will and Linda to see the ring, but the couple just gazed at each other smiling.

"Were you surprised?" asked Will.

"Stunned is more like it. Are you sure, Will? I mean, I really, really don't want you to change your mind, but are you really sure?"

"I am so sure that I've already asked your parents for your hand in marriage and I want a short engagement. Say, maybe only a few days at most. I'd like to marry you here, before the end of this family reunion. Is this too soon for you?"

She shook her head smiling. "It's not too soon for me."

Will released a breath, taking her into his arms again.

"Okay, so now I have two of my girls to give away?" Chuck moaned without heat.

"I'm afraid so, Dad," Linda said still smiling at Will. "What do you think, Mom, Nana Sylvia? May I wear your wedding gown to marry Will?"

Vivian nodded as did her mother, their smiles full of emotion as Vivian and Sylvia formed a ring hugging their eldest daughter. "It's an honor and a pleasure to see you start the next phase of your life in a dress that brought your father and me together as husband and wife. Your grandmother wore it before me, and her mother before her. It brought your Nana Sylvia and me so much happiness that it can't fail to do the same for you." The tears that fell from the eyes of three generations of women were tears of joy.

Chapter 20

The sun was pretty hot on the man's back as he walked slowly through the acres of the Summer County Fair Grounds. He wasn't accustomed to this strong, summer sun and would definitely have a tan or a sunburn before the day was over if he wasn't careful. He was there since eight o'clock that morning, waiting in line until the grounds opened and talking with an older man and his wife. The elderly gentleman was former military and he and his wife of sixty years would be admitted to the fair grounds free of charge. They admitted to being excited about the scheduled Sock Hop, putt-putt golf, and pig races. They had their great-grandchildren with them who, because they were under ten years old, would also get in free. The children were more interested in the carnival attractions, Ferris wheel, merry-go-round, and wackee paddleboat rides on the Santee River adjacent to the fair grounds.

There was a breeze blowing, too, but, in this moist heat, it carried the scent of farm animals, pink spun candy, blooming onions, and barbeque. He wore a hat, sun shades, a white T-shirt, shorts, and leather sandals, but still, he wasn't feeling the best in the heat. With bottled water in hand, he was slowly making his way to the rodeo ring where Dena was scheduled to ride Starfire, her beautiful, midnight-black stallion, in the first race and Quick Silver, her quarter horse, in the barrel races. At a distance, he watched Dena weigh-in, holding her gear with other jockeys. Others of the Montgomery children were out early putting their horses through their paces to compete in other races while their parents and grandparents looked on from the shaded grandstands.

Now, the man noted, Chuck and Vivian and their oldest son, Brian were at the horse auction buying livestock no doubt for their ranch here and the ones in Maryland and Pennsylvania. Brian, after college and grad school at Penn State came home to manage all three family farms. By all accounts Brian was doing an admirable job of it.

The man had to do a double take when he spotted Chuck's father, Stephen, with his arm around Harriet Jackson's shoulder and kissing her by a fence. *Well*, he wondered, *when had that happened?* There were more Montgomerys and Jacksons near them but they didn't seem at all surprised by the intimacy between Stephen and Harriet. He moved cautiously, avoiding accidentally coming in contact with anyone who might recognize him.

There were so many people out at the fair moving from one exhibit to the next he didn't fear being discovered, and there was so much to see and do that it boggled the mind. In one section with the antique cars, it looked like a city of ten-by-ten tents in a grassy parking area. Gregory Alexander was there with his own much larger tent sheltering five fully restored vintage cars that were drawing quite a bit of interest, much to several of his nephews' and nieces' dismay. Though some weren't old enough to drive yet, they apparently had visions of owning one of their uncle's reconditioned, vintage cars. Gregory gave two cars away to two nephews, twins, Justin and Jarrett Alexander, on their sixteenth birthdays. He'd bet real American money Gregory would continually see to it his siblings' offspring would have a vintage car on his or her sixteenth birthday. That's the kind of loving uncle Gregory Alexander seemed to be. On Linda's sixteenth birthday, she received a 1965 Pontiac GTO convertible in pumpkin orange with a white ragtop. Though it was stored in her uncle's garage, Linda was so often away, she rarely had opportunities to drive it. When they had time, he wanted to ride somewhere with her in that car.

Moving on, the man laughed during the greased-pig competition where Linda's brothers, Darren, Derrick, Jr., and Spencer repeatedly fell in the muck and mire while the pigs squirted out of their grasp. The water from several hoses raining down from overhead added further chaos to the misery of the grimy chase. The mud was so deep and thick some chose to go barefoot for fear of losing a shoe. It was their cousin, Cecelia Dixon, a girl of Violet's age, who actually caught and held onto a fat, little pig to win the competition. She would get to keep the pig as her prize. Though she was covered from head to toe in mud, her parents, James and Janice Dixon, both Ph.D.s in science, and Linda's cousins, hugged her, praising her victory with the pig still squealing and squirming in her arms between them. Cecelia's brothers, James Junior, Alton, and the baby boy Kent danced around her proclaiming their only sister's victory.

By noon the man had witnessed the chili cook-off, seen the fine arts exhibits and handcrafts, watched the children at the petting zoo, taken a hayride around the grounds just to get off his feet, and noticed the men and women working to open the carnival for later that afternoon and night. The home-and-garden show in a big blue tent showcased many new and interesting gizmos and gadgets. He didn't think he'd know what to do with most of what was on display, yet many others were buying at an impressive rate.

At the beer garden, he sampled several different beers, but none were as hale and hardy as the dark lagers he shared with his Da and Mum in an old pub in his hometown in the Province of Munster in County Cork, Ireland. *They hadn't visited there in quite a while,* thought the man, as he tasted another beer. *He considered he should do that, go back to his home in Ireland when his business with Linda was done and he could take her with him. It wasn't too much to ask she share his home with him.*

The man moved on to the pie eating contest and then to the baked goods match which included casseroles as well as delicious looking desserts. The Jackson side of Linda's family arrived just a little ahead of him yesterday. They and Chuck Montgomery's sisters and sisters-in-law were really good cooks. He tasted their food last year at the country fair in Monroe County, Pennsylvania. He was tempted to buy one of the strawberry shortcakes that one of Linda's other aunt's, Sheila Jackson Montgomery, baked. However, it would mean trekking all the way back to the parking lot to store it in his rental car. He didn't think that was a good idea in this heat with the sun just past the noon hour.

While he was there in the tent, near where the Jacksons were making a name for themselves with their home-made jellies and jams in pretty glass jars and pots, he got out of the heat. There were big ceiling fans which created somewhat of a breeze. He continued strolling through the 4-H whole food tents full of fresh fruits and vegetables. It was a souped-up farmers' market more beautifully displayed than he found in Londonderry, Ireland.

The Alexanders and Dixons were the owners and operators of Alexander-Dixon Industries (ADI), hydroponics farms where they grew fresh fruits, vegetables, and flowers in water troughs and in glass-enclosed buildings. They also had a fishery which, in addition to trout and other specialty species of fish, included shrimp, lobster, and other shellfish. They held tours on weekdays through their facilities where the produce was grown, harvested, and shipped the same day to boutique stores and restaurants both near and far. Angelique received daily shipments of the ADI produce to serve fresh in her restaurant the same day it was received. He had actually taken the tour and been impressed with their operation. Of course, when he could manage to get a reservation, he'd eaten in Angelique's restaurant.

Alexander-Dixon Industries wasn't stingy with sharing its success. They took on students through their Summer County Academy who wanted to learn and implement the business of growing crops in water instead of soil. The father and son team of Romelo and James Dixon, Linda's uncle and cousin, ran the family business and funded the Summer County Foundation with the excess profits. The Foundation primarily supported higher education grants for graduates of the Summer County Academy. The man studied the annual report of ADI and was a regular anonymous donor to the Foundation. He liked what they did and how they operated.

As he moved further through the large tent full of fresh produce, there were herbs galore at Madeline Montgomery's stand; some he never heard of. He wondered whether his mum would like some of the American ingredients to add to her kitchen garden. He purchased an assortment of twenty from Madeline, Chuck's older sister, not really knowing anything about food preparation, but the pretty young girl, one of Madeline and Chuck's nieces, Esther Lynn, assured him these were the basic components for any meal. She had an incredible welcoming smile, much like her grandmother, Esther, used to have before her death. He accepted a business card from Esther Lynn though he didn't need it. He knew every one of the Jackson family members and Chuck Montgomery's side of the family, too.

The herbs smelled good in there and the air was much cooler. He felt a little better as a result, so he continued to go from one stall to the next. His shopping bag of goodies was filling up fast. He needed to rest and would soon have to make his way to his car in the building heat. Global Warming was a real thing, to his way of thinking. He planned to go to his car and turn on the air conditioner right after he watched Dena in the horse races.

He thought ahead and, always two years in advance, snagged a room at The Summer House, a huge bed and breakfast in a three-story, beautifully-restored, antebellum mansion. It was owned and operated efficiently by one of Vivian's cousins from her mother's side of the family, Satarah Josephine Johnson, who everyone called SaraJo. He had breakfast that morning at six and SaraJo herself welcomed him back to Summer County. She even remembered him by name since he began staying at her B&B just after she opened it for business five years ago and every year since.

SaraJo gave up her career as the head emergency room nurse at Summer County Hospital and married the County Fire Chief, Douglas Johnson, a transplant from Richmond, Virginia. They had four boys between them from previous marriages, and two young daughters under the age of five. If the baby bump he was too embarrassed to ask her about was any indication, Doug and SaraJo Johnson were expecting again.

SaraJo had no inhibitions about gleefully announcing she and her husband were expecting the birth of their son in another few months. She was insisting they name their new son Douglas Edward Johnson, Jr. Her husband thought they could do better than that, so they were still in negotiations. She told him smugly Doug was a pushover; putty in her hands. So, she was confident she would win the baby-naming challenge.

He added that tidbit of information to his files before he left for the fair grounds, with a "have a good day," call out from SaraJo. He had seen how big, strong Douglas Johnson looked at SaraJo, so he was betting she'd have her way and the new addition to the Johnson household of eight would be named Douglas Edward two point O. She was returning to her kitchen to create more fabulous meals for her other guests, most of whom were her relations in town for the family reunion.

When he turned from his musings and mindless strolling, he was face to face and nearly chest to chest with Will Hamilton. Linda was at his side, as were his brother, Drew and Dena Montgomery. Tucker Cavanaugh and his fiancée, Whitney Ivy Alexander, and Gregory Alexander, and his fiancée, Angelique were right there, too. He had been careless and let down his guard when he should have been vigilant.

Immediately he turned his head, offered a quick apology, and tried awkwardly to move away as swiftly and unobtrusively as possible from the knot of people jamming the aisles. Fortunately, he still had on his ball cap and his sun shades, so he thought he had gotten away cleanly. Then he heard Will's voice say something to Linda.

The guy who nearly bumped into his chest looked very familiar to Will and a bit out of place at a county fair in South Carolina despite his shopping bag and loose-fitting, stylishly fashionable, but clearly expensive clothes. This was not one of Linda's security team members he knew. She taught him to spot her protectors in a crowd. This man's exposed skin tone, face, arms, and legs were almost a clear shade of alabaster despite the heat as if he didn't get much sun. He must not have worn sunscreen because he was working on what was looking like a sunburn on his exposed shoulders. He was a tall, well-built man, not quite six-four, but appeared to be attempting to make himself seem smaller; not quite as noticeable.

Will's eyes drew together in concentration trying to remember where he had seen the man before because he was sure he knew the part of that face he could see from somewhere. He stopped walking and turned around to watch the man's rapid departure from the tent.

"What is it, Will?" Linda asked, when Will stopped and turned around bobbing and weaving to watch someone.

"I don't know. Wait here with your uncle. Don't leave his side. I'll be right back," he said and then shouldered his way through the thick crowd. As he moved as swiftly as possible, he remembered Tucker's cautionary words about keeping a vigil where Linda's safety was concerned and increased his pace. There was something at the back of his mind but he wasn't sure what it was. However, given the haste the man was making to leave the area, it wasn't normal.

"Excuse me, sir," Will called out when he was nearly on the man's heels. When the man didn't stop, Will reached out and put a hand on the man's arm to stop him. "Excuse me," Will said again, this time louder.

"Yes?" the man said but didn't fully turn around to face him.

Curious and more curious, thought Will, so he walked around to squarely face the man. "I think I've seen you before. Have we ever met?"

"No," the man said and tried to sidestep Will, but he wasn't quick enough.

By then, Linda and the rest of the group had caught up with Will and the man.

"Will," Linda called out. "It's okay. Let him be. He's not a threat to me."

Will looked up sharply at Linda perplexed. "I've seen this man somewhere before."

"At Indulgences," she supplied. "He's a member there. It's okay, sir," Linda said addressing the man directly while moving to Will's side. "Don't let us detain you. Enjoy the fair."

"You know him?" Will asked incredulously. "He shows up in South Carolina of all places and you're not concerned for your safety?"

"No, I'm not. He's an avid fan whose name is Brad, Bradley Connor Smyth, II. He's a computer whiz kid who has homes in County Cork, Ireland, and Manchester, England. Recently, he followed me from Paris and bought a condo on the same side of the street where I live, diagonally across from where Indulgences is located in New York and set up shop. My security team is aware of him. He sometimes follows me to countries where I perform."

At that, the man looked up to see her smiling at him, took off his shades looking into Linda's eyes. He was astonished she was aware of him and even knew his name, and apparently, had for quite some time. His heart raced and pounded in his chest, his ability to breathe impaired. He started to speak when spots seemed to come from nowhere and blur his vision. He felt himself begin to crumble and heard Linda's concerned shouts just before everything went black.

Chapter 21

"Here, bring him in here," Chuck demanded, opening the door to his in-home medical office and infirmary while Will, Drew, Tucker, and Gregory carried the young man in.

"This isn't necessary, sir. I'll be all right. I just need to rest a bit . . ."

"No, you're beyond just needing to rest, son. You're in crisis and you're seriously ill, aren't you?" Chuck asked while he and his mother-in-law started checking his vital signs. He used a penlight to check the young man's pupils, then stood up and crossed his arms over his broad, muscular chest. "I know it's warm outside, but when you collapsed, it wasn't from heat exhaustion. Your lips, gums, and nail beds are pale as your skin. You're experiencing weakness in your limbs and joints. I'll bet you're sleepy and tired all the time. Right now you're spiking a temperature above 101°F, an increased heart rate, shortness of breath, and, from the pain I see in your eyes, one helluva headache. You have aplastic anemia, don't you, son?"

Brad's moss-green eyes widened in surprise. He looked around the room at the concerned faces of Linda, Will, Drew, Dena, Gregory, Brian, Vivian, and Linda's grandmother, Sylvia Alexander. Mrs. Alexander, a registered nurse, was hooking him up to monitoring equipment and making him comfortable, his toned upper body slightly elevated by the hospital bed. He closed his eyes briefly and nodded his head against the cool, fresh sheets in resignation. "Yes, sir. I was diagnosed when I was in my early teens."

"What treatment have you undergone?" asked Chuck.

"Immunosuppressive drugs, either anti-lymphocyte globulin or anti-thymocyte globulin combined with corticosteroids and cyclosporine."

"You're under thirty years old, maybe as young as twenty-six. How about hematopoietic stem cell transplantation?"

Bradley shook his head. "No, sir."

"Why did you ask that, Dad?" asked Linda.

"Stem cell transplants are used to replace bone marrow that isn't working or has been destroyed by disease, chemo, or radiation. In some diseases, like aplastic anemia, and certain inherited blood diseases, or diseases of the immune system, the stem cells in the bone marrow of the patient don't work the way they should."

"Honey, I've never heard of this," commented Vivian, concern obvious in her voice.

"Aplastic anemia is a rare disease and, as I said, bone marrow and the hematopoietic stem cells that reside there, are damaged. This causes a deficiency of all three blood cell types: red, white, and platelets. Aplastic refers to the inability of the stem cells to generate mature blood cells. It's most prevalent in people in their teens and twenties. That's what's happened here to Bradley. It can be caused by heredity or immune disease, exposure to chemicals, drugs, or radiation. Normal bone marrow has thirty-to-seventy percent blood stem cells, but in aplastic anemia, these cells are mostly gone and replaced by fat."

"Chuck, this sounds life-threatening. What can be done to help him?" asked Gregory.

"This is not my area of expertise, but at a minimum, I believe he needs an immediate stem cell transplant," he said in answer to Gregory's question, then he asked Brad, "Why haven't you had the transplant?" and then he knew. "Your blood type is rare, isn't it?"

Brad nodded, still somewhat awed by Dr. Montgomery's speedy diagnosis. "Rh-null," he answered.

"Damn it!" Chuck cursed vehemently.

"What does that mean, Dad?" asked Linda, concerned at her father's distress. She knew her father rarely cursed.

"Bradley's blood lacks any antigens in the Rh system. As I recall from med school, there are less than ten active donors in the world who have Rh-null blood. More have the antigens but are not donors." He looked up into his daughter's eyes. "Your blood happens to have those traits, too, babe."

Shocked, Linda shook her head in confusion and disbelief. "How can that be?" she asked quietly then looked at Brad for an answer.

He closed his eyes. He didn't want to tell her like this or at all, but everyone was standing there around the hospital bed waiting. Then he felt Sylvia Alexander's hand placing a cool compress against his achingly feverish forehead and her other hand in his like a lifeline. He held on and took a deep breath. "My biological father has the antigens. You have it, too, because you're my biological sister. We share the same father."

Stunned even more, Linda's brows bunched as she searched Brad's face, noting the pretty, dark-green eyes, long dark lashes, dark blond, thick, wavy hair, and porcelain skin tone. He was, indeed, a very handsome man under the sickly pallor of his illness, but, to her mind, except for the dark-green eyes, which seemed to match hers, they looked nothing alike.

"How did you come to this conclusion?" asked Vivian, protectively putting an arm around Linda's shoulders for support, while Will reached for and held Linda's hand.

Brad raised his eyes to her. "My parents never hid from me the fact I was adopted. In fact, they love me so much they offered to do whatever I wanted them to do to help find my biological parents. I was adopted as a baby, literally days old. My parents are wonderful people who were past their childbearing years when I came to them. They had given up on having children of their own. When they took me in, they didn't know anything about my biological parents because I was left at the doorstep of a fire station at two o'clock in the morning about two hundred miles outside London, England, in Manchester. My Da used to volunteer at the fire station. I wasn't discovered until about five in the morning when a fire alarm startled me awake and I began to cry. My Da found me and took me home with him to his wife who became my Mum.

"Years later, when I became aware of the circumstances of where I was found, I didn't really want to know who my biological parents were, so I never asked. I had a wonderful childhood with people who love each other and me and took good care of me. I had all of the advantages I could ever want, but I was never very healthy, so my parents home-schooled me.

"When I was diagnosed, I started searching for a familial match on various medical websites but got nowhere. Then, several years ago while still in my mid-teens, I started searching websites with DNA profiles for a match. That's when I found an old file for a little girl in America, but the file was confidential, and I couldn't find a legal way to open it.

"My adoptive Da is a scientist and taught me to use a computer before I could talk or walk," he said, smiling at the memory. "In my adolescence, I was very good at reading and writing computer codes and could hack computer programs and systems.

"While I was at college at Cambridge, big business and government entities hired me to legally hack their systems to determine where they are vulnerable and find ways to close gaps in their firewalls. Sometimes I'm hired to trace other hackers and report them to various law enforcement officials, like your American FBI or CIA, the British MI5, and the Israeli Knesset. I've even worked for your NSA and Homeland Security. I have an ongoing contract with Interpol and other entities I am prohibited by contract from mentioning. So, I have nearly unlimited access to databases and put my skill to work to answer questions about my ancestry and who the little girl is I'm related to. It took time, patience, and a lot of effort, but I finally pieced together who I am." He stopped talking for a moment looking into Linda's eyes. "Also, who I'm related to.

"An Englishman, a respected, but lower level member of the British Royal Family, a scoundrel in his thirties, had sex with a young girl, a very rich British diplomat's daughter in Iraq, who was barely fourteen at the time," Bradley continued. "The young girl never told her parents or the authorities who the man is who impregnated her because the silly twit thought the man was in love with her and herself to be in love with him. However, being a good Catholic girl, her parents convinced her to give up her baby for adoption. She agreed, but when the baby was born at their home in a very posh section of London, her parents took it and drove over four hours to a fire station outside London and left it there on the doorstep. They told their daughter they'd found a nice, young couple to adopt her baby and he would be well taken care of. It was all a lie. Clearly, they didn't want to do an adoption the legal way because they wanted no paper trail connecting their under-aged daughter's scandalous behavior to their family's good and respected name or their position in the Catholic Church. They could have done worse and buried the infant somewhere no one would have ever found it. However, their hypocrisy only went so far.

"I am the baby my good Catholic mother and grandparents gave away twenty-plus years ago. When I went to see them, they thought I was trying to blackmail them and wanted their money. I didn't tell them that I have more money than I could ever spend in five lifetimes nor did I explain my condition to them. I already knew my egg donor's blood type, but I needed to confirm who I believed my biological father to be. When I had the information I needed, a sample for DNA testing, I made them sign a non-disclosure agreement. Then I thanked them for throwing me away, laughed in their still stunned faces that I had found them after all these years, and left.

"I repeated the process by going to see my sperm donor, but I will not go into the reception I received from him. Suffice-it-to-say, it wasn't an amicable meeting. Still, his somewhat brute of a wife demanded he own up to his paternity, sign the agreement, which he did obediently and gave me a sample of his blood and saliva for DNA testing. Once I was able to fill in the blanks of my ancestry, I was done with them.

"John Lewis was not your biological father, Linda. Yes, he was married to your biological mother at the time you were born and, yes, he fathered your deceased younger brother. However, while she was in Iraq working as an interpreter and married to John Lewis, your mother had a long-term, intimate affair with the same Englishman who sired me. I was born almost exactly a year before you were. Our DNA matched nearly one hundred percent except your mother was an extremely beautiful American of African descent, while mine is Caucasian of Scandinavian descent.

"Fortunately, to the best of my knowledge, the Englishman has no other children, legitimate or otherwise. Apparently, after learning from your mother and/or mine, he fathered a child, he had a vasectomy. He didn't want children and married an heiress who is seven years his senior and didn't want children either." He stopped talking as if that was the end of the story or he was awaiting a reaction.

"There's more, isn't there?" asked Vivian, perceptively. "We have no secrets in this family, Bradley."

Bradley studied her for ponderous moments before nodding and then looking at Linda again. "Your mother is correct, Linda. Although John Lewis was presumed killed in Iraq, he survived and had severe facial and other injuries. Because he was at the British Embassy on business the day of the terrorist bombing attack, he was mistaken for the British attaché he was meeting with. The real attaché stepped out of his office to use the restroom but didn't survive the attack. When the first responders found John Lewis unconscious and in a coma in the attaché's office under the rubble, they assumed he was the British attaché.

"After several surgeries, including plastic surgery on his face, he was in a hospital until after your mother and little brother were killed in the auto accident you survived. Using a photograph of the real attaché, the surgeons remade his face to closely resemble the British attaché's as possible. They had fairly similar facial bone structure. John Lewis signed into the Embassy and, because the man found in the hall was crushed under fallen debris, the authorities reported that John Lewis was dead. I never got the straight of it, but, somehow, the real John Lewis learned of his wife's infidelity and with whom she was having an affair behind his back. Really, it probably wasn't too hard to obtain that kind of intelligence. Caucasian foreigners in Iraq are a small group and information about them and their activities can be bought from household servants for little or nothing.

"Apparently, since his unfaithful wife and his son were dead, you weren't his biological daughter, and he was presumed dead, he moved to England, stepped into the dead British attaché's shoes, so-to-speak, and began another life. He purposefully sought out and married the young daughter of a very wealthy banker who used to be a diplomat in Iraq. As the son-in-law of the banker, he has become a very wealthy man. Through my research, I pieced together most of the facts and only needed to have them confirmed. They spilled the beans, so to speak, for fear I would publish their indiscretions and taint their worlds. They couldn't fathom I didn't want my name, my Da's name, associated with them."

Linda closed her eyes and shook her head. *"Wait!* You're telling me the man I thought was my biological father, John Lewis, is still alive and living under an alias in London, and was, in actuality, my stepfather? He is my biological mother's husband, and he married your biological mother?"

"I am, yes, that's the way of it," he said, his British accent pronounced, "but the injuries John Lewis sustained caused him to be sterile so he and his wife, my biological mother, have no child between them and I have no siblings to be concerned about from them. Still, John Lewis got retribution over the Englishman by having an illicit affair with the Englishman's wife; cuckolded the pervert, he did. An affair that's, apparently, still ongoing. I will tell you the names and addresses of these people, particularly the name and location of your stepfather and your biological father's name if you want. However, I should tell you John Lewis knows who you are. He's seen you perform more than once. He is aware you don't know about your parentage because you still carry his last name. Yet, in all of the time, he never reached out to you.

"Having met and talked with the parties in question, I believe it's totally irrelevant at this stage. None of them are nice people, Linda. Certainly not nearly as nice and supportive as the people who raised you, love you, and have been around you for most of your life. The only thing we share with the Englishman is the color of our eyes. However, the eyes I look out of do not have any connection to the man who sired me, not what others may see about our resemblance to one another."

"Oh, what tangled webs we weave when first we practice to deceive," commented Dena. "Did you stalk Linda for more than half her life because you want something from her, like her stem cells?"

"No, I did not," he said, vehemently, looking Dena directly in her eyes. "I've known who and where Linda was for many years. I could have come to her at any point to tell her who I am, who she is, but my purpose was not to ask her to sacrifice herself for me. I first saw her perform when she was still a young teenager as was I. She is a phenomnal star and, from what I've learned about her over many years of research, a very special young woman." He turned from Dena and looked into Linda's eyes so like his own, his expression softening. "I've followed you around the globe just to witness your skill as an artist. I just wanted to know you, to have a connection to someone. Not because of your wealth, your celebrity or for anything you might do for me, but because you're my younger sister and an innocent in all of this.

"I'm young, too, but I'm a very wealthy person. As wealthy, if not more so than you are. I'm paid extremely well for what I do, and in my last will and testament, you're my sole beneficiary. I've insured my parents are set for life because they are precious to me. I did this through your Uncle Gregory's Wall Street institution without his knowledge. All of my funds are invested there. I've found him and his partners to be extremely competent and forthright. You and your family invest with him, so I had no reason not to do the same.

"I admit, although my parents love me, I'm too often alone and . . . lonely sometimes," he confessed with tears flooding his face. "I have no friends to speak of or family beyond my Da and Mum. What I do is usually a solitary task where I don't meet people and spend most of my time alone. Because of the secrecy of what I do, I cannot talk with anyone about it. Still, I never would have told you any of this. I just wanted to find a way to meet you and strike up a conversation. Maybe get to know you, have lunch or dinner with you a few times. Each time I planned for that to happen, someone or something got in the way. I didn't want to scare you," he said and laughed a bit, "but I certainly didn't realize your security team found me out." He took another deep, weary breath before continuing. "I don't want anything from you, except to know you as a friend before my life is over."

Linda had to bat tears away, too, and take a deep breath before she stepped forward, sat on the side of his bed, and hugged Bradley. With tears on her cheeks, she held his hands in hers, and smiled tremulously at him, at her stepbrother. "Then as your younger sister, big brother, I demand the right to share my stem cells with you. My parents have given me a lot of siblings to love and care for, but you're my first older brother, even if it's only by a year."

Brad vehemently shook his head, his face stern. "No, I won't accept that. The risks to your health are unacceptable and your talent belongs to the world, Linda, for as long as we're privileged to have you dance or ice skate for us. Even if you are my bratty younger sister," he joked, choked with emotion by her acceptance of him, "you won't bend me around your little finger because I'm in awe of you and your talent. You are not to consider doing anything about my condition. In fact, you are forbidden from taking any action at all.

"Now, go away because, as your father told you, I'm tired and need to rest. Take your family with you because you have a family reunion going on. If you don't hurry, Dena will miss the start of her race and you don't want to disappoint Eugene and Violet, do you?"

"I'll go for now because I do as my father instructs me, but you haven't gotten your way with me. Now that you tell me you and I are members of the Royal Family and in line to ascend to the Throne of England, we have much more to discuss. I've danced at a command performance with the Royal Family in attendance, but I wonder whether we'll be invited to afternoon tea or presented at Court if our ancestral lineage were known to the King and Queen?" She smiled into his tear-filled eyes. They held each other's face and kissed each other on both cheeks as is common in Great Britain.

"Lady Linda, the fifty-first Duchess of Edenburgh and Duke Bradley Smyth, the daughter and son of a charlatan. What a pair we'd make."

"We will, Sir Bradley, but for now, rest."

He nodded and closed his eyes, his body weary.

Chuck helped to usher everyone out of the room but stayed behind with his mother-in-law, Sylvia, to monitor Bradley's vital signs. He looked away while Sylvia held Bradley in her arms to help him quell his racking cries and dry his tears. When sleep finally came, Bradley looked exhausted, he and Sylvia agreed. Chuck worried he wouldn't be able to find a way to help this gravely ill young man before it was too late. When he was assured Bradley was sleeping soundly, he and Sylvia left only to find Linda sitting with Will outside by the door to the room.

Linda rose quickly when her father and grandmother left Bradley's room. Searching their eyes, she asked, "Dad, Nana, how serious is this?"

"This is going to be a hard hit to your gut, babe, but it's bad," said Chuck. "I won't hide the fact he's a gravely ill young man. Your grandmother and I are surprised he's made it this far, but I'm an emergency room doctor. I don't specialize in blood disorders and we don't have anyone on staff here at Summer County General who does. Nevertheless, I'm going to do some research and find out who the eminent authorities are and consult with them. I'll do this quickly and I'll know more in an hour or two." He brought her to him for a hug and kiss on her temple.

"For now, he's resting," said Sylvia, as she ran a comforting hand down her granddaughter's arm. "That's the best thing for him right now. Your father and I don't want to give him anything to change his blood chemistry, especially if we need to fly him to a hospital today. If we can get someone on a video conference link, we will know more about how to help him, if he can be helped. For now, however, it's okay if you and Will want to go in and sit with him for a while."

"Thanks, Nana, Dad," she said hugging both of them in turn.

Chuck wrapped her in his strong embrace and kissed the top of her head. She didn't have to verbalize what she was feeling or what he knew she had in mind to do. He knew his children, all twenty-eight of them, and was proud to have helped raise them to be the compassionate, responsible, and dedicated people they are. "I'll be in my office here at home and call you as soon as I have some information. It shouldn't take me long to figure out who I need to consult." He kissed her again, then he and Sylvia left her in Will's capable arms.

A little over two hours later, Chuck, Sylvia, Vivian, Linda, and Will stood in the media room at the Montgomery's estate in Goodwill,

Summer County, South Carolina. On a large split screen were the faces of the brothers Brooks, Mark and Vaughn, both doctors. Mark was a general practitioner currently in an African village somewhere not indicated on any map while his brother was lounging on a floating raft in the pool at their family's palatial estate in New England.

Mark, a former Marine, and a close friend of Douglas Johnson, also a former Marine, and now the Summer County Fire Chief, was a friend to the Alexanders and Montgomerys, and married to a cousin of theirs, Satarah Josephine. Mark, at Douglas' request, used to live in Summer County for nearly a year to assist with establishing a medically-staffed ambulance service for the fire department. Once the service was up, operational, and staffed with medics Mark and Sylvia Alexander trained, he returned to the Ship of Hope, a floating medical facility, to travel the world helping wherever his curative expertise and talent was needed. With him in Africa was a young registered nurse he met in Summer County, a distant relation of the Alexander-Benson family.

Mark's younger brother, Vaughn, a hematologist and surgeon, was one of the foremost authorities who specialized in diseases of the blood and bone marrow.

Chuck was briefing his family on what he learned from Dr. Vaughn Brooks. "A blood and marrow stem cell transplant works best in children and young adults with severe aplastic anemia who are in otherwise good health and who have matched donors. Young adults are less likely to have complications after the transplant. The transplant replaces damaged stem cells with healthy ones. During the transplant procedure, which is like a blood transfusion, Bradley will get donated stem cells from Linda through a tube placed in a vein in his chest. Once the stem cells are in his body, they will travel to his bone marrow and begin making new blood cells. Blood and marrow stem cell transplants may cure Bradley's aplastic anemia, but he must receive the treatment very soon."

"Dad, I've never heard of this process. What else do you know about it?"

"This process is often called bone marrow harvest," interjected Dr. Vaughn Brooks. "It's done in an operating room, while you, as the donor, are under general anesthesia to put you into a deep sleep so you don't feel pain. The marrow cells are taken from the back of your pelvic bone. You will lay face down, and a large needle is put through your skin and into the back of the hip bone. It's pushed through the bone to the center and the thick, liquid marrow is pulled out through the needle. This is repeated several times until enough marrow has been harvested. The amount taken depends on your weight. Often, about ten percent of your marrow, or about two pints, will be collected. This takes about one-to-two hours to complete in an operating theatre. Your body will replace these cells within four to six weeks. Your father has already taken blood from you and will give it back to you after the procedure."

"After your bone marrow is harvested, you'll be in recovery while the anesthesia wears off," Chuck said, picking up the briefing. "When you're fully alert and able to eat and drink, we'll bring you back here and I'll stay with you. You may have soreness, bruising, and aching at the back of the hips and lower back for a few days. Over-the-counter acetaminophen or nonsteroidal anti-inflammatory drugs are helpful in dulling your discomfort. You may feel tired or weak and have trouble walking for a few days, but you're in excellent shape to tolerate the side effects.

"Despite the reinfusion of your own blood," Chuck continued. "You will probably have to take iron supplements until the number of your red blood cells returns to normal. Knowing your dedication to your workout routine, you'll, no doubt, be back to your usual schedule in two-to-three days. However, it could take two or three weeks before you feel completely back to normal."

Dr. Brooks continued. "There aren't many risks for you, but I want to caution you that, although serious complications are rare, bone marrow donation is a surgical procedure. Atypical complications could include anesthesia reactions, infection, nerve or muscle damage, transfusion reactions or injury at the needle insertion sites. Problems such as a sore throat or nausea may be caused by anesthesia.

"Once the cells are collected, they are filtered through fine mesh screens. This prevents bone or fat particles from being given to the patient. For an allogeneic or syngeneic transplant, the cells may be given to him through a vein soon after they are harvested."

"Vaughn," said Mark, "get your ass up out of the pool and on the family jet right now or I'll come home just to kick your narrow butt. These are people I care about, and they need you there now," he directed.

"Damn it, Mark, I have tickets for the ballet tonight," Vaughn groused. "This is my first night off in two weeks. I've been waiting for months to see this performance."

"The stem-cell donor is the prima ballerina Linda Lewis. Do you really want some hack working on her?"

That got Vaughn's attention. For a black man, the color nearly drained from his face. "You're *shitting* me! *The* Linda Lewis?" his voice awed.

"I kid you not," declared Mark.

Linda stepped forward to be clearly seen by the video camera. "Dr. Brooks, I am, indeed, The Black Swan, Linda Lewis, and if you will come and stick a needle in my ass right now, I can promise you free of charge, front-row, center seats to any performance in any theatre in the entire world on any date you desire for the rest of your life. You will be given back-stage access for each and every performance so that you can meet the performers and be treated royally. I may even name my first born after you."

Vaughn didn't bother to cut the video connection as he raced out of the pool while grabbing his cellphone and screaming for the pilot to fire up the jet.

"Thanks, Mark," said Chuck.

"Don't thank me yet," he said laughing. "I love my brother, but he's a snob and a royal pain in the ass most of the time. Still, he's one of the best hematologists and surgeons in the business. He dare not be otherwise. Our mother is a pediatric surgeon and Vaughn's boss. Our dad is the head of Medical Services at the Townsend Medical Center in Boston's Back Bay. I wouldn't trust Linda's care to anyone other than Vaughn. Get her prepped, Chuck. Vaughn will be there in under four hours if he has to get out and push the jet himself. He's a ballet theatre groupie who believes your daughter walks her pointe shoes on water without getting her feet wet."

Chuck laughed. "I appreciate the courtesy considering everyone in your family is a doctor. I've never visited the Townsend Medical Center, but I understand that your three times great grandfather started the center. It enjoys a stellar reputation."

"Everyone in my family except my cousin, Michael Rodgers, and I work there. How Michael escaped MCATS and medical school is considered the eighth wonder of the world in our family. Still there is hope. He managed to get his wife, Kayla Hill, pregnant, so the possibility that they could be raising the next generation of Townsend family doctors isn't a complete lost cause," he said laughing. "After all, medicine is the family business. In order to get married in this family, the intended has to have a medical degree and pedigree."

Chuck laughed. "We hadn't heard the news about Michael and Kayla. Thanks for the update. Come back to us soon and bring Mary Ella home with you, good buddy, ya hear? You're missed," said Chuck.

"Later," Mark said with a tip-of-the-hat motion before disconnecting the transatlantic video conference call.

"I hope he does come back," said Vivian looking up into her husband's eyes. "Mary Ella hasn't been home in years, but we'll talk about that later. You have work to do now. Our baby needs you." She rose on her toes and kissed Chuck's mouth.

Chuck squeezed his wife to his body and then said to Linda, "All right, Princess Mine, let's head 'em up and move 'em out."

Linda nodded her consent. "All right, City Cowboy, one more hurdle to jump."

Chapter 22

When Bradley's parents, Bradley and Abagail Smyth, Senior, arrived, they first were taken in to spend time with their son before Sylvia Alexander directed them to a salon in the Montgomery's home to sit with her husband, Bernard, Linda, Will, Chuck, and Vivian.

To Linda's eyes, the Smyths looked like the aged Flower Children of the sixties she saw on film of the era of Woodstock. Bradley Senior wore his age well with his long, salt-and-pepper, wavy hair loose and curling around his shoulders. Love beads and chains hung around his neck and his loose-fitting clothes were reminiscent of the era of Free Love. He and his wife both wore Birkenstocks on their feet.

Abagail Smyth had rosy cheeks, a wrinkle-free complexion, and calm, robin's-egg-blue eyes. Her burnished reddish-gold hair was in thin braids with ribbons, beads, and colorful string woven through them and hung below her bottom. Moon, sun, and star earrings in silver climbed the lobe and shell of her right ear while a diamond stud winked and matched the one in her husband's left ear. Her long, floor-length, A-line dress was a muted, psychedelic array of colors like a tie-dyed cloth.

Abagail Smyth took a tissue from her hidden pocket and pressed it to her pale eyes while her husband, Bradley Senior, rubbed her back comfortingly. "No," she said gathering herself and sitting up straighter on the sofa, "my Braddy wouldn't a want this from me. He wouldn't a want tears on me face." Her Irish ancestry whispered through her voice. Wiping away the evidence of her anguish, she smiled tremulously at her husband of more than forty years while rubbing his knee.

"No, the lad wouldn't a want it. I won't tell him, if you don't," he said caressing her face.

"He's such a little git, he'd suss it out, me Braddy would. No, I won't cry and let him see me eyes red and swollen with bags under them thick as lunch pails when he wakes. He'll be cross with me if he does." She turned to regard those assembled. "I can only thank you for bringing us here."

"The lad didn't a want his Mum and me to see him suffer. He's a good boy, our Braddy is, but a stubborn tike when he puts his mind to something."

"Takes after his Da, does our Braddy. He's been that way since he was a wee babe. Had to walk before he crawled, that one. Talked a blue streak like a magpie; always thinking and doing," Abagail said smiling. "Sharp as a whip though, he is."

"Pure genius, our Braddy is," said the senior Bradley proudly, his eyes alight, but tearing. Turning his head, he looked at Linda. "When he discovered he had a real sibling, the light in his eyes . . ." he paused choking back emotions.

Abagail patted his knee, held his hand, and picked up where her husband faltered. "We actually took Braddy to see a performance of The Nutcracker in London by The Royal Ballet Company one Christmas when he was still a teen. He wasn't keen on the idea until he saw the pretty girls. Then he wanted to know everything about it and studied until he was an expert on every classical ballet."

He looked up into Linda's eyes. "You were the star of the show. You brought the light of interest into his eyes. We didn't a know at the time you were his kin."

"Years later, when he found out your connection to him, he came home nearly busting a gut. He had someone of his own." Abagail shook her head smiling. "He told us all about you and your extraordinary family. He couldn't sit he was so excited. He just marched back and forth in me garden raving about you while we had our tea and crumpets. We knew when he came to be ours and his sickness was found . . . he was not ours to keep. It was only a temporary blessing. He's been ours, but we . . ."

"We're glad to share him with you even if only for a short time," continued Bradley Senior, when sufficiently recovered from his emotional distress. "You see, we pushed him to come to you and tell you who he is, but he wouldn't a do it. He's usually not a shy one, but he's been rejected by the arseholes who created him. He didn't a want to be rebuffed by the only other person he shares blood with."

His wife nodded in agreement encouraging her husband to continue, but he couldn't as tears welled up in his gray eyes.

"He didn't a want to be pitied or cause you to feel obligated . . . He wanted to find another way. We studied together, he, I and his Da, to find a cure. Our Braddy and we gave a lot of money to programs and helped children in need get well, but we found no medical program, no plan, no research able to help someone like him with his special blood type. He wouldn't a come to you, you see? If you hadn't a found him, he wouldn't . . ." She stopped speaking and took a deep breath. "My lad, my *son*, would not have interfered in your life. This is not his way. We are glad to know in his final days, he's been happy because, unlike his twat and wanker, sperm-and-egg donors, you befriended him," she said angrily.

"Now, now, Abbey, don't be getting your dander up."

"Well, I be giving them the truth of it," she fussed. "And himself not needing nor deserving the meanness he found when talking to those who made him. They are shameful people, the lot of them!" she huffed.

"Dr. Smyth, Mrs. Smyth, I am not going to lose him now that I know who he is, who I am to him. We," Linda said, looking around at her family and Will, "are not going to lose him. You have Power of Attorney to say what happens now. I want your permission to disregard his instructions and provide the bone marrow he needs to try to save his life."

"He didn't a want that and made us promise when it came his time, we would let him go. You see, he made peace with the inevitable."

"I'm more stubborn than he is. My family knows this to be true and they helped to make me this way." Turning her head, she looked into Will's eyes. "The man I love very deeply understands me and what I need to do." She turned her head to look into Vivian's eyes. "My mother is an excellent attorney and US Supreme Court Justice. If I ask her, she will move heaven and earth to find a way to grant permission for me to make decisions on behalf of my brother. My mother would risk her career because she loves me," She looked at her father. "My father loves me to distraction and he's an excellent doctor. He will do what is necessary to assure we don't lose Bradley." Then she looked back at the Smyths. "I am going to do this because your Braddy is mine now. He's my big brother and I'm not through being his bratty, little sister yet. My parents adopted me and by connection they've adopted Bradley, too. That's how it works in our family. So, I ask you to be my step-parents by adoption as Bradley's sister and let me do this for *our* Braddy."

Epilogue

Linda stood outside the glass partition on the sixth floor of her school and watched Eugene and Violet go through their routine with others for this year's featured ballet named Goodwill. It was a two-hour piece and featured only young children as the stars of the show. The anticipation was building in the entertainment industry for this new ballet. School-aged children who never had an interest in ballet before were clamoring to see it. It was trending up on social media sites. Goodwill promised to become a classic even before it debuted.

She couldn't keep the smile off her face as the children executed each movement she choreographed with precision, style, and energy. Goodwill was a story of a group of young people's triumph over their devastating beginnings in a Fairyland world. Matt Kennedy and Trey Kennard collaborated to score the music and, with her, were the executive producers of the show. The set decorations were magical and ever-changing thanks to the support she received from silent benefactors who promised the production would be well funded for its first season on Broadway.

When an arm circled her upper body and kissed the top of her head, she didn't jolt. Rather she lay her head back against a firm chest and sighed pleasurably. "Are you finished with work for the day?" she asked.

"Probably. In any event, I couldn't focus because I wanted to come watch the rehearsal. How long have you been on your feet today?"

"Nag, nag, nag," she groused. "You're worse than my husband."

"Where is boy-o anyway?"

"It's nine inches of snow outside, so he and Uncle Greg went to play eighteen holes at Golf Manhattan."

"Humph," he scoffed. "That's not *real* golf."

Linda chuckled. "Don't try telling them that. We're glad to see the back of them for a short time. They're like glue around Angelique and me," she said rubbing her rotund belly.

"May I?"

Linda took Bradley's hand and placed it on her extended belly where her and Will's son was most active.

Wonder lit the twinkle in Bradley's pretty green eyes and a smile slowly bloomed on his handsome, dusky-colored, unshaven face. His hair was long and tied in a queue at the nape of his neck. What his sister called his work mode. "I can't wait for this bugger to get here," he said grinning. "I have to teach him to write computer code ..."

"His father wants him to learn to hit baseballs with a bat and your parents and mine want him for long periods of time without any interference from me, Will or you."

"We'll have to negotiate that agreement. Your parents have nearly thirty offspring ..."

"Correction, *our* parents, brother-of-mine. Chuck and Vivian are in Manchester as we speak visiting Bradley and Abagail Senior."

"Are they, now? I must have lost track of time again. I didn't think Chuck and Vivian were going until next week. Maybe I'd better ask, then. Who's coming to dinner?"

"Well, let's see. Angelique and Uncle Gregory, of course. Dena and Drew, Will, you, me, and your latest heartthrob ..."

"*Whoa!* Natalie Portman? How did that happen? I mean I've seen her socially, but I didn't invite her to join us."

"No, you didn't, but when she found out Uncle Gregory's relationship to you, she wheedled an invitation from him. She's in the financial industry and knows Uncle Greg. You didn't think she was coming to all of those games just to see her friends' son play baseball, soccer, basketball, and football, did you? Especially, since she always manages to get you to walk her home after lunch. Then you don't show up for hours and hours, sometimes not until the next day. Remember, you're still recuperating. You're really not up to full speed yet, boy-o. A woman like Natalie, a cougar, can wear even a young man out."

Brad's white complexion noticeably colored. "Well," he said palming his face as Linda giggled at his chagrin. He loved to hear his sister laugh and didn't mind at all it was at his expense. She saved his life and then stuck to him like glue. He was a groomsman in Will and Linda's wedding in Goodwill, South Carolina. The memory of how she and everyone in her family incorporated him and his parents into their clan, removed all of the sadness he ever experienced as an unwanted and abandoned baby. Now he was a part of a pretty big, extraordinary family and proudly wore the gold chain around his neck to prove it.

He was also about to become a real uncle in a few more months. He saw Linda every day since he still lived right down the block from her. She and Will gave him keys and code access to their place, and he was usually expected to join them for meals, outings, and events. His inclusion in every aspect of their lives was a foregone conclusion. Life, he realized, as Linda held his hand over her motion-filled belly, was good and now, because of his and her shared ancestors, he had time to live it.

About the author...

Ann Jeffries, the critically acclaimed author of the Family Reunion—Wisdom of the Ancestors Series, is a native of Washington, DC. As an only child, she enjoyed the benefits of a private school education at Allen in Asheville, North Carolina, and a public education at the University of Maryland. Ann began writing fiction for her own amusement.

Ms. Jeffries is the recipient of many awards for leadership and public service. A keynote speaker at colleges, universities, conferences, and conventions, she has extensively traveled the North American continent, Asia, and Europe. Among other endeavors, she is an entrepreneur, an avid supporter of public television, a genealogist, and a voracious reader.

Her pride and joy are her family, particularly her Fabulous Four grands. She lives in Maryland and South Carolina.

Follow Ann on her website: www.annjeffries.net, Facebook: @ Ann Jeffries, on Twitter @Ann Jeffries and her publishing house site: www. newviewliterature.com. Her novels are available in e-book, paperback, and audiobook formats. Her autographed copies can be found through www.annjeffries.net and also un-autographed on Amazon.com and barnesandnoble.com.

Audiobooks are also available through her webiste, Audible, iTunes, and Amazon. For bulk sales, contact Ingram Book Group Distributors.